Among the Bieresch

THE
SEAGULL
LIBRARY OF
GERMAN
LITERATURE

Among the Bieresch

KLAUS HOFFER

Translated by Isabel Fargo Cole

LONDON NEW YORK CALCUTTA

This publication was supported by a grant
from the Goethe-Intitut India

Seagull Books, 2021

Originally published as *Bei den Bieresch* by Klaus Hoffer

First published in English translation by Seagull Books, 2016

ISBN 978 0 8574 2 840 0

British Library Cataloguing-in-Publication Data
A catalogue record for this book is available from the British Library

Typeset by Seagull Books, Calcutta, India
Printed and bound by WordsWorth India, New Delhi, India

Contents

PART ONE

Halfway

The industrious hands are at rest. Nothing stirs, the air is smooth as a mirror. Elsewhere, perhaps, a crime is in progress —all things are so nameless, so nerveless. 'What is my name?' you ask. And the answer is this humming, this rushing. It is the rustle made by the world's hair as it turns over in its giant bed.[1]

From the scriptures of the Bieresch

Zick

I spent the summer in one of the inaccessible provinces in the east of the Empire, with an older relative now living on her own.—In this district, flat as though burnt to the ground, the days seemed short, fleeting, almost beyond recollection when the dry, cold nights began, nights when the skin of the dying cracks like pottery glaze.

My daily tasks, which I soon performed as though in a dream, did not occupy my attention, but only my right hand, while the left, often clenched in a fist, rested like a stone in the pocket of my uniform trousers. The trousers had belonged to my uncle, the brother of my father and my new hostess, who had just died of a stroke while performing his job as a postal clerk.

A custom of the barbaric inhabitants of this desolate region, only negatively affected by the amenities of civilization, required the oldest, closest male relative of the deceased to don his clothes for a year's duration. This lot fell to me. My uncle and aunt had gone unmarried and childless; I was the third of four children, the only child from my mother's second marriage. My father had died in the war before my birth.

Now, wearing the much-too-large outfit that fluttered about my chest and legs, held together round the waist by a cord used to tie postbags, I was to carry on living my uncle's snuffed-out life; perhaps the inventor of this degrading arrangement had promised it would exorcize the malevolent spirits, or he had believed the souls of the dead would sooner find their peace if in that first difficult time after death they could visit their old haunts now and then and see that all was well.

For this first year after death, the bereaved were forbidden on pain of physical punishment to lock the doors and windows of their dwellings.—This usage, it was explained to me, followed logically from the aforementioned custom, ensuring that the soul, now homeless, could enter without impediment: the house was to stand open, with a bed freshly made for the deceased, a simple rice dish, fruits in season and a piece of cold roast meat waiting on a plate in the pantry.—In fact, though, this stipulation was the stunted fruit of a law—at one time no doubt quite progressive—that systematically advanced the non-violent redistribution of wealth by declaring the estate of the deceased to be ownerless property for the space of one year. In that time all, in their natural freedom, could seize it, and all could regard it as their property—while preserving its substance—and enjoy its usufruct without restriction.

Under the beguiling auspices of a senseless custom, the impoverished population thus took turns to ruthlessly exploit the original intent of the law, lining their pockets with the meagre estates of the deceased until a death in their own family rendered moot all their rights of usufruct.

ONE

Arrival

Three houses stood empty when I arrived in Zick. In a fourth house, the family was just equipping itself with the bare essentials; a fifth house and a sixth still lacked tables and chairs, the main furnishings. On the floors, mattresses awaited bedsteads and bedsprings.

My arrival in Zick was the prelude to the looting, for until the 'proxy' came, or the 'caretaker', as the heir was called with ingenuous irony, the house of the deceased was taboo and the raids could not begin until the night after his instatement.

At the station, which seemed from outside to consist of the remnants of a shantytown, drummed up and carted in for the sole purpose of letting me disembark, not only my aunt was waiting, a wheelbarrow parked beside her on the tracks as a welcome gift, but also the heads of the six families involved along with their followers, perhaps to gauge their future adversary's strength, perhaps to intimidate. My aunt stood by herself off to the side, and the tears flowed down her face as she spied me on the step of the moving train, clutching my small, black pasteboard suitcase held together by a cord. I jumped down and waved at her, and even as I hurried over the conductor gave the green signal for the train to continue on its journey.

I put the suitcase in the wheelbarrow, whose handles were delicately worked, ending in two wooden human hands, and laid the black umbrella with its ornate horn handle on top. I embraced my aunt, we kissed each other on both cheeks, I was introduced and named my name to the man who seemed oldest and greeted me first—he turned away briefly towards the wheelbarrow to look at my luggage, the umbrella on top and the suitcase underneath, turned back to me and said with a short bow that slightly disarranged his full, parted, combed-back hair: 'I'm honoured to meet you, Master Caretaker!' At that he fell back one long step into the row of people, making way for the next oldest, who greeted me as well, hands at the folds of his flared uniform jacket, head slightly inclined. This procedure was repeated four more times until at last I had been introduced to all the 'godfathers', as they called the caretakers who remained with their families after their grace period had elapsed. I was struck by two in particular who were clearly much younger than I, but all of them, old and young, displayed an unwavering, solemn courtesy which set them and their behaviour strictly apart from the rest of their families.

After a brief pause, in which we stood gazing at one another in silence while the other family members vented their feelings with senselessly darting hands and inscrutably gulping mouths, the eldest godfather took his leave with a bow, followed by the others, and the families' procession vanished in the shadow of the station exit, arched over by a heavy frosted-glass awning.

I took the wheelbarrow—where, due to the afternoon heat, my aunt had put her thin, transparent rain cape—by its handles, and they slipped easily into my hands, letting me weave quickly through the tables and chairs of the station waiting room which had been converted into a spacious saloon. My aunt's acquaintances thronged the tables, some giving us barely perceptible nods, and, in a small alcove separated from the rest of the room by a coatrack, I recognized several people from my first visit as a little boy: a strapping young lad with a jute-coloured woollen jersey and a bristling moustache, his sleeves pushed up above his elbows and his elbows propped on the table, kept passing his right hand over his face as though to brush away memories, while a second man, whom I remembered for the way he kept closing his eyes and rolling them under closed lids as though to fend off some fright, told him a story which kept getting drowned out by the laughter of a third, unfamiliar fat man, dressed in black and with the look of an altar boy.—I was about to stop and watch them and perhaps catch and return the gaze of one of the ones I knew, but my aunt tugged vehemently at the sleeve of my jacket and said in a hushed, angry voice: 'Don't look over there!'

She carved us a path between the chairs of the pub guests who barely took note of our presence, merely leaning forward abstractedly or, if necessary, shifting their chairs a bit further under their tables when my aunt, in an almost tender gesture, placed her hand on their shoulders.

We stepped out into the open. The station door swung shut behind us. The pale, broad road leading from the station was filled with potholes which, after the last heavy rain, had collected a brown, oily, caustic-smelling liquid. My aunt walked to my right, always one or two steps ahead, turning back to me now and then as she talked.

'Your uncle was an exceptional personality, so it won't be easy for you to step into his shoes and replace him. But that's what they'll expect from you, not I—you can never replace him for me!—but the others. They don't expect much: a little sensitivity, common sense, *esprit de corps*. Join in, and you'll do well, as we say. Life must go on, we hate all novelty, each novelty brings more of the same. We don't need change, we have no time for it. It takes your whole life to grasp the least little thing. This may seem strange to you—you're from the city!—City people count for nothing here. They're easy to mislead. You're no different. Didn't you think I was crying just now?—Does it look like I'm crying?' asked my aunt, and jerked her laughing, somehow depraved-seeming face towards me, impudent dark eyes gleaming. But then she turned sober again and went on speaking with a rhythmic cadence underscored by her swift, sure steps: 'You see, you're still a child. You let yourself be fooled. No, don't contradict me. I've been testing you.—Just take the second godfather. You saw how his left eyelid hangs askew across his eyeball, no matter, it's a squinty eye, and a squinty eye doesn't see. But I know this was all you noticed while he was talking to you. Everyone does that, he counts on it. Watch your step!' The road dipped slightly and, focused entirely on the wheelbarrow so as to circumvent the potholes with the small wooden wheel, I had nearly plunged my left foot into a knee-deep hole. 'He counts on your staring at his left eye, but he sees with the right one. We've known him a long time, we circle and come from the left when we speak to him. That gives us a slight advantage. He's a wildcat!'

We walked side by side in silence for a ways. Once my aunt took the umbrella from the wheelbarrow to test its pliancy. 'We'll have to find a good hiding place for it!' she said, putting it back into the wheelbarrow, but took it out again a moment later. I didn't understand what she meant, and didn't ask. Instead I pushed the wheelbarrow cautiously down the steeply sloping road while my aunt strode on ahead of me, seemingly lost in thought.—Here and there, though, she poked around under the turf with the tip of the umbrella, lifting the clumps of roots slightly. I had to restrain the barrow from running away from me down the road;

sometimes, when it got rather too fast for me, I imagined that the wooden hands on the wheelbarrow handles were gripping my arms above the elbows to keep me from falling.

'First of all, we've got to fix you some clothes to wear. These here won't do!' she said, lifting the tails of my flamboyantly patterned coat with the tip of her umbrella.—'And the hat you've got on!' she laughed tauntingly. It was a broad-brimmed sun hat; I wore it on doctor's orders because severe anaemia made me sensitive to the heat, quick to faint in the sun. 'Give it to me,' my aunt said. But as I leant over to set down the wheelbarrow, she plucked it from my head and put it on herself. In a jiffy she'd folded down the brim in three places so that it looked as though made to measure for her. The material, once stiff, now yielded, and the brim bobbed along with each of her long strides. I was astonished at her facility in bending objects to her will, and, as though in response, she turned around again, laughing, and said in her haughty, mocking voice, 'You have a lot to learn!'—And I wanted to laugh as well, for I believed I was beginning to see the light about her, and I wanted to learn, too, but my hands were still sweating on the handles of the wheelbarrow, and, as though in self-defence, as if to dodge a blow, I half-turned my face to the side.

My aunt walked somewhat faster now. Wordless, she swung the umbrella far ahead with each step and leant on it heavily when it landed. Sometimes she quickly turned her head, as though to call to me in her sharp, commanding tone, but then, perhaps thinking better of it, she looked ahead once again and took still longer strides, so that the distance from me to her increased to several yards. I steered the wheelbarrow after her in an effort to keep up but the many potholes, which I had to skilfully avoid so as not to get stuck, made this impossible.

The sun was in the west. When I looked up, or my aunt raised the brim of her hat, it shone straight in our faces.—Perhaps her stubbornness was meant to provoke me into speaking, but I said not a word, which no doubt was why her strides grew still longer; I only redoubled my efforts, pushing my load precariously along the pits and holes whose depth I no longer feared but whose treachery, on the other hand, I did not underestimate, as they were clayey and soft at the bottom. I gasped after her, and the front wooden wheel squeaked in time with her steps. When I looked up from the ground, I saw, a bit ahead of me, her long skirts swaying to and fro with the almost urban elegance of her movements. She had pushed back my hat until it covered her chignon. Her shapely legs bent like willow wands as she set them down, but suddenly her right leg buckled and she bent down to rub her ankle. With her head at her hem, near the hollows of her knees, she gazed up at me from below and asked with a coaxing sigh, 'I'm so tired, can't you give me a ride?' I merely nodded and slowed my steps until I reached her. As though too exhausted to stand upright any longer, she collapsed backward into the wheelbarrow.

'I have faith in you!' she said again in her former tone after pausing to arrange herself in the wheelbarrow.—'Just now I thought you were already losing hope. It wouldn't have surprised me—you city folk keel over in the least little breeze. You're snivelling, indecisive, scatter-brained.—Didn't you notice, even the children were making fun of you because you don't know what to do with your hands? —It drives one batty just to watch you!—"Just look at him!" I said to myself, "he's at his wits' end!" —When this is just the beginning!' my aunt added, turning around to me in her wheelbarrow, so that I could hardly keep my balance and now really did skid down into a pothole brimful of water. 'But I'm starting to believe you'll make an effort. Turn to the left up there and take care, it gets steep!'—She held the umbrella in her left hand, the suitcase across her lap, handbag on top. In time with her words, she jabbed the umbrella at the ground which had a tamped-down appearance, cracked in places because the brief rain had followed a long dry spell. 'You have one advantage,' said my aunt, 'and if you're clever, you'll use it: they take you for a fool. Don't say a thing, I know it's so.—Your chequered coat, that crazy hat, your luggage, your umbrella—they're only surprised you didn't rent a draisine! Didn't you notice how brazenly the first godfather homed in on your luggage?—Before the train arrived we all went to the station pub. A parting drink, that's a tradition we have. And do you know what we talked about? You. That's unusual (you don't speak of the winter when it's knocking at the window), but one thing was clear as day: the ridiculous figure you'd cut!—And so it was: one foot on the step, the other in the air, a suitcase in one hand, the other on the door handle. City boy on weekend visit to country relatives. It's enough to make me cry. Next turn to the right.'

My aunt spoke without turning around to me once. Her legs dangled long past the edge of the wheelbarrow, the heels of her shoes striking the front side by turns. Only once did she turn half to the side, still speaking, to rummage for a while in her handbag. Finally she took a small, rectangular photograph from an envelope and held it up with the picture facing me. 'Do you recognize this?' she asked, suddenly quite conciliatory. It was a group photo; though I leant all the way forward between the handles as I pushed, I couldn't make anyone out. 'That's your uncle, with the first godfather standing next to him,' she said, pointing her forefinger at a freestanding figure while the umbrella rolled dangerously back and forth on the edge of the wheelbarrow. 'This is me, this is the second godfather, and this here,' she pointed at something my uncle held in the crook of his arm, 'do you know who that is? That's the sixth godfather. I nursed him myself!' She reached up and pressed her hands to her breasts. For a year, following a miscarriage, my aunt had been the village wet-nurse. 'And this—look here!' she said, taking another photograph from a different envelope in her right hand. It was too dark and too far for me to see a thing except a patch of white in the middle of the picture. 'That's your father's house. Remember? I'll show it to you when we get to the village.'—'How far is it to the village?' I asked. The landscape before me stretched endlessly to the horizon, and when I turned around the steep ridge we must have descended seemed more like a long cloudbank, a strip of haze parting sky and earth. 'Another two hours,' my aunt said. 'If you like, we can have a little rest.'—But she said this so dismissively, and so busy with her handbag, now extracting envelope after envelope stuffed with photographs, that I didn't dare park the wheelbarrow and pushed it on dully between what always seemed the same two frail little trees, onward towards a sad sunset.

'Faster, faster!' my aunt said with sudden vehemence though still hunched over the photographs, her face close above their blackly gleaming surfaces, holding them at a tilt to the sinking sun to catch more of its light. 'I can hardly see a thing now, don't you have a torch?' But without waiting for my reply she said, 'You'd better keep to the streambed from now on, then you can't lose the path.' We'd now come with our conveyance to the bank of a dried-up creek, which I vividly recalled, having bathed in it frequently during my first stay in Zick. Once, on a bathing trip—the men had driven their cars into the creek to wash them and the women sat on the bank with their silk petticoats rolled up above their knees—two boys had see-sawed like mad on a very long beam which they'd scavenged from a washed-out bridge and laid across one of the boulders. All at once the beam had begun to move in a circle as though of its own accord and, unnoticed by the boys who heeded only the impact and the rebound, shifted so far to the side that at last one of the two, the lighter boy, a scrawny half-grown child with a pigeon chest, which tapered off nearly to a point in the front, and an enormous hump, struck the stone with such force that a flap of flesh was torn from his foot and toes and the joints glimmered white amid the slowly pooling blood.—Now little dark puddles lay here and there in the recesses of the streambed between the pale stones, left from the heavy showers of the past few days. But wherever the loamy ground lay full in the sunlight, ankle-deep cracks and fissures had formed once more.

I pushed the wheelbarrow down the middle of the dry creek-bed, and at regular intervals the useless jetties above us cast broad shadows across the deep channel as the sandy banks now rose vertically to the right and the left. Shallow ruts in the ground showed that it had been used before by heavier vehicles than ours.

'We'd often go bathing here!' my aunt said, suddenly animated. Then she fell silent again and finally returned a large stack of photographs to the handbag that lay open on the suitcase in front of her. 'You remember Oslip,' she said—more a statement than a question. She was quite calm again, gazing straight ahead. I knew she meant the boy I'd just been thinking of, so I waited in silence to hear what she would tell me. 'We often came here together, you, Oslip, your cousin and I. Oslip had an enormous hump. And a nose like this!' she said, drawing a great arc in the air with the index finger of her left hand. Then she laid the finger motionless on the edge of the wheelbarrow and used it to steady herself. 'He was my lover.—Back then, three days after you left, we came here together, down there by the weir, where the millrace branches off. Don't turn around when I'm talking to you—how often do you need to be told!' she said sharply, but went on at once in a conciliatory tone. 'In one of the two sluices, there was a hole the size of a kitchen hatch. You kids would always dive through there. Even back then the water flow couldn't be regulated. Once a bridge pile got wedged in this hole, and when one of you boys tried to dive through, his head got stuck. At first no one paid any mind, why should they, it was always the same silly game—dive through, let the current carry you downstream and climb out of the water into the bushes a bit further down, so that no one could see you and they'd think you'd drowned. Oslip was the next to dive, and found him.—No matter. You had just gone home, and I took Oslip swimming,' my aunt recounted. She seemed beside herself now, sliding back and forth in the wheelbarrow. 'The boys played for a bit, and suddenly one of them had the idea to take a beam from one of the washed-out bridges and build a see-saw.' She made a dramatic pause, turning towards me furtively as though to gauge my reaction. Rather than look at her, I closed my eyes. It made me faint with rage—less that she had caught me again at my memories than that she had tried to destroy them and turn the tale of the bathing accident into a memory of someone else's story. Behind my closed lids I felt sick, and I clutched the wheelbarrow hands so hard that I broke both thumbs at once from the wooden handles. In my mind I counted my steps to make the feeling go away, but with relentless clarity her words cut through this haze to my ears.

'Oslip fetched the beam,' my aunt went on, turning to face forward again, 'and sat on one end, across from the other boy. The two see-sawed so madly that we all got up and went over to watch them. It merely goaded him on to see me among the spectators.—When the beam touched down, Oslip pushed off with his right foot only, making the see-saw turn in a circle, more and more wildly, swinging up and down as though it had gone berserk.—What are you doing!' my aunt cried. Her story had put me in a trance, the terrain around me rose and fell like heavy swells and the wheelbarrow swerved back and forth in their midst. 'I feel sick,' I whispered, but she wasn't even listening;

instead, entirely caught up in her memories, she intensified the wheelbarrow's sway by clinging to both sides like a child and rocking from side to side. 'You don't like Oslip, that's what's driving you crazy!' she said shrewdly. 'You only like your friends the caretakers, those fine gentlemen! Do you think I didn't notice how you were drawn to their table in the waiting room? Go ahead, rush headlong into disaster, I won't stop you!' She leant all the way back in her wheelbarrow and stared upward vaguely, arms folded under her head. The silence was unbearable, and I flinched when an object—a frog?—struck the water with a splash up ahead. 'I'll spare you the rest,' my aunt said. 'From then on, we met upstairs every day in your father's house.—Your uncle didn't notice. No one noticed a thing, do you hear!' she said triumphantly. I straightened up as though someone had been beating me and now all the blows had been delivered. And even as I stretched out between the wheelbarrow handles to dispel the sense of being at sea, I felt that outside me and around me the entire terrain was stretching, all the water returning into the ground through cracks and fissures, the banks arching over us to collapse and make way for a primeval monster that sloughed off all these crusts and waddled on ahead of us down the narrow defile to the village.—'Oslip is dead!' said my aunt. 'It's all over. You can tell everyone.'

TWO

In the Dance Hall

We had parked the wheelbarrow at the edge of the creek and left it there. My aunt strode on ahead of me, poised and erect, the tip of the umbrella, hip-high, levelled at the village. Now and then she struck it against the rubbish bins that stood by the side of the road, clanging metallically under her blows, dark and dull or bright and ringing depending on the height of the impact.

We took a narrow path leading along the creek and up into the village. A little slope—on which the bins waited, some open, some closed—separated our path from the gravel road. In the dusk it was like a milky white length of fabric laid out on a meadow to dry.—'Washing day,' I said to myself, but so softly that my aunt, who kept striking the bins with her umbrella and talking to herself unintelligibly, couldn't possibly hear me. '*The washerwomen in the rain showers*,'[2] I said under my breath, and, 'White-washed row houses.'—'Tulip beds with Dutch maids,' I said, noting whether my aunt struck her umbrella on the top of the bins or aimed her blows further down, on the barrel.—Further ahead I observed several men in dark overalls in an open garage, holding strangely bent wrenches and spray guns, busy about a jacked-up wrecked car lacking wheels and headlights. The light in the garage was glaring and yellow, and the men inside looked like miners in an old photograph.—When my aunt aimed her blows at the lower halves of the bins, I accompanied her with deep, dark, drawn-out vowels, seeking the higher tones for my words once she raised the umbrella to swing it down on the lid or against the upper rim.

'He has ophthalmia,' I said, trying to anticipate the rhythm of her blows with my words. Sometimes two blows fell on one bin, and often I failed to predict which part of a bin would be struck next. I whispered 'Abnormalities in antimony mines,' but that was wrong, and the more complex my utterances, the rarer the correspondence between the pitch of a word and the blow. I said 'The radio-gramophone producer's carcinoma' and achieved only one correspondence. 'Sundays and Mondays,' I said, and each tone fit perfectly. 'No, only Mondays,' I amended, stepping over a puddle, 'closed on Sundays!' I said, swinging my little black suitcase, 'never on Mondays!'—'Chimeras after camel caravans,' I said, but nothing fit. 'Equestrians!'—and once again the primary stress was correct. 'You're such a weathercock,' I said. 'In winter weather the mountains are white with snow!'—'God knows!' I said emphatically as even the secondary stresses fit.

'What's that you're mumbling about?' my aunt asked, turning towards me. Her dark eyes gleamed reddish as the light of the first streetlamps struck them, and her hair, too, had an almost red shimmer in the artificial light. She was an albino. Refusing to take her seriously at this masquerade, I said nothing, even when she repeated the question and impatiently struck the bin beside her.—'We're there!' she said then with finality, as though this declaration made everything else immaterial. She raised the umbrella and pointed the tip at a low, square house reminiscent of a village school.

The house marked the centre of a square that spread out before us, the rows of houses shrinking back into the dark on both sides. Its facade was unlit; above the entrance, reached by a too-narrow flight of stairs, two lamps rose on curving arms. Further back, on the left side of the house, light burnt in several windows, and through the closed shutters and doors music filtered as though from a fair, mingling with the distant caterwauling of drunks and the babbling of the nearby creek, which emerged here from a duct and flowed under a little bridge. For a time we stood mutely by the house, attending to the sounds, I with my right hand on the bridge railing, my aunt with the umbrella in one hand and the cape over her other, bent arm, pressed protectively to her chest. I was gazing up to the house's shallow gable when suddenly the light above the door went on and I read the words 'Dance Hall' on a broad swag beneath the gable. The words' twice-repeated *a* had the striking form of a ladder with two crossbars, rising to a point.—Like me, my aunt stood still, as though arrested by this miracle. Then she turned quickly, strode towards the stairs and with a hasty, barely noticeable motion stowed away the umbrella in the dark opening which the builder had left beneath them.

Only upon mounting the first step of the stairs did I realize that the arms of the lamps were indeed human arms of pitch-black wrought iron, growing from a powerful torso cut in relief into the masonry. The hands clasped spherical glass lampshades, aiming them at the torso in such a way that the light fell straight upon the front door. It was a wide door, tapering off at the top in a shallow arch. High up, just above the shoulders and a very short neck, a sun wheel was sculpted into the plaster where the head should have been.—When I took a few steps back to get a better look at the image from further away, it dissolved, and I had to draw closer again to take in the artful execution of the relief and the details. Only from a certain distance did you have the proper impression, as though the whole thing were the work of a myope. If you stood too close, the image blurred, and an obscure force seemed to tug you towards the door; too far, and it dissolved again. Meanwhile, at the bottom of my pocket, my right hand clutched the two wooden thumbs I had broken from the wheelbarrow handles and secretly tucked away.—These wheelbarrow thumbs in my hand and the lamp arms above me on the wall, the correspondence of these two phenomena, their correlation and unrelatedness—all this suddenly struck me as a joke whose underhanded punch line was aimed at me but which I failed to comprehend. Fist clenched in my trousers, I quickly followed my aunt through the front door into a narrow, brightly lit corridor where the first godfather greeted us with the words: 'You certainly took your time!'

'He keeps dawdling,' my aunt said, annoyed at having to make excuses for me. 'There, just look what he's getting up to this time!' she said, pointing back at me; I had stepped into a little niche to stare at a pale patch on the darkened wall. Once it must have been hidden behind a mirror in which the dance-hall guests had surveyed their outfits. 'He's an incurable dreamer!' my aunt said angrily, taking the suitcase out of my hand and parking it in the niche.

We walked down a corridor which made a sweeping curve, with massive doorways set into the walls every few yards, some of the openings blocked off by all sorts of equipment, some of them walled up. These, as I soon learnt, led to a small stage which had once been used for theatre and ballet performances.

The lowest door at the end of the corridor was open, and stooping to pass through it we entered the dance hall, inadequately lit by the glow of several scattered candles on the tables. These tables, simple wooden planks placed on sawhorses like those set up in pub gardens in the summer, stood along the left-hand wall, and there, sitting together in groups, I discovered the families of the six godfathers. Further away, at the back wall, sitting apart from the others, I saw the three lads from the station pub. They looked as though they'd never left their places there: yet again one was telling his stories, and the moustachioed lad, who reminded me of a friend in my hometown, kept passing his hand over his face, while the altar boy—half-turned away from the other two—stared across the room, his torso often shaking with laughter.

Zerdahel

At the furthest table, to the left of the lads, I spied an elderly farmer who'd pushed back his traditional hat with its short green feather and stared at his beer glass, which stood in a large puddle on the table in front of him. He must have been dead drunk, for a group of six- to ten-year-old children stood around him, plunging their hands into the pockets of his coat with impunity, pulling out all sorts of things and putting them in their pockets. Now and then the drunk would emerge from his paralysis and pound his clenched fist on the table—he'd curse, stub out a cigarette butt in the ashtray in front of him or gingerly lift one of the wine glasses and put it down again elsewhere as though according to some plan.

The talk and music fell silent for a moment as the first godfather led us into the hall. Briefly all that was heard was the deep hum from a bulky, old-fashioned radio-gramophone on the right-hand wall, but the monotonous singsong of men's and women's voices soon drowned it out again. On the floor next to the radio-gramophone stood several crates of beer and wine bottles, about half of them empty. The godfathers must have taken a different, much shorter route from the train station and arrived long before us, for a great deal had been drunk.

The empty bottles were lined up along the wall, arranged in groups by shape and size. One spinning bottle formed the focus of the game several children played, squatting on the floor. They, too, must have been treated to a drink, for several of them lurched about giddily, turning mad circles with their arms stretched out to the sides until they grew dizzy or keeled over from exhaustion, often banging their foreheads or the backs of their heads on table edges or hard armrests.

The adults seemed unconcerned with the children's condition or with their games. Only when they felt their conversation had been disturbed by the reeling bodies would they raise their hands, still talking, and dispense indiscriminate slaps in the face, not distinguishing between culprits and victims.

I stood there a while marvelling at these goings-on.—After my aunt's previous admonitions, I didn't dare to join the three lads at their table, but to be closer to them, and drawn by the playing children now thronging the old man—who sat there as though unconscious, his arms hanging limply at his sides and his forehead sunk to the tabletop—I went over to his table and sat down at the corner across from him. Otherwise the table was empty, though the one next to it was overcrowded, thronged by the third and fifth godfathers with their families.

As I watched the children play, I shifted my chair closer to the next table to eavesdrop discreetly on the two godfathers' families. But they divined my intention, put their heads still closer together and began to whisper.—Soon, it seemed, they had come to an agreement—the fifth godfather stood up with solemnity and strode softly over to the radio-gramophone, propping one hand on it as though to hold a speech. He cleared his throat, seeming to call for attention, but then he merely bent down, opened the cabinet doors and put on a record with a bulging rim, no doubt left too long in the sun. The static surged and subsided accordingly, sometimes drowning out the instruments, chiefly bagpipes and percussion, which played endless variations on the same monotonous Scottish military tunes. And the needle danced on the bulging record surface, sometimes vanishing like a little boat in the wave troughs. The godfather seemed to like this music—first he turned the radio-gramophone knobs in time with the needle's ups and downs, amplifying the record's static when the needle swished down into a trough and decreasing the volume when it rode up the wave crest.—Then he waved over the third godfather, a bit shorter than he, leant on him, laying his arm across his shoulders, and imitated a cripple, dragging a stiff right leg in time with the music and repeatedly making his right leg buckle. Meanwhile the third godfather, who had put a bracing arm round the other's hips, occasionally reached his free hand with an exaggerated gesture into the vest pocket under his lapel, pulled out a large, filthy handkerchief and wiped the cripple's brow.

During this performance the fifth godfather kept turning around to me obtrusively to the laughter and encouragement of those around him, signalling to me by making inviting motions with his head or—emphatically closing his eyes and opening them again—giving sardonic winks.

First Lengthy Conversation

'Don't look over there!' the drunk man at my table said suddenly without looking up. 'If you don't look, maybe he'll stop.'—'Why is he doing that, anyway?' I asked, confused, gulping air in agitation. 'He's my nephew, "Petty Theft"—here everyone has a telling nickname!' he added in explanation, waving my question away. 'Petty Theft is the third godfather. I'm known as Zerdahel, "the stutterer". I used to stutter at one time. Still, the name is misleading. No matter.—These are colloquial names, not family names. When a Bieresch makes his first house call (when he has his initiation as a godfather), the other godfathers give him his name.—What you see here, incidentally,' he said, making a sweeping gesture with his arm, 'is what we describe as "making a house call". Petty Theft got his name the first time he accompanied the others to Rák.—Rák means "crab", a Hungarian name, from the Slavic while for the Bieresch it also means "the other verdict".—I'll have to explain that. Perhaps you've heard of the Histrions.[3] They're a sect, still powerful in this region, which was founded back in the third and fourth generations. The Histrions hold the view that for each misdeed there are two guilty parties, the evildoer *and* the victim. They justify their view with the story of Cain and Abel. "The victim," they say, "proceeds to the deed, the evildoer proceeds to the butcher's bench." Abel, it's said, is the one who called Cain (for it is written: *Sin lies at the door, and its desire is for you*),[4] and Cain merely carried out the verdict which Abel passed upon himself. Each misdeed, the Histrions maintain, is but the atonement of a past wrong and, becoming manifest, weighs more lightly than its cause, which remains hidden. "How gravely," ask the Histrions, "must Abel have sinned, that only a murder could expiate his deed!—And on the strength of this exegesis, once a year (by calculations inscrutable to the uninitiated) we condemn to death the victim of a crime, symbolically for all, while the culprit goes free.—Rák, as I said, means "the other verdict". It is said to go crabwise, for as you may understand better now, the Histrionic laws say that each verdict "contains a second verdict". This verdict partly or completely rescinds the first.'

The drunkard tipped his beer glass and stuck in the pudgy forefinger of his right hand to remove something. Then he took a small tin spoon and stirred the glass until a bit of foam had formed on the surface.

'Petty Theft,' he continued his story, 'brought back nothing from his first visit to Rák but an old, tarnished mirror, hence his name.—These four,' he interrupted himself, turning around impatiently to point at the group of children standing to his right, 'are "Petty Theft's" family.—Scram!—The others'—there were five in all—'belong to the Naghy-Vág clan, meaning "the unicorn". Rák is the fourth godfather, Naghy-Vág the second. His name comes from the fact that he squints and his squinty eye sees next to nothing.—We call the fifth godfather "Stitz", "the milksop". "Stitz" is our word for certain milk pitchers without handles, and Stitz, as you'll have noticed, has no ears. The sixth godfather is called Lumiere or "the bulb"—that's a corruption. Lumiere's last name is Limier (that's French). Rák knows French and rechristened him Lumiere due to his large head.—So much for the ascending order. Among themselves, in descending order—and this is a catastrophe whose full magnitude one barely grasps at first—the godfathers have different names for one another. The exception is the first godfather, whom everyone addresses as "First Godfather". Petty Theft addresses the Unicorn—due to the cast of his eyes and his bird's head—as "Crossed Beak". Rák never calls

Naghy-Vág anything but "A Backpack Full" for his hump (which, by the way, all his children have inherited), while calling Petty Theft "The Mirror"—it's obvious why. Stitz calls the Unicorn "Prussian Blue" for the colour of his eyes. For him, Petty Theft is "Fool's Silver on the Way from Him" because of the mirror affair, and Rák, due to a minor speech impediment (he can't pronounce a "sh"), is "Running Water". Lumiere, a superb chess player, calls the Unicorn "Long Castling" for his bulging eyes (the "castles") and their cast, while referring to Petty Theft as "Queen Sacrifice" due to an old story (in which your aunt, incidentally, played the main role). For him, Rák is "River of No Return" (for the "other verdict" which the verdict conceals is said to "swallow up" the misdeed while the verdict itself only avenges it).—Since Lumiere's only loss in chess came at the hands of Stitz, who turned the seemingly hopeless game to his favour by sacrificing a knight, he calls him "The Trojan Horse".'

The drunkard paused, took a large swallow from his beer glass, passed his hand over his face and went on.

'But that's not all.—All these names, you see, are traditional epithets, passed down from generation to generation. For instance, according to an old tradition, the first godfather was addressed as "Župan" (which is Croatian and means "chief magistrate"), or "Ispán", which means the same thing in Hungarian.—Certain names go out of style from time to time (my grandfather, one of the last initiates to know all the genealogies by heart, was addressed as "Shadow at the Window", a very fine name which no one bears at the moment), but just you wait, in a generation or two one of us will suddenly recall a seemingly long-forgotten name and bring it back into use. Then the others start to remember, and suddenly all the old names crop up again, names which no one had thought of any more but which had never been quite forgotten. Of course it also happens now and then that someone or other, just to put on airs or have his fun, claims to vividly recall a great uncle of his mother who bore the name "the Giblet Altar", a corruption of the place name Gibraltar, actually called "Jabal Taher" by the Spanish Arabs. And as no one is prepared to demonstrate the falsity of the claim—on the contrary, everyone is prepared to believe everything—over time many false names gain currency which in fact have no tradition whatsoever, though even that cannot be claimed with any certainty, as each of us has practically limitless powers of recall whose light often penetrates even the darkest chambers.'

The drunkard paused, lit a cigarette and continued.

'Whatever the case may be—as a rule the names we're all given are original, and to this day there's a game in this region whose aim is to combine all the names in a Bieresch community in a sequence that makes one single, self-contained, logical narrative. Were this to succeed, an old prophecy promises, we would be delivered, disbanded, and each (that would be the deliverance!) could go his own way.—Of course it will never come to that!'

Shielding his eyes with his hand as though to ward off blinding light, the drunkard looked at me for the first time. Now I saw that he had very pale, water-blue eyes and a long, handsomely curved nose from whose wings two sharp, deeply incised arcs descended almost to the corners of his mouth, undersized as though by an oversight. But his ears were disproportionately large and stood out like wings far back on his head.

'In periods of recovery from droughts or catastrophic floods, it often happens that all names—in what seems an act of providence—promise to fall into place, and each new name is like a long-sought puzzle piece. When you actually piece it together, however, everything fits beautifully on the whole, but in the end you're left with two or three pieces which you simply don't know what to do with. If it were a game—' silently the drunkard made an obscene gesture, clasping his thumb between his index and middle fingers, 'you'd pocket them unseen!—But it's not a game! And no one, having begun, will get up from the gaming table and go to the pub now. On the contrary—when the hopelessness is greatest, you cower still lower in your chair.

'In the view of various scholars, and I won't deny that after all my experiences this has a strong appeal for me,' said the drunkard, leaning back in his chair, stretching out his clasped hands and gazing at the ceiling, 'it is utterly out of the question for a single individual to find the solution to this problem, though there is a solution—always and at all times, we all agree on that!—In this interpretation, the solution is found in the circle of the family on long winter evenings, while weaving baskets, honing knives or churning butter. You sit together, one person begins, the second carries on, you fit pieces together, joining one to another, and suddenly you know, everyone knows—it is finished. You rise to your feet, you stretch, you go up to one another with congratulations and hugs and sit back down again to write it down, for this, too, is part of the game. But you fail. You refuse to believe it, trying again, starting from the beginning. In vain. It's over with.—"In the face of nothingness, say: It was nothing",[5] one of our old proverbs goes, and so it is.—You give up and speak of other things, but you can't look each other in the eyes. You know the mark of Cain is on your brows, visible even to the blind.—Only one incorrigible person, called "Anochi", meaning "I", devotes his entire life from then on to the reconstruction of the story. But he fails as well, and his efforts are like clumsy hands, inextricably knotting the clew they're meant to untangle.'

Top That Spins You

'There is an account from the fourth generation,' said the drunkard, picking up a beer coaster and tapping it on the table as though to music I couldn't hear, 'the story of the Anochi Gikatilla. I'd like to tell it to you. It's short, and it's entitled "Top That Spins You".—"*The*

Anochi Gikatilla,” the legend goes, “*always lurked where children played. And when he saw a boy with a top, he’d lie in wait. The moment the top began spinning, the Anochi would chase and catch it. He paid no heed as the children clamoured and tried to keep him from their toy. When he seized the top as it spun, he was happy, but only for a moment; then he tossed it to the ground and went away. For he believed that the knowledge of any trifle, a spinning top for instance, sufficed to know the universal. Thus he did not concern himself with the big problems—that struck him as inefficient. Were the smallest trifle truly known, all would be known, and so he concerned himself only with the spinning top. And whenever preparations were made to spin the top, he hoped that now it would succeed, and when the top spun, in his breathless pursuit of it hope became certainty, but when he held the dumb piece of wood, he felt sick, and the children’s cries, which he hadn’t heard till now, chased him away; he teetered like a top lashed by a clumsy whip.*”’[6]—‘That is the story,’ said the drunkard, ‘it is the truth.’

He interrupted himself to fetch another beer from one of the crates. Then he sat down at the table, pushing back his hat, and went on.

‘The legend dates back to the fourteenth century and is said to have come down to us unaltered. Some even make the persuasive claim that it is an authentic testimonial, that is, one of the combinations which successfully captured the complete, unaltered, unfalsified history of the Bieresch community rendered solely in the names of that community’s members at a certain point in time. According to others—the aforementioned Histrions, who hold the notion that *every man is two men, and that the real one is the other one, the one in heaven*[7] (and in their view only this person has the right to bear a name)—the account is inauthentic because it mentions the Anochi Gikatilla by name. And indeed no expert in the books can help but be struck by this fact.—I personally don't attach such weight to it, however. This Anochi achieved immortal renown for all times, and the naming of his name can be seen as a singular tribute to this outstanding personality.

'Be that as it may—the fact is, at the time the legend of the top was written down, its authenticity was unclear. This relativizes it, depriving it of all value as a solution. Yet in the studies of all subsequent generations it has become a uniquely significant source of knowledge for every Anochi, in more respects than one, as you'll immediately grasp.—First, the legend explicitly warns the Anochi against losing himself in his inquiries (for here one of our most incorruptible thinkers makes himself the laughing stock of the very children). Second, it encourages him to search on tirelessly, for many, surely with good reason, regard the very words that seem to crush all hope—"he teetered like a top lashed by a clumsy whip"—as a metaphor for the dawning of knowledge. Third, the legend's substance warns, as it were, against the reading of it (the narrative moves along like a clumsily struck top), admittedly a warning which you only understand once you've thrown it to the winds. And finally, all without exception see it as the first, crucial step on the road to knowledge, for it says that by knowing you block off this very road, as the fruits of the Tree of Knowledge are inedible, whereas its shade redeems the promise of the fruits when you lay yourself down in it.'

After these words the drunkard rose, excusing himself, and disappeared for a moment. I took advantage of the interruption to step over to the half-open window behind me. At my back the radio-gramophone blared out louder in the sudden silence. The three lads at the next table paused in the middle of their discussion to look over at me, and the godfathers and their families also seemed to have interrupted their conversations for a moment. They reached thoughtfully for their beer coasters or played with the bases of their wine glasses. The fourth godfather's wife, a tall, bony woman with dark skin and a broad face, produced a long, high, melancholy tone by running her forefinger round the rim of the glass. I stared out into the darkness of the town and breathed deep, dazed by the alcohol fumes, the smoke and the drunkard's stories.

The drunkard reeled back to the table holding a new bottle of beer which he raised as though in greeting and swung between his fingers. Seeing that I was watching him, he winked at me. We sat down again, and as he elaborately lit a new cigarette, he went on with his story.

'After his grace period, the first godfather will have nine different names to choose from. Four of them were given him in descending order, while he received the other five in ascending order, for even when a name has been agreed upon jointly, those whose suggestions were rejected by the other godfathers always stick to their epithets in secret. A stubborn trait of our race!' Zerdahel added. 'The first god-father's names are: "Fish Who Can't Swim", "Sharp and Swift" (that's what the rest of us called him), "Water Coming Home", "One Step Back", "the Lesser Light" (as the Bieresch call the moon), "Found and Not Lost", "Corrective Injustice", "Headfirst" and "Hardly Begun".—Some of these names may strike you as cumbersome, but they aren't, since nearly all of them are translations from the argot, in which they have no more than three or at most four syllables.—That's why you may hear the first godfather (he won't be godfather much longer, then his year is up) referred to at some point as the "Jackal". The reason is this: the name agreed upon after the godfather's first house call was "had kal", translated as "sharp and swift". "Had kal" was corrupted into the "Jackal", the same thing that happened to me and my name. The original word is still known but, whether from impatience or lack of understanding for tradition, it is translated not only by meaning but by sound—evidently "Zerdahel" proved impossible to pronounce and got turned, no one knows how, into "Stöttera" (a place name, like "Gibraltar"). The word has held its own for one or two generations, but even today some people wouldn't think twice if one of my nephews suddenly claimed that his stepmother's brother was actually called "the Stutterer".'

The Blurring of the Words

'The old chronicles tell us of this. One has the impression that its sole purpose is to empty a word's meaning from its receptacle—metaphorically speaking—remould the vessel and pour in a new meaning. The Bieresch call that "filling old skins with new wine" and laugh about it, though it is precisely what the scriptures warn against. Of course, our ill-starred language is also to blame, since it knows no pure meanings, only images, and thus invites interpretation.—Besides,' said the drunkard, using his coat sleeve to wipe away the ash his cigarette had dropped onto the table, 'it's so continental here! It's a sickness. In all these hot days and cold nights the meaninglessness is impossible to bear—a game of patience *we* still practiced from an early age.—The letters are signs, and each sign carries its old meaning. *Sometimes*, it's said, *the droplet closes around just one or two sounds that words contain—a precise, titillating gesture of which lips and tongue partake when articulating, a skeleton in the shifting sands of the word's meaning, suddenly stirring my memory.*[8]—We'd spend hours listening to the tone sequence, the changing sounds and the path of the tongue, and savouring them. "Sucking a word dry", as one of our old proverbs goes.—But nowadays no one believes, no one listens, no one can take it any more. People show off with new, invented names, new meanings—and now,' his fist crashed down on the tabletop so hard that it bounced and the glasses jumped into the air, 'we can start all over from the beginning!'

The False Doctrine

Unsure what the drunkard hoped to achieve with these lies—for I knew full well they were lies—I tried to stand up. But as I braced my hand on the tabletop, he quickly reached for it, held my wrist and said, 'Don't go yet!' Gradually the malice vanished from his gaze. I leant back on the hard, uncomfortable chair, and the drunkard recommenced his story.

'It's time someone established a false doctrine!' he said. He raised his beer glass to drink to me and winked.—'We are assured that at all times six enlightened ones exist, their light too strong and steady to be seen. Listen to what an old prophecy promises:

Oh, a sleeping drunkard
Up on a bench in the park,
And a lion-hunter
In the jungle dark

. . . .

And a Chinese dentist

. . . .

And a British queen—
All fit together,
All fit together

In the same machine.
Nice, nice, very nice;
So many different people
In the same device.

'As you may have noticed, the hymn is incomplete. It is the 53rd Calypso (a corruption of the Jewish word "klipot"), ascribed to Bokonon ("Yohanan!").[9] The "klipot" are "the Shells", said to hold the power over the scattered, sunken soul-sparks of the first human beings.

'The Anochis of each era have waged countless disputes over the text's incompleteness, with just as many failed attempts to complete it. One opinion that has stubbornly survived, catching on again at recurring intervals, is that the two missing links must be two so-called "false prophets" whose names were intentionally omitted to preserve the truth of the rest. According to the Histrions (the aforementioned sect), each person may inscribe himself and his other part, the one in heaven, into the lacunae.

'However, a schism runs through this camp as well. Some believe you must place your earthly self in the first lacuna and your heavenly self in the second, for the base must precede the exalted in order to announce its coming. The others hold exactly the opposite view. They maintain that the earthly self derives its existence from the heavenly self which must hence be named first in all circumstances. They designate the earthly self as the "Shekhinah", meaning "the lessening of the moon", for originally, it is said, the moon was just as bright as the sun but then was lessened by God.—This second faction, to which I feel I somehow belong, believes that the earthly self vanishes entirely in the heavenly self's radiance, and thus (except in the state of astronomical opposition, when its silhouette can be made out) cannot be named at all.—You'll understand better when you consider that, for the Histrions, the relation between the earthly and heavenly selves parallels the relation between the moon and the sun. Thus they say that in opposition the heavenly self performs actions completely counter to those of the earthly self—while the earthly self lives in total abstinence, the heavenly self runs riot in debauchery (or vice versa).[10] This state corresponds to the lunar eclipse, and the actions of the heavenly self completely negate those of the earthly one (and vice versa).—Incidentally, "And Vice Versa" is quite a common name for us.—On the other hand, the earthly and heavenly selves find themselves in complete accordance when closest together (applied to the heavenly bodies, this means: in the event of an annular solar eclipse). Then all deeds weigh doubly, for they are performed doubly, and yet their weight is nothing and less than nothing, for though the moon shines almost as brightly as the sun then, it does so on the far side from the earth, so that to us here all appears bedimmed and the streets and squares are swept clean of animals and people, who flee into the darkest corners.

'Whether you are to fill in the lacunae with two false prophets, or think of them with your own two names, it all comes down to the same thing. If you inscribed your names in the blank spaces, you would expose yourself as a false prophet (*for the truly enlightened one knows nothing of his enlightenment*, as they say). Moreover, the earthly self is to the heavenly self as the false prophet is to the truly enlightened (or as the moon is to the sun), and what, besides lies, could the false prophet say about the truly enlightened?—And so you have your choice!' the drunkard said and continued again immediately:

'"Reach in, and you'll have it—but what?" goes an old proverb of ours. "Only rarely does an enlightened man reveal himself—it's the moon!" goes another. We know nothing of the enlightened. We don't know who they are and where they are, but we know—they are, they exist.—"Light Emerging from the Shadow" is the translation of an old name, meaning "an enlightened man reveals himself". But another translation of this name is "total solar eclipse", which in turn means "when an enlightened man reveals himself, he blocks the light", and all we can expect from such an enlightened man is—a false doctrine. "Do everything twice!" is the basic proposition of all false doctrines. "When you lie, lie a second time. They'll believe you" is one proposition. "When you strike your brother, strike him a second time, he'll thank you for it" is another. And in times like ours, when there's nothing left to look forward to, we're saved by the words "Do everything twice!"—It's no coincidence that I took my name just now to illustrate what we're experiencing these days. Zerdahel is a name that comes from the argot. The translation "the stutterer" isn't bad, considering what Zerdahel really means— "Do everything twice." Do everything twice.'

Another Legend

This talk frightened me, and I wanted to go. But the drunkard clung to the end of my coat sleeve with both hands and pulled me back down on my chair. As he did, he hissed at me in a manner I'd never heard in my life. 'The Anochi Gikatilla's son was a lifelong cripple,' he hissed between pursed lips, 'and once, when his visitors asked him yet again to tell a story about his immortal father, he said, *My father always said, there's no sense in telling stories if they alter nothing. All the same, as hospitality dictates, I will tell you a story.—My father was a very pious man, and whenever he lost himself in contemplation, he went into such a rapture that as he prayed, without noticing it himself, he began to dance and leap.*[11] And as he told this story, the son of the great Anochi went into such ecstasy that he, the cripple, tossed aside the blankets in which he was wrapped, got up from his chair and began to dance and leap. All present thought it was a miracle, some doubted their own sanity. But when the cripple had finished his story, he stood there and kindly motioned his guests to leave.—He had lost his speech. Do you hear? He was not firm enough in his belief, and so he lost his speech!'—I tore myself away from the drunkard, who at his last words had seized my upper arm with both hands and kept squeezing tightly, and I said, dying of agitation, 'Let me go, you're out of your mind!'

THREE
De Selby

My aunt had instructed me to pick up the wheelbarrow next morning, which we had parked at the edge of the creek above one of the small, grass-grown jetties, take it downstream to Inga's general store, which also housed the public telephone, pick up the post and deliver it.—De Selby, the altar boy from the day before who had laughed so heartily in the station pub, stood some distance from the house as though waiting for me, watching as I stepped outside. He was still wearing the light, black coat. As I nodded and turned onto the already familiar path that led out of the village, he approached me in a friendly manner, introduced himself and asked if he could join me. I invited him to come along, and after exchanging a few more initial pleasantries—neither of us, it seemed, wanted to start the conversation and this awkwardness soon threatened to smother the most innocent forays—he set forth, suddenly resolute, his theory of the one-way system, whose quintessence lay in an observation I had often made myself: that all roads can ultimately be taken in one direction only.

The One-Way System[12]

De Selby proceeded to define 'Ways There' as those roads between the places A and B that were designed to lead from A to B (or vice versa). You could tell them by the fact that you'd walk them with ease, even when taking them the very first time. On a Way There, De Selby explained, time seemed to fly, while Ways Back and Wrong Ways led through rapidly shifting, seemingly cobbled-together scenery. On Ways There you are at home, he declared. The road taking us out of town was a Way Back, which I might easily tell by the fact that the surrounding landscape receded as we advanced but then suddenly lay behind us, fully justifying the nameless feeling that our orientation system was about to collapse.—To substantiate his theory, De Selby related two incidents that had occurred in the region long ago. In one case, a Bieresch, surprised by darkness while conversing with his neighbour, attempted to reach his house by taking a shortcut across the meadow that lay between it and his neighbour's. He never arrived home, however; after searching for hours his wife found him in the village pub, drunk out of his senses. Despite everyone's cajoling, he could not be convinced to return home.—'The other case is no less tragic,' said De Selby. 'It, too, is a legend. As it's crucial to my theory, I know it by heart. It's called "The Everyday Confusion",[13] in its very title laying claim to universality. It teaches us never to take shortcuts, for even an inch's deviation from the right Way

There can lead straight to disaster.'—Often, De Selby explained, small, well-worn paths accompany a Way There, misleadingly running alongside it for a long, senseless time, seeming to make for easier, freer walking. But though their subtle deviations were invisible to the naked eye, these paths led away from the Ways There and straight into perdition. Glancing up from your thoughts, you suddenly found yourself in utterly unfamiliar surroundings. 'Wrong Ways, then,' said De Selby. 'Something shifts, swift and ruthless as a slip of the tongue!'—Now all at once you had regrets. You looked about, listened, stopped in your tracks. Everything seemed suddenly deranged: rises in the road suggested declines, a valley that looked broad and sweeping in the distance proved on approaching to be an impassable cliff crevice. 'Mountains dissolve into thin air. The ground gives way beneath the wanderer like a rotten jetty,' declared De Selby, the sexton. 'He grows dizzy, he staggers, he clings to a railing.—He has "seasickness on solid ground"[14] as we call it.'

He paused. Then he said, 'Ways Back are foot-traps. The legend tells that the wanderer, conscious of his confusion, tried at once to follow the wrong Way Back in the opposite direction but, try as he might, he couldn't find the path. Before the wanderer's eyes, tells the legend, a ribbon of fog rose into the air and dissolved.' Once again De Selby lapsed into pregnant silence.

'Ways Back—I'll admit it despite all my caveats—' he continued, '—Ways Back have their advantages all the same. I, too, am often enticed into using them. But I give in to the temptation only when I'm in company.—Then you can help one another out by telling stories. Of course, this redoubles the exertion, so on these paths—in contrast to the Ways There, down which you rush, sharp and swift, as though in a stream—you make but stumbling, plodding progress. But then they take practically no time at all,' he cried. 'You take them *across* the flow of time, as it were, not *with* the flow of time like a Way There.—Just remember yesterday!' he said emphatically, flinging his arms into the air. 'Those of us who'd stayed behind in the station pub decided to reach the village by way of the "Sign of the Green Wreath" to ensure that we'd arrive ahead of you.—On your road (I have to say, this was thoughtful of your esteemed aunt!) you probably felt you were flying. We embarked on the adventure of the Way Back—actually, you must have heard us singing as we passed you,' De Selby interposed. 'We risked it, and though we set out half an hour later than you and put in a stop at the "Green Wreath", we reached the dance hall well before you.—And while waiting we took advantage of your red wine,' he said with a laugh.

'I was watching you just now as you left the house. You may have noticed. You looked about, then set your sights on the goal.—I knew what you were thinking,' he cried.

'So decisive, so bold—only an all-round expert could act as you did. At first I wanted to make a bet with myself, but then I didn't bother, because it was clear that you'd choose the Way Back. Of course you didn't do it knowingly, but isn't the one who harbours the fear the one who unwittingly takes such pains to avoid the peril?—Eyes on the goal, the chasm in-between surely won't be too wide, one leap—and you're across. That's the right approach!' he said with a loud snap of his fingers. 'That's where I'm different—I think first of my health and convenience. And I reach for the hand that holds out a Way There. I go straight ahead, however far it may be, and I talk straight as well. But you, you're all for inconvenience.—When someone reaches out his hand to you, you clasp yours behind your back and turn away. Quite right! Who really knows who a hand belongs to! Better a dangerous Way Back, you think, than the well-travelled high road.—I'm sure you'll like Inga. So: off to Inga!'—De Selby was quite out of breath. Flustered from all his talk, he kept waving his arms even after he'd stopped speaking, and when we'd reached the place where I had parked the wheelbarrow the evening before, he flopped exhausted onto the grass.

I didn't find the cart where I expected it.—Someone had pushed it over and down the bank. It lay in the creek bed as though butchered, bottom up, legs stretched in the air. I plunged down the bank. The wooden hands had broken from the handles and lay next to the conveyance on the dry, cracked clay.—As though these hands had something to do with what De

Selby had been saying, at the sight of them I felt dismayed by the low esteem in which the inhabitants of this region held other people's property. Perhaps I wasn't quick to grasp outstretched hands, but I didn't lop them off either.—People were more keenly aware here of the community of effort that comes together in a piece of work—the many artful ornaments seemed but the most incidental sign of this—yet nowhere had I seen this work treated with such indifference and scorn. The fruit of an effortful, time-consuming game had been ruined in the wink of an eye. A child had been allowed to destroy what all had given, allowed even to be proud of his destructiveness, for—to mock everything!—after his deed he had climbed down the steep bank and in a crack in the wheelbarrow's bottom had planted, like a topping-out tree, a peculiar hazel branch, its end spread out in spokes and grown together in a wheel, a 'monyorókérek', which means 'circular hazel bush' or 'the Wild Hunt' and is worn here tucked under the hatband on certain occasions in place of some other trophy.

As I freed the wheel of the barrow and laboriously pushed the vehicle up the bank, De Selby gazed down at me, his palms planted at his sides in the grass as though he were poised to leap. 'You're good at what you do,' he said. 'If I were your aunt—and who knows, maybe I am!' he added laughing, 'I'd never let you go again!' He got up and shook out his trousers, to which a few dry blades of grass clung.—'I haven't even explained who Inga is!'

'"You people are always explaining!" he'd say now. Explaining, explaining. Inga's right—we don't live, we explain life. And for most that's quite enough. Not for Inga. Inga's the keeper of the general store where your uncle always picked up the post. You'll be doing that now.—I knew your uncle well. We walked many a Way There together—and most of all, many a Way Back!' he said, laughing again.—'Am I talking too much for your taste?' he asked, probably because I'd glanced up from my fruitless attempts to fit the slipped wheel back into its mount.—But like my aunt, De Selby was not one to wait long for an answer when he'd asked a question. And yet: Had the sexton heard my thoughts? Had I looked up before he asked me his question? '"Inga swings from yesterday to tomorrow—and vice versa, hence his name," says Zerdahel. God knows what he means by that. He always talks in fancy phrases,' De Selby said.—'"You Histrions," Inga always says. "You're like tightrope walkers. You're always explaining. Your words rig ropes to keep the world from flying away!" he says. That's how he talks.—Of course we explain things. Our entire history is nothing but a succession and repetition of false explanations. "A knot that ties itself when loosened," they say.—"That's the strange thing," says the wanderer in the legend I spoke of just now. Suddenly he stops in his tracks and says: "Astonishing—it seems that everything repeats, and yet comes as a surprise to me!"—He is a Bieresch. We say, "It comes like a blow that was meant for another. What on earth did he do?" We act, yet it seems we lack the larger context. And Vice Versa draws these connections—he does nothing twice without doing it differently the second time.—"Repetition," he says, "is either a folly or a feat." It's a different matter for us, who believe in repetition because we seek salvation in it. And thus there's no greater disgrace for a Bieresch than to be asked: "Are you repeating yourself?"—Of course I'm repeating, and I intend to do so again. But to be doing a thing behind my back, so to speak, without noticing it myself, that's what's shameful.—The river of history, our history, has carved indelible channels, basins and meanders in our brains. These are well-worn waterways in which the boats of our thoughts float silently downstream, if you'll permit such an image. You load your boat, stow the freight and lash it down, you set the sails—but in the end it's someone else who jumps in first, unmoors the boat and pushes off.'—He interrupted himself, looked at me, laughing, as I hunched helplessly over my wheelbarrow, and said, 'It seems to me you're repeating yourself!'—Then at once he turned serious again and went on: 'We are humble people. Our climate permits agriculture on a small scale. Lettuce grows here, beans, spices and some wine. In the south there's even bamboo.—The winters are mild, while the heat of the summers oppresses even us. The sprouting grain can wither then in a single night. Such nights are rare, but they occur. And it's said that once a Bieresch walked out his door in the morning, and the mere weight of his footsteps made all the luxuriant growth collapse upon itself. "Mulch for the next year!" we say when something goes utterly awry.—We don't expect great things, how could we,' said De Selby.

Having finally fit the wheel of the barrow back into its mount, I picked up the conveyance. 'We don't want great things,' De Selby repeated. 'But neither do we look down in envy and derision upon the backward idyll of our ancestors.—We are our own ancestors!' he said, and added, as though by way of a joke, 'But which ones, that's the question!—We're stuck in one of time's blind alleys. The story I told you before is the story of the Bieresch. The bypath the wanderer takes is a Way Back. It leads nowhere. And we've been standing there for centuries now.—In metaphorical terms, we're stuck in the future perfect: our present is the past of our people—"the great past of our great people," Zerdahel would correct me. Whatever the case may be, we move in place, haunted by the sense that an irreparable error has been made.—We eat, we drink, we talk to one another. We act like anyone would after surviving a great terror. What terror, and when did it befall us?' said De Selby, ducking exaggeratedly. 'A thousand years ago? Yesterday? A minute ago?—What did I just say? Have I repeated myself?' As part of his game, De Selby glanced about anxiously. Then, calm again, he went on. 'To be sure. But in what way?—At some point in our development, a giant leap occurred. A leap to the side? From the safe Way There to one of the countless Wrong Ways and Ways Back which beckon coaxingly to each of us?—Did this all happen when I was born? Is it happening to me now? Do we seek something others lost in another life?—A Way Back is like the way to church blocked by a woman's inviting body. A temptation, one might wrongly say. Rather, a wrongly placed punctuation mark that destroys an entire meaning. A senselessly spat-out word that startles everyone nearby.—"He goes his way," the legend says, "and all at once—bang! To him it seems the sudden commencement of a universal, unending fart, mixed with the shrieking and wailing of children."—It's revolting—like seating yourself on a half-inflated balloon. A light, barely noticeable wind of madness, passing through the sluices and chambers of our brains and out again. "The breezes kiss," our people say. *"Ireland is a fine country,"*' De Selby suddenly said without rhyme or reason, '*"but the air is too strong there!"*'[15]

'Be that as it may,' he went on, smacking his lips. Then he touched my arm and warned in a low voice, 'Talk like that drives Inga crazy.—"Nothing is as it may be," he says, and starts harping on the same theme: "There are no repetitions!"—He says the only thing that repeats is our folly. But even we've got more foolish since the last time. That's how Inga talks. Nothing else goes for him. And yet everything does repeat. Do you know French?' he asked me. I shook my head. '"Tout le nouveau c'est plus du connu," they say in France.—"Everything new is more of the same old." Limier is a Frenchman. Inga is Hungarian and means "the pendulum". He swings from yesterday to tomorrow. *Tick tock, tick tock, is three and four,*[16] the children call after him when he swings by on the street.—May I? I'm feeling a bit tired already!' With an airy movement, De Selby parted the tails of his coat and sank into my wheelbarrow like a feather. I protested.—He begged pardon with a bow and returned to my side. 'Wheelbarrow-riding brings good luck,' he said in explanation.

'So, Inga doesn't believe in repetitions. Inga counts. He counts while eating, while walking, while sleeping. But doesn't counting mean repeating yourself, and hoping that everything will repeat one day?—"Inga's tongue," says Zerdahel,' said De Selby, waiting for me, for he'd quickened his pace as he spoke and was almost out of earshot now. '"*His tongue,*" says Zerdahel, "*warns him against each number. Each number, before letting him pronounce it, looks around in all directions, as it were, the combinations of figures shatter before his eyes, he sees their insides, they rustle like leaves in a forest!*[17]—But what is it Inga's counting? you'll ask," says Zerdahel.—Don't ask,' said De Selby. His tone had become quite grave and confidential. Everything seemed slightly deranged. 'Some people think he's counting his steps, and they tease him by saying, "He's walking funny because he keeps losing count!" But just ask Zerdahel! He claims, "Inga *doesn't* count."—"What then?" you ask.—"Inga numbers" is the answer. "And that means?"—"What it says!"—Aha. So it's the umpteenth table in Inga Benyul's life, the umpteen thousandth person, the umpteen millionth morsel of bread. That would be nice and simple. But it isn't like that. Because when Inga thinks no one's listening, he counts freely and out loud. And when you listen to him, you notice it at once—he counts differently from you. Often he counts by fits and starts, skipping a few thousand numbers, sometimes backwards, then again doubling a sum or multiplying a number by itself.—Maybe, you say, he's counting things, or is it the names of things: What he sees, or what he thinks? Or he's simply tallying out loud what he silently thinks, and adding this to what he says. Or he counts what he sees *and* what he thinks.—Sometimes he closes his eyes while counting, and then he counts on regularly, as though breathing, number by number. Then you sense: now he's at peace!' De Selby stopped and brushed off a leaf that clung to his coat. 'It's as though he's relieving himself,' he went on. 'Each new number he excretes seems to be the new thought that he's thinking and that he must count. Perhaps he's praying? Perhaps he's thinking his numbers the way we make music? They unfold and rise within him, and once he's seen what they are, he slips on another numeral.—"And then, you'll think,"' said De Selby, '"the new thought forms out of the last number, and this thought is given a new numeral—he enumerates the numbers, then, and one number is the occasion and pretext for the next numeral, and so on?"—That's what you think.—Far from it! Inga is different.'

De Selby paused. He was tired. It was clear that all this talk exhausted him. He was sweating heavily. His hair hung over his forehead, his sideburns were plastered to his cheeks.—'Inga's numbers are *his* ropes between thoughts, to put it in his terms,' said De Selby. As he walked, he passed a feeble hand over his face. It was as though the words were cursing within him.—'But you don't really know. All you know is—he doesn't want you to know he's counting. And he's not bad at hiding it. But sometimes it has to get out. He'll be sitting across from you at the pub table, suddenly his hand flies to his mouth, and behind that hand he furiously hisses out a number at you.—"He counts as greedily," one of my friends says, "as though he'd like to gobble back up the words he spits out!" It sounds indecent. It's a splutter like someone blowing his nose behind your back. And indeed Inga tries to cover it up by honking into his handkerchief a moment later.—And what's Zerdahel's view? *He's looking for something he lost in another life,*[18] he says. A fancy phrase, naturally. But maybe he's right. Only—who actually believes in another life?' asked De Selby, giving me a keen sidelong glance. 'Do you?—The other life, the other shore: those are Zerdahel's fairy tales for children. We're repeating ourselves, our lives burning out in the klipot.

“A year after you’ve died, you’re dead,” say the Bieresch. Everything else stays the same. You and I,’ said De Selby, ‘Zerdahel and Inga—we don’t even exist. We are what the scriptures call the “foul-smelling discharge”, the “rotten teeth in the great, eternal jaws of the Bieresch” that have bitten themselves bloody on the world.—It’s the same old story: Yesterday my older brother Oslip died, today it’s your uncle. Soon I’ll be called “Door to the Mountains”, and you “Talks Inward” or “The False Explanation” or “Walks between Two Windows”. And as long as we didn’t know who we are, we were happiest. The brief dream of youth is dreamed, and the widest valley is the wall you knock your brow bloody on in the dark. There is no “Door to the Mountains”. I ought to be called “Laughs without Reason” instead,’ he said sadly.

Ablaking

De Selby collected himself and went on in a firm voice. ‘Do you know the feeling? Often when I say something, some phrase, my name, a word—I feel that it’s not *me* speaking. The children play that. We call it “ablaking”.’—He’d turned sad again; meanwhile, this remark, which he’d seemed to toss out innocently, unthinking, struck me like a blow—we’d played this game as children, and I had thought *I’d* invented it. With us, it meant imitating strange voices.—When you were alone, you spoke to yourself in another’s voice and replied to it in yet another. Of all the people I’d introduced to this game, my little sister mastered it best. Often she'd play it for hours. The others of us would watch her from some hiding place, then suddenly jump out and grab her. Two of us would hold her tight, and she'd have to ablak for us till it was too much to stand, and we leapt to our feet and ran away, beside ourselves with pleasure, fear and then pleasure again.—'It's not *me* speaking,' said De Selby, stopping alongside me for a moment, 'another person *in* me opens a hatch to my mouth and says what I say. He takes my voice, speaks a few words and closes the hatch again. And before I can say any more, to correct what was just said in my voice, another window, another "ablak" opens up inside me, and another voice speaks a phrase. And so on. It's so sordid! As though I were filled with windows, torn open and slammed shut by turns, and between each opening and shutting someone yells a curse word at me.—Do you understand?' De Selby was nearly screaming in pain. 'There's so much filth in the world,' he sobbed. 'Sometimes I think I can't go on.' He'd stopped in his tracks, raising his arms and dropping them hopelessly. Taken aback, I said nothing. What did he expect from me?

Then we walked side by side in silence for a time. The grass was thick here, bristly as a beard. It stood up straight again after each step. It hid another world—the world of beetles, spiders and snails.

De Selby had taken off his shoes and rolled up his trouser legs. He walked barefoot alongside me. His white, hairless legs gleamed in the sun as though greased with a bacon rind. He looked like an old man. Sometimes he raised his right hand, holding his shoes, to wipe the tears from his eyes. He'd stopped speaking as abruptly as he had begun. I felt wretched. It was as though he'd erased the whole world with his last words, and as though this had to hold true for me as well. Was that allowed? Was it so hard to do?—Now he was walking a bit ahead of me again. From time to time I heard him sigh. His sighs sounded like falsely placed punctuation marks—'as though another were taking the voice from within him and using it to sigh'. Sometimes, as he walked, he spread his toes wide like a child and ran them over the grass as through a shock of hair.—Now *I* would have liked to tell him a story. But what kind of story? One from my home? A comedy of city life?

It was years ago that I'd first come to Zick. At ten I'd fallen in love with a dark-haired twelve-year-old from the village.—Her father, an old man, nearly deaf, had leased the 'Sign of the Green Wreath' and installed the village cinema in what at that time was still a crude annex to the building. In the behind* of the long farmyard he'd installed a carpentry workshop, and the air prickled the nose with the warm, dry scent of sawdust and seasoned wood. The old man liked me. Whenever

* The term the Bieresch use for the back portions of their farmyards, adjoining the sleeping quarters and often housing subterranean stables and storerooms.

he spoke to someone, he used the plural. 'The lads play hooky,' he'd say, patting me on the shoulder. 'And the lassies won't wash up,' he'd say kindly to his daughter. It was a soft, melodious dialect. It was holiday.—Sometimes in the mornings I'd sit with the girl on the hard folding wooden seats in the dark, empty cinema. The theatre was cool and smelt pleasantly of the oil used to varnish the dark wooden floor. The cinema doors stood ajar, and through the crack a beam of light fell white to my friend's white socks. And she slid her foot into this ray as though to warm herself. I sat beside her, very still, and waited.—That was a fine story. It would surely be good in the telling.

FOUR

And Vice Versa

'Let's get something to eat,' said De Selby, as if to put that all behind us. And added, as though this were not a contradiction but an explanation, 'Inga's sure to be waiting already.'—Next to the general store's entrance, a broad portal with a basket-handle arch, several steps led down to a long, narrow pub above which the faded words 'London Inn' could be read. In the middle of the taproom stood an unusually small billiard table, and next to it a rangy man of about forty-five. He had wavy ginger hair which he wore parted in the middle. The light shed from above by an old-fashioned pulley lamp with a white enamel shade surrounded his head with a nimbus. A billiard stick swung loosely between the man's thumb and forefinger. De Selby turned around and motioned towards the man with his head. That, then, was Inga.—He had an interesting face with closely set eyes and a coarse, broad mouth whose drooping upper lip was adorned by a Spanish moustache with twirled ends. A large Adam's apple dangled from his long neck as though in a sack. Inga was incredibly thin, the effect amplified by the low billiard table whose bathtub feet ended in lion's paws. His old, dark trousers with wide-set needle-stripes were girded by a broad waistband, over which dangled the long, slack, tapering tails of his waistcoat. When he leant over the table to play a move, these tips trailed inaudibly over the green-lined rail cushions. There was no one in the taproom but the three of us, though the proprietor could be heard behind the Italian bead curtain, probably in the kitchen, busy with pots and silverware. De Selby asked me what I wanted and shouted our order to the proprietor.

As I stepped out from behind him, And Vice Versa bounced his stick on the floor several times, as billiard players do after an especially felicitous shot. De Selby nodded in greeting, I greeted him out loud, and then we sat at a table in one of the alcoves, whose walls were covered with cheap imitation leather. Lamps with red plastic shades were mounted at regular intervals on the walls, and their light gave the copper tabletops an unnatural glow, like embers in an artificial fireplace. The sagging wire over the bar formed two garlands of alternating red-painted light bulbs and mock chilli peppers. The beads of the curtain tinkled as the proprietor, wearing a plush dressing gown with a crude orange flower pattern, emerged from behind the bar. He served De Selby's cabbage soup in a clay vessel. At my place he set down a handle-less china cup of Turkish coffee and next to it a glass of chilli schnapps, which De Selby had recommended. I took a sip from the glass. The schnapps burnt fiendishly.

Meanwhile And Vice Versa went back to his game at the billiard table. Before each shot he seemed to carefully consider the direction, the force of impact and the side spin, tilting his head slightly as though watching himself play. He took the cue between his legs and rubbed the stick's leather tip with a blue cube of chalk which he took from the side pocket of his vest. Then he propped one buttock on the edge of the table, poised the stick behind his back like a violin bow and, from this awkward position, gave the cue ball a light, well-aimed blow. Spinning, the ball travelled almost parallel to the cushion, touched the corner, changed directions and slowly returned to the other two balls. Then he held his cue almost perpendicular to the playing surface and aimed his shot in such a way that the cue ball, after touching the red, automatically returned to the black ball and struck it with a click as soft as a kiss. The shots seemed extremely complex, but once they were executed and you saw the balls race away, you nearly clapped your hands in wonder at their clear-sighted conception.

Mental Rigour

'This is the ninety-third shot in this series,' said And Vice Versa, rubbing the tip of his cue with blue chalk again. He turned to De Selby and asked, 'Don't you want to join me?'—'No thanks, not today,' said De Selby, nudging me under the table with his knee. 'He's counting,' he whispered.—'A pity,' said And Vice Versa, preparing for his next shot. Torso twisted over the table, glancing at me sidelong, he added, 'De Selby plays by feel.' This time And Vice Versa's aim was off; the red ball bounced from the playing surface over the rail and darted like a small animal under one of the copper tables in the back of the pub. 'That's because of the abrasion,' he explained, though at first I didn't understand what he meant. He straightened up and from his trouser pocket conjured a new red ball which he weighed in his right hand, then placed on the table with the others. 'De Selby gropes for the ball's path like a blind man. He's incapable of calculating. Three combinations are the most he can do,' And Vice Versa said. Coming from him, the name De Selby sounded like 'the selfish'. 'I can make it up to thirty, a relatively high number, even for a strategic player, and yet that's nothing.—Come here for a moment,' he said, waving me over. I stood up. And Vice Versa pointed to the balls. 'Look at our distribution here. The shot is of average complexity, requiring nine calculations—namely, shot direction, shot force, force of impact, first deflection and trajectory of the struck ball, reduction of velocity at the cushions, that is, frictional resistance, second impact and deflection, transfer of spin and rolling path, not counting, as you were able to observe just now, abrasion of the ball surface, or air temperature and humidity, which affect the baize and thus the velocity of the balls.—The ABC of billiards, you'll say. Quite right. And yet, the position of these three balls,' said And Vice Versa and blew his nose, 'allows an average player approximately twenty-five directions of impact. If in addition he commands an unusually strong force of impact, this number doubles or triples, though certain configurations would inevitably match, especially towards the end of the trajectory.' And Vice Versa interrupted his lecture and went to the bar. He poured sugar from a glass container into a small cup of coffee, eyeballing the amount, stirred elaborately and emptied the cup in one swig. 'This stick, incidentally,' he said, raising his cue, 'is one I ordered specially from Paris. It's hollowed out in the middle, with a platinum-iridium rod inserted in the cavity, so that I'm not at the mercy of weather conditions.' With a quick motion he tossed me his cue so that I could take a closer look at it. The thick butt was carved into the body of a pregnant woman with enormous, bulging breasts. She held her swollen belly with both hands. 'My contribution towards the propagation of the Bieresch,' said And Vice Versa with a laugh. He took the cue from my hand and pointed it at the ball. 'Of the aforementioned twenty-five possibilities, a good player now rejects twenty to twenty-two from the outset because they would unnecessarily complicate his calculations for the further course of the game or create unfavourable starting positions for the following shots. This leaves three possible shots, providing for an as-yet-unforeseeable number of further manoeuvres.—But is a man a good player if he can choose from three variations for each shot? Just try cubing this number! By the time you calculate the third shot, you'll be faced with no fewer than seven hundred twenty-nine positions. That's when things get complicated. Ask De Selby!'—Again And Vice Versa spoke the name as though he'd said 'the selfish'. De Selby sat with his head leant back and eyes closed, as though asleep. 'And so in fact there is no alternative,' said And Vice Versa, propelling the cue ball with his right hand so that it circled the table once before gently bumping the red ball, then the white ball with the black dot that looked like a stain. 'At the very first shot you must reduce the possibilities to a minimum. The minimum is one. To combine three in one, that, as the Jews say, is pilpul, it is both hard and easy.'[19] I stole a sidelong glance at De Selby, whose head had slid down sideways on the synthetic upholstery. 'For such an act of force, and it is an act of force, for ultimately there is nothing behind it but a hypothesis—my certainty that with the pertinent knowledge of geometry and dynamics it should be possible, actually possible, to aim each shot such that the balls come to rest at the precise point from which I launched them—for such a physical and mathematical act of force, then . . . ' and now, actually hissing—it sounded as though, almost from underneath his words, he were tossing onions into boiling fat—he spat out a number at me. One hundred eighty-four thousand forty-one! Then he immediately continued, ' . . . you need first of all a cool, calculating mind, then mental rigour and finally powers of recall that untangle into the future.—The emotionalist,' And Vice Versa averred, blowing his nose, just as De Selby had predicted, 'has none of these. Rather than organize his thoughts, he relies on the strength of his intuition. He hopes that his brain will remember and belch, as we say. That is why he always lacks precision. And yet these shots, which all have something vague and dreamt-up about them, cast an incredible spell.—And what does the strategist do?—I force my mind into these balls, or the other way around, I force these balls into my mind. I myself become a ball the moment I see the field stretch out majestically before me, all the way to the horizon. This, then, I must cross, I say to myself. I am ready. Cue, strike! Now I travel, slowly at first, then picking up speed. And as I travel, the playing field unrolls before me, yard by yard. It's like slow motion, my senses dim. I cross a past path for the first time—a train of thought has carved its course into the playing field, the future paths outline themselves before me on the baize. I flit beneath them as under bridges. The conceptions of the twelfth, twentieth, thirtieth shots lie clear before my eyes. But then, suddenly: a crack, as though the balls were breaking in half. The swoon of the brain. Stasis. Imagination and memory no longer obey your will. Why?'—'Because you're on the Way Back!' cried De Selby. He half-straightened up, drew his legs up on the bench, and lay down on it with bent knees. I glanced at him. Had he been following everything? He lay there open-eyed, gazing at the ceiling.—'That's De Selby's consolation,' And Vice Versa said, and as though to fulfil my expectations, it sounded as though he'd said 'the selfish consolation'. I looked over at him again, but he didn't stir. 'The consolation of the emotionalist is that here even the keenest calculations lose focus and break down. But why?' Apparently De Selby's explanation didn't rate a mention from him. 'After all, I always proceed the same way,' he went on. 'With each shot I winnow out the three optimal possibilities. In so doing I brace myself as best I can against the numerical flood of possible combinations that surges up from behind. I utilize the pendulum effect—like a connector I rush from the outermost outposts of the numerical series back to the roots extracted from them. From the second numerical series to the second node, onward to the third series, back to the second node, from the seventh node to the twenty-ninth series. "The dog returns to its vomit,"[20] as they say, so I return. And then it happens—a cogwheel breaks, the spring jumps back to its resting position, something inside me whimpers and lies down. The swoon of the brain. The Way Back.—Has the gap between the number of my nodes and the actual possibilities grown too large? Is the number system breaking asunder?—I see its insides. Twenty-nine is a prime number, and prime numbers are difficult—perhaps that's it?'

'No matter,' And Vice Versa went on. 'In the attempt to stop the numbers' proliferation, my capacity for projection collapses. And then I stand before this table's green abyss, and the web of the balls' paths on the surface, as clear just now as a web of sewing patterns, easily legible to any tailor's apprentice, begins as it were to sag and unravel. Now the balls are no longer moving on a plane, they're hurtling through the depths of my perceptual space. An echo follows in their wake, a whistling escapes my right ear, I'm standing where dimensions intersect. A feedback effect, then. *At this point I must break off and close my eyes.* I look up. The balls lie there as though nothing had happened—dead eyes, the green surface winking at me.' And Vice Versa spoke in extreme agitation, turning and pressing the cue between his hands as though to wring it out. 'If only my brain,' he choked out, in the cadence of a prayer, 'if only my brain could perform this one last leap—I'd set aside the balls for ever, or invent a new game.—And my brain is *grinding away* at a new cue!' he said, accompanying this with the vulgar gesture I knew from Zerdahel. 'It's brooding over a cue that could do everything I need. Is that the whistling sound in my ear?—What will the Vice Versa bird say when he sees his egg?' he said laughing, and with these words all the tension seemed to leave his head and flow into the ground. With light steps he went to the wall and leant his queue against it almost tenderly. He brushed the chalk dust from his hands and clothes. He took his raincoat from the coat hook and flung it over his shoulder. 'Off to new shores, Hans!' he cried. He meant me.

Parting

I looked at my watch. It was eight on the dot. A new day had begun. A light rain fell. And Vice Versa took a large bunch of keys from his coat pocket and unlocked the door of the shop. I waited outside with my wheelbarrow while he set up crates of vegetables and lettuce, already slightly wilted, in front of the shop. 'Just look at that!' he cried, pointing at the sky. 'A splendid shower! That'll make for nice fresh vegetables. Inga, the rainmaker!'—Over his suit he donned a green smock with the emblem of a supermarket chain and put on a dusty, plate-sized beret. 'Here, catch!' he said and tossed me a blue cap, the uniform cap of the postal clerk. It was my uncle's cap. A greasy sweatband, a broken post horn in front. A dead man had lived in it. I sniffed it and removed a long, black hair. Was that how the dead smelt?—When I was fifteen my grandmother had died, and under a relative's supervision I'd had to kiss her lips. How had that tasted? I'd always believed that the bereaved had to eat of their dead. The flesh of the dead—it smelt and tasted like raw chicken meat. Once I had tasted my urine. 'The brain belches,' say the Bieresch. They have an explanation for everything. I was the dead man's pale shadow. 'Uncle is dead!' my older sister had cried, bursting into the dining room. Everyone knew what that meant. Mother went pale and lowered the spoon full of soup to the tablecloth. White rings formed around my brother's eyes, gradually growing until all the blood had fled his face. In the kitchen my little sister howled in pain. In her fright she'd spilt a pot of boiling water over her hand. She came running into the room. I saw her hand, and before my eyes the reddened skin puckered into delicate, coarse-grained burn blisters. Now I screamed. Doors slammed, the drawer with the medicine bottles crashed to the floor. I stared at the forgotten soup spoon; it looked as though it were to blame for everything.—Then my suitcase was packed; my mother placed the folded clothes inside neatly, carrying in each piece like a dead child cradled in her arms. 'You won't need any of it,' she said each time she put something in the suitcase, as though she wanted to rid the world of it.—'They're robbing him of his future and me of my life,' I heard her moan hopelessly behind closed doors on the eve of my departure. I lay awake in bed, her words lashing me like electric shocks. At each sound I felt as though scissors were cutting blood vessels, tendons, nerves at random within me. I remembered a passage I'd once read in a book. *Every intellectual being has the duty*, it said, *to open a woman's belly to find out what's inside, and if he finds a child, you see, then there's been hanky panky going on.*[21] I stood up in the darkness, my head knocking back and forth with pain. I looked for a candle and pinched off a bit of wax to put in my ears. I went back to bed, made myself small, curled up, crawled away, lay there as though in an opened womb.—On the bus ride to Vienna, where I caught the train, I vomited onto my mothers lap. It was a whitish soup, the soup from the day before. The spoon was to blame. My mother sat without noticing a thing, absent-mindedly putting her arm round my shoulders. The people on the bus were outraged; we had to get out and flag down a passing car. When we arrived in Vienna, she refused to get out. 'They can't take my boy away from me,' she kept weeping. The driver wrapped her in a blanket, took me to the platform and put me on the train. He stood there waving until he could see me no longer. Then he must have gone back to the woman in the car, who was now his property.—That was yesterday.

A Legend

—And what do the Bieresch think about memory?

— 'The brain belches,' as the legend has it.

'*"One day, I am told" the Anochi relates,*' the legend says, '*"one Anochi Yglemech went to Anochi Tam (a short form of the name 'Strem', which means 'water that flows') and asked him, 'Tam, tell me, what day is it today?'—Tam replied truthfully, 'Why do you ask, Yglemech? You know it's Tuesday.'—'I thought so too,' Yglemech replied, 'but suddenly it dawned on me—look at the sky, Tam, look at your brow, your cheeks, your hands—it dawned on me: Today is Monday.'—'Oy,' Tam cried, 'it's forbidden to curse. But first, won't you sit down, Yglemech, brother?'—The other persisted, refusing his offer, 'Today is Tuesday, today is Monday. The two things are all one!' He could not sit again, he explained, until the ground had ceased burning beneath him.—'Do you see the fire, Tam, emeth (that is, "the truth")?' And he picked up a handful of sand by way of revelation. Indeed, at once it went up in flames.—The next day, I am told," says the Anochi, "Yglemech came back and said, 'It's doomed, Tam, I won't celebrate the next Sabbath. Look at the air, hear the humming of the sun. The time machine has broken asunder. Today is Monday too!'* [22] *To prove he could not stay, he scooped a handful of water from the well. At once it turned to blood and formed a crust on his hand.—A similar thing came to pass on Friday. 'The clocks have stopped, Tam!' Yglemech cried in greeting. 'Believe me, it's Monday.—I've learnt in a dream that we're lost and outcast. There are cracks in our air—you can fall out of time through them. There are things that should not be. We are the sons of Ishak (that is, "Isaac"), the mocker!'—In a dream, Yglemech reported, the Anochi Gikatilla had appeared and said to him, 'The corner of the world you live in is accursed. It is an obtuse corner, but the curses of the sharp angle rest upon it. For the circle you describe is round, but its arc is a straight line!'—'My eyes,' Yglemech cried, 'return to my vomit as the dogs do. We are the tops that wind themselves up as they spin. If we dipped candles, the sun would shine all day. If we wove shrouds, no one would ever die again. The balance wheel has broken, the clock hands show not the time but the place. This place is Monday. A crack echoes through its eternity.'"—At that,'* the legend tells us, *'Tam resorted to extreme measures and cried, "Try not to go forward, go backward, Yglemech, meth (that is, he is dead)!—And verily, he returned to his former state (as lifeless earth)."'*—'The brain belches,' says the legend, 'and memories force their way through. What was is; what is will be. Alas, poor us!'

Third Lengthy Conversation

'The lesser uncertainty relation,' And Vice Versa called over to me as I sat on a low workbench in the small back room, sorting the post that had arrived that day. There was nothing but junk mail and flyers labelled 'Current Resident'.—'They call it "the lesser uncertainty relation",' And Vice Versa said, 'and what they mean is the transition from one ego-state to another. In proof they cite our scriptures, which say: *Looking away from myself, I move closer to myself.* De Selby, who has sensations of this kind, compares them with shifting states of matter. "Something within you turns liquid when you see yourself," he says, and, "Look away from yourself, and you're solid again." I don't sense that as strongly, that is, in me nothing shifts. I am Inga, and Inga I remain. "It's like watching your hand in the glow of a fire," De Selby describes, "a callous grows, closing over it like a jungle canopy. Birds begin calling beneath it!" I have little use for such images. They contribute nothing, they only confuse things further.—For how can this social system even function if everyone has a different, secret name for himself? How does

Zerdahel picture that?—He calls me "And Vice Versa", well and good, but deep down inside I'm still Inga. I swing between yesterday and tomorrow—and vice versa,' he said, and laughed. He held nothing sacred, not even his own name. '"Let us have this one little unfreedom," says Zerdahel,' And Vice Versa continued. '"Let us be foolish and happy at least by this little fire!" He thinks he can ridicule me. He mocks what we rightly call the "Histrionic Lie". He has no sense of honour.—And yet we accept the fundamental system of the Bieresch that's woven around the legend of the names. More than that—the Bieresch precept that *iron bones containing the finest marrow are cracked only when all the teeth of all the dogs bite together*[23] is sacred to us. It is our creed, one we wish to shout in the faces of all the Anochis and Zerdahels who ever lived. For it's enough to hear the name of that fine organization Zerdahel's cobbled together.—"Free Sons of the Bieresch"—what does he mean, "free"? No Bieresch is free, and it's a scoundrel who gives more than he has. On the shortcuts you meet the lazy ones, and Zerdahel is taking a shortcut. With his claim that we are our own ancestors, that we don't need to know ourselves and can simply leave our naming to the others, he releases the individual from his obligation to seek his place within the system. *"He seeks not, he is found,"* he cites, bastardizing the scriptures. And with a sigh of relief everyone takes this apocryphal path. Just think of De Selby, how tormented he is. We owe all this to Zerdahel's heresies!—We Monotomoi,'[24] And Vice Versa said with sudden pathos, as though before an assembly, 'We Monotomoi profess the two great precepts of the Bieresch, the dog's return to its vomit and the collective cracking of the bone. Like all rational people, we welcome the fact that for us there's no progress, that we can't spin the top of history without it spinning us in turn, that our small community's structure and its relations of production have not changed in the course of the centuries, that everything we do not only reflects us but also reproduces us, so that the semblance of our collective life is clearly limned in our works, that we breed work and it us, and that it will beget children upon us who will become what we once were. Because we are surrounded by *things that stare at us, always from the same angles*, as the poet says, because we regard this immortalization of ourselves in work, and this resurrection of our qualities, relations and relational variations from work, to be the only opportunity for knowledge, we welcome what the chess player, in that famous image, calls "the stalemate of the Bieresch". *Enlightenment*, the fable instructs us, *comes even to the greatest fool*![25]—We are not the *people made dumber by harm*,[26] as is claimed of us. And it is the historic certainty of the Monotomoi that we who for centuries have tossed and turned, racked by pain, in the Procrustean bed of history, will reap knowledge of our error in reward for our torments.—How but as challenge and consolation are we to understand the incontestable apodeixis of the scriptures that the eyes are like the dogs and, in murderous nostalgia, are unable to turn from life and its abominations? But we emphatically reject the Histrionic Lie that would make us credulous, that would lull us to sleep by preaching that we *are* our own fathers: I, "And Vice Versa", you, "Walks Between Two Windows", highwaymen of history, in other words, pouncing greedily on passing physical husks and usurping them.—I'm not an Ashkenazi like Zerdahel, who *steps on the face of God*[27] and *lets the wheel fall before the cross*![28] I am not "And Vice Versa"—do you hear? I am Inga!'

A Postcard of Stonehenge

I had hardly been listening. His orator's pose—I could picture him sitting out there on his flour sacks, legs crossed, accompanying his thunderous words with frowns and clenched fists—repelled me. Zerdahel didn't strain so much for effect, though his speeches might at times have sounded more confused.—I went back to my work. In the heap of circulars before me lay a postcard. It was hand-coloured and showed shaggy Neanderthals performing a grotesque dance at the Celtic sanctuary of Stonehenge in southern England. In this depiction, the outer and inner stone rings, both in ruins today, were still fully intact. I turned the card over, curious to see who here was getting post. The address was written in clumsy, childish letters and in English. 'To the Great Bear of Zick,' it said. That was all. The message was in English as well: *Replacement part being rushed with all possible speed.*[29] Beneath it was a drawing of two fingers spread in a V—the victory sign? 'Life is a thread,' they say here, 'always running through the same old convolutions, the same old unravellings'—who then could think of victory? Who was 'Great Bear'? The name evoked a Wild West novel. Who could the sender be?—Viktor? Veronika? Vilma?—I felt homesick for my former world, where things hadn't been so difficult. Here everything seemed so wilfully artificial. People didn't act like people with their own personal desires and urges. It was as though they'd shed these things thousands of years ago. Nothing simply *was*, everything had meaning.—But wasn't it part of life that at least sometimes you were simply there, alive and ignored—as an implement, a natural phenomenon, a punctuation mark? Couldn't you even breathe without being eyed, packaged, labelled? Who was I: 'Great Bear' or 'Walks Between Two Windows' or 'Laughs Without Reason'? Could I keep up my resistance in the long run? If not—what means would I develop to deal with these problems? Numbers? Balls? Names?—All was null and void.—'Replacement part being rushed with all possible speed'—this simple phrase seemed able to solve more things than all the speculations of the Bieresch put together.—'I asked you a question,' And Vice Versa suddenly said very loudly beside me. I gave a start. He was standing in the door. 'What are you doing there?—Reading other people's post?' He took the card out of my hand. 'Oh, for Urs,' he said casually and slipped it into the pocket of his smock.

'Zerdahel, then,' said And Vice Versa, leaning on the door frame, 'holds that the community of the Bieresch has remained unchanged since its beginnings. As proof he cites the large number of writings providing a detailed and historically accurate picture of the Biereschek, accounts that indeed are as fresh as though written today. We recognize our life in every single one—any one of us could have written them, even if they're a thousand years old. This leads Zerdahel to conclude that not only the working conditions, customs and social circumstances have stayed the same, the people have as well. He sees not only the predispositions and character traits as the constants that reproduce themselves through work. The individual itself—a combination of these qualities never to be repeated, unique, unambiguous, and impossible to misconstrue—does too. Our social system, as he rightly says, is frozen within our work, and not only have we swallowed up our products, it is a two-way channel—our products swallow us up as well. I agree with him there, too, and I do so even when he claims that each new individual is a sign meant to help us understand ourselves in a new, old way, and that, accordingly, each death withdraws from the game a piece of information that has become superfluous, has gone unused. And I also believe it's quite right that our children should die by the hundreds long before they've found themselves, though the next hospital is only five miles away. Our society is a self-regulating process—I say process and not cycle!—and each superfluous child would create a redundancy of information, adding one more torment to our martyrdom. "The only good child is a dead child!" says the cynic, and he's right about that.—But I don't believe that our fate is inescapable. If I did, I'd have to give up on everything. After all, over the course of our history we've taken the subtlest sophistries to their extremes! If even a single generation of Bieresch had repeated itself and yet failed to solve this riddle, I would regard it as eternally unsolvable!—So I say to Zerdahel, "How can your system be right when the first thing to come to mind when I think of myself is the name Inga? How could De Selby's ablakok sensations come about?"—And what does Zerdahel reply? Zerdahel says, "It's the lesser uncertainty relation! The names are like the relief at the entrance to the dance hall—if you're too far away, it dissolves, if you stand too close, it swallows you. But you're a Bieresch, because you see it, and only a Bieresch can do that!"—I say, "You and your uncertainty relation! Assuming I was in fact And Vice Versa, and you're so proud of your hand-carved evidence—who would benefit? Who could manage to write down this cursed story when everyone's sitting around thinking of someone else? You thinking of 'And Vice Versa', I thinking of Inga."—And Zerdahel says, "It's the fault of the spurious etymologies. Ruins of meaning gape at us from inside the language. The lesser uncertainty relation: you're And Vice Versa, but once you begin to think of yourself, your shape turns uncertain, you blur, you're swallowed, become Inga."—"I don't blur," I say. "If I do turn uncertain, the only reason is that everyone calls me And Vice Versa when in fact I am Inga. When I think of myself, as you put it, I'm thinking with you, so to speak. My initial response to my thoughts is, in keeping with my nature, Inga. Only then do I turn uncertain!"—"The system is reversible," says Zerdahel. "Think of And Vice Versa first, if you like, what do you think will come out in the end?"—I say, "Inga!"—Zerdahel says, "Of course. But the rest of us aren't to blame, what's to blame is the fact that the names haven't come down in their original forms, that from the many fantasies woven about them two extremes have evolved and ossified into antitheses."—"That's the bad thing about you," I say in the end, "that you mix truth and lies and ultimately the web becomes impenetrable."—"There you have it," says Zerdahel (he always has to have the last word), "And Vice Versa has talked just like that for the past three thousand years!"—The circle is complete. But we aren't reborn. I know it. Let's assume there've been a thousand generations of Bieresch and all of them were reissues of the first three or four—even a random number generator has its limits. At least one single time in our long history it should have been possible to complete the puzzle! The mutational leap should have happened. Long ago someone should have jumped up to avow, 'Yes, I really am "Fool's Silver on the Way from Him"!' Then the puzzle would have completed itself, and we'd no longer sit around, evening after evening, on these ugly, hard, uncomfortable pub chairs, racking our brains over riddles.—But we do, precisely because I'm not And Vice Versa, precisely because I am Inga. I am."—"And Vice Versa has been saying that for the past three thousand years," says Zerdahel.'

Peach-Pit Carving

As he spoke, I stacked and bundled the batches of circulars to deliver. And Vice Versa took a packet of flyers from a low, hand-turned whatnot and put it on the workbench in front of me. They were the flyers he used to advertise his business, bearing a nonsensical slogan: 'To eat, use the fingers, to shop, *come to . . .* ' Below that stood the words Esch McForditott. I asked him what that name was supposed to mean. He replied that it was a parody of his name, meant to annoy Zerdahel. And Vice Versa was 'és megforditott' in Hungarian. I shook my head. Senseless, inscrutable games were being played here.—I looked around. My work here was done for the day. Now the bundles had to be loaded into the wheelbarrow and delivered. Just as I was getting up to leave, my eye was caught by a vice attached to the far end of the workbench. It held in its jaws a meticulously polished peach pit, into which the unclear contours of a head were carved. I went around the table to take a closer look at the work. Blurred, as though under water, my deceased uncle's face gazed up at me. 'It's the locket for your aunt,' And Vice Versa said, 'go ahead and take it out.' I loosened the vice and extracted it with my thumb and forefinger. 'It's your uncle.—That's the custom here,' he said unconcernedly. 'When it's finished, you can open it and there'll be a photo of you inside. Do you like it?' I shook my head again. I couldn't say a word.—So even he, who grandly proclaimed with every sentence how far he had come from the superstitions of the Bieresch, was completely captive to them. And he didn't even notice!—'I have to do it,' he said, 'that's how I make my living.' I looked at him. He shifted uneasily. 'I know,' he said as though in apology, 'it's a superstition, but do you think those measly groceries out there could keep my head above water?—And if I did stop, who would shop here any more? Besides, I do it better than anyone!' He said it defiantly, like a child. Then he paused. Once again, I felt the wretched sense of inescapability De Selby had given me. 'And who do you think is going to carve the new hands for your wheelbarrow?—If your aunt finds out . . . !' And Vice Versa was triumphant. He'd got himself in hand again.—'Then you must have done the relief for the dance hall entrance, too?' I asked. I was prepared for anything.—'Hardly,' And Vice Versa said light-heartedly, 'that's a hundred and twenty years old!—And besides, you're starting to talk like Zerdahel!' And Vice Versa sat on the workbench, turning towards me. His long legs nearly touched the ground. 'Historically speaking,' he explained, 'peach-pit carving has nothing whatsoever to do with the Histrions. It's a custom of the Monotomoi.—Incidentally, do you know how the Vulgata begins?'

The Vulgata

He went to the whatnot and pulled a tattered paperback out from under the heaps of flyers. 'Here, read this!' he said, handing it to me. From its looks, it came from a lending library. The cover and spine were missing; on the first page, in great Gothic flourishes, stood 'The Vulgata', and beneath it and beside it the previous owners had apparently written their names on the yellowed paper. Some of them appeared several times, yet all but Inga's had been crossed out again. I turned the first page; the paper was pleasantly rough. I read the heading: 'Section One'. Beneath it stood in smaller letters: 'Brief Summary of the Creation Story / The First Six Days / GOD Creates the World and Mankind / The Monotomoi / The First Day.' I began to read.

'It was a leap day. GOD sat at his workbench, yodelling. HE had learnt it from the turkeys stalking through the tall grass around him.—Of all the things and animals HE had so far created, HE loved the turkeys the best. But most of all GOD, the Father of the Universe, loved his larynx. And as HE had no one HE could have spoken to, and since even the turkeys merely gobbled excitedly when HE addressed them, HE took out his larynx, Adam's apple and all, and looked at it under the magnifying glass. And GOD was content. HE cut up the larynx and put it back together again. But HE forgot the Adam's apple, lying on the workbench beside HIM. When HE saw what HE had forgotten, HE took HIS Adam's apple and held it up to the light. It looked like a peach pit. GOD spat to the side, took a penknife from HIS trouser pocket and got to work. A portrait emerged beneath HIS busy fingers, resembling HIM in many ways . . . '

Disgusted, I snapped the book shut and handed it back to And Vice Versa.—'See,' he said reproachfully. 'I told you it has nothing to do with the Histrions. Quite the opposite—they've banned and burnt this book for centuries. Mainly because of the first two sentences.—Though it's them I find so appealing. They exude a cosy serenity: "God sat at his workbench, yodelling,"' And Vice Versa quoted. 'It sounds like the chiming of bells.—If you like, I'll lend it to you.' I gave him a look. He understood. 'Too bad,' he said. 'The writing is quite engaging, and it's an excellent introduction.—So I suppose even now you can't bring yourself to join us?' I didn't know what he meant.—Then I understood. 'There's a membership application,' And Vice Versa said unperturbed. 'I'll give it to you just in case. You don't need to commit yourself yet. Think everything over at your leisure and decide as you see fit.'

The Selfish

Those, then, were the 'new shores' we were heading for.—When he laid the slip on the workbench in front of me, I wanted to tear it up before his eyes. I felt besmirched, betrayed, deceived. A gigantic hand, inescapable, reached for my head and pushed it under water. I struggled for breath. Slowly, as the hand and the water bore down for centuries, gills, as it were, unfurled from my throat and strained in a scream. It sounded like the squeak of a rat. I had to talk to someone. Right now. Outside, at the door, De Selby might have been waiting for hours in the rain. I would tell him everything. How helpless we'd been, at the mercy of this cynicism's subtle machinery. But that would change now. I stood up.—And Vice Versa reached gently for my arm and thrust me back into the chair. He began to speak again, binding me with new secrets.

'There's one more thing you must know,' he said, as he saw that I submitted unresistingly. 'Over the centuries we Monotomoi have suffered much injustice. For instance, various people, especially Zerdahel, have called us the true masterminds of the redistribution of goods. This charge—however easy to refute by logical means, since our concept of constant qualities crystallizing into unique clumps of personality is incompatible with notions of ownership and possessions, while Zerdahel's apocryphal notion of the rebirth of the Bieresch would be compatible indeed with the graspingness of the rapacious godfathers, as you'll soon see—this charge, now, has lodged itself in the brains of the Bieresch, those who have a brain, as an ineradicable prejudice against us. And yet it doubtless arises solely from the fact that our movement has existed since times immemorial, that without interruption there have always been Monotomoi, forced to stand by and watch as houses were plundered, possessions destroyed, the indivisible divided, the sacred defiled. We are the Esau of this story, cheated of his birthright. Endowed with the right of primogeniture, we've had to stand by as generations of treacherous brothers robbed us of hearth and home before our very eyes and gambled away our fathers' blessings. *Your hand is hairy, but your voice sounds high like your brother's* [30]—thus begins the first verse of one of our folk songs. And so we are taken for someone else! How could we not be!—Isaac himself was nearly sacrificed on the altar of Abraham's stupidity! What do you think he said to his father when he realized it? He said, "*Father, when you have burnt me as an offering, take the ashes that are left of me, bring them to my mother Sarah and say to her: This is the smell of Isaac!*" [31] Isaac means "the mocker",' And Vice Versa said.—'For centuries, without cease, we've been persecuted, taunted and trodden underfoot. Zerdahel can brashly profess the degrading doctrine of rebirth, that apologia for human misery—we reap the rebukes.—For this reason, and no other, I have compiled and organized all the evidence to present at our next gathering. Now the pendulum will swing the other way for once, I promise you! I've spent hours refining the phrasing of all the thoughts, conceptions and insights that have shaped our mindset over the centuries. I can now refute, point by point, every single charge ever made against our movement. And this here is my witness!' And Vice Versa laid two fingers in an oath on the Vulgata. 'De Selby, for one, will help me in his own way,' he said hoarsely. Now I had heard it quite clearly: And Vice Versa had definitely said 'the selfish one' instead of the proper name. It had sounded strained and distorted, but there had been no mistaking it. Was it the symptom of an illness that he had to count compulsively, compulsively distort names? And Vice Versa took his handkerchief back out and blew his nose. Somewhere inside the house a kettle whistled, immediately followed, in a slightly lower register, by the village siren. It was twelve o'clock. The noon train I'd taken yesterday would arrive in the station now. I listened. The rain streamed down the windowpane. Somewhere, far away, a dog yowled. Then steps were heard outside, an object tumbled to the floor, someone wiped his shoes on the doormat. The front doorbell rang briefly, the door opened, the noise of the rain grew louder. It sounded like a bored audience, listlessly clapping. Then De Selby stood in the doorway, drenched. Tears ran down his cheeks. 'What happened?' And Vice Versa asked. 'They killed my dog,' said De Selby, racked by sobs, 'They ran him over with their train, the bastards!'

FIVE

At the Knackerman's

The way to the knackerman who would bury De Selby's dog was long and arduous, though the road descended smoothly and the wheelbarrow rolled on ahead as though untethered from me. But this time I knew the pitfalls of these roads, it was all the same as yesterday—and so I easily dodged the potholes, now brimful of water following the rain.—I had volunteered to load De Selby's dog, a cross between an Alsatian and a St Bernard, into the wheelbarrow and take it along, if a blanket were thrown over it and I could put the post to be delivered on top. If it hadn't all fit into the wheelbarrow, I could easily have stowed some in the small rucksack my uncle had always used when there was a large amount of post. De Selby declined my offer, however; though it was covered with blood, he picked up the dog's corpse which he'd thrown down by the doormat outside Inga's shop. The body sagged like a heavy sack in the sexton's arms.

The world was licked clean of moisture. It was hot, and a strange hum filled the air, its origin impossible to pinpoint. At times it seemed so close that you turned involuntarily and, seeing nothing, thought the noise came from yourself.—The industrious hands are at rest, says the legend. Nothing stirs, the air is as smooth as a mirror. Elsewhere, perhaps, a crime is in progress—all things are so nameless, so nerveless. 'What is my name?' you ask. And the answer is this humming, this rushing. It is the rustle made by the world's hair as it turns over in its giant bed.—I didn't want to be the first to speak, and De Selby was silent. There was only the wheelbarrow, digging its softly crunching way through gravel and coarse sand. And so we dozed, more asleep than awake, between the white houses of the Bieresch, which—they, too, concerned only with themselves and their own affairs—lay scattered amid often-stunted fruit trees. Their fronts gleamed forbiddingly, the wooden doors were shut. The reed-thatched, mud-plastered granaries looked like exotic sepulchres. The distance between the scattered, largish farmhouses and their outbuildings was uneconomical and exhaustingly long, and our gravel road led in-between as though utterly unconnected.—Sometimes one of the houses showed us its backside, as though at loggerheads with the others. Everywhere the turkeys gobbled softly, the sacred beasts of the Monotomoi. It was a world bewitched, but already it seemed I half-belonged to it.

The first house we stopped at was a small, white-washed hut; its door agape, like that of a gypsy dwelling, it seemed to consist of a single small room.—In front of it a half-dressed man waited in the sun, wearing baggy blue work trousers with an open fly and, otherwise motionless, snapping the suspenders now and then against his bare torso. He smoked a cigar, at intervals raising it to his lips in a sweeping gesture, as though to wipe them.

The house stood close to the road on a low hill through which our path cut like a ditch. Next to the house stood a pile of stacked-up boards with a light, high-wheeled motorcycle leant against it.—The man, the second godfather, I realized as I drew near, propped his left hand against the house and watched us approach, now and then turning his head casually to the side as though to keep someone in the house appraised of the goings-on outside. A small portable radio in his pocket emitted the squashed sounds of folk-dance music, light, quick tones like tossed-out words that no one takes seriously.—Today, without a cap on, the godfather seemed greatly altered. His head was shaved smooth, and his deep-set eyes, with their marked squint, roamed steady and sluggish, never seeming to rest on any one thing in particular. This and the rest of his appearance—the small, bulging button nose, the open trousers and the steep hump—was somehow flagrantly brutal.

I parked my wheelbarrow on the side of the road and took out the circulars for this address to deliver them to the godfather. Ignoring my outstretched hand with the post, he fiddled with the radio in his right-hand trouser pocket to turn down the volume. There were a few bursts of static as he lost the station, followed by a steady buzz which he silenced with a smart blow. I stood to his left, as my aunt had recommended, and his eyes darted to and fro as though he were reading, searching the landscape for me line by line without finding me, perhaps since I stood too close. But then he did turn, briefly looked at me and past me and said: 'Throw this junk away!'—A voice came from inside the house. 'Leave him alone!' a woman yelled. A moment later she appeared in the door and asked me for the advertising flyers as though to apologize for the godfather's insult. I knew her as well—she was the fourth godfather's wife, who'd been sitting at the next table with the others last night, making the plaintive music with her forefinger on the wine-glass rim.—The sleeves of her blouse were rolled up, her arms fat and fleshy, with pale erect hairs. I gave her the post, and with a gesture of finality, as though now I'd seen enough, she let down the sleeves of her blouse and closed the uppermost, open button. She seemed both sturdy and cowed, her shoulders sunken forward like an old woman's, her steps determined as those of a drinker, yet hesitant and uncertain. She went back inside her house, followed by the second godfather, whose movements, in contrast to hers, were sneakily quick and measured. 'Had-kal', 'sharp and swift', might be the first godfather's future name, Zerdahel had said. The name suited this man better, who now turned once more before vanishing into the gloom of the house behind the woman, and said to De Selby, intentionally drawing out his words to wound him, 'A real dog day, isn't it?'—He underlined his taunt with a provocative jerk of his head, turning up the music on his pocket radio in accompaniment.—'It was you! You killed him!' the sexton cried, beside himself. 'You're a murderer, yes you are!' And like the public prosecutor in person, he lifted up the dog's corpse to show it around.—Was he beginning to understand?—The very way he yelled was proof he hadn't grasped a thing. His pathos was ludicrous at a moment when the other man had openly admitted everything and now abandoned him again to his own absurdity by going back into his house without a word, merely shrugging his shoulders and hump.

I stood there indecisively: inside Rák's wife was talking to the second godfather in an excited whisper; outside De Selby sobbed uncontrollably, his face buried in the dog's fur. It was both pitiable and repellent.—Then the woman's whisper rose to a wail.—'My God,' she cried, 'they'll bring us misfortune!' The godfather snarled at her roughly—for a moment there was silence, and then it started up again, her voice climbing an ever-ascending scale of misery until at last it cracked. 'I told you to leave them alone,' she cried, as though now all were over and done with. The response was a blow, resounding like a slap and somehow liberating. But like someone who knows he's in the right, a right he'll never cede now, she began again, escalating until her voice, up high, jarred and jangled the nerves. The godfather mimicked her menacingly, but though I couldn't understand what he said, I sensed the great fear of an irreparable mistake that was about to happen, or had happened just now. Plates clattered—'So dishes were being washed,' I thought, gnashing my teeth, yet approving.—'Stop!

Stop!' the godmother cried, now in extremis.—'I will not!' the furious godfather defied her. And as though to destroy fate with his words, which he thrust out one by one, seeming to drive the woman across the room with them, he pounded his fist on the tabletop. Glasses clashed together, something—the radio?—a broom fell to the ground. Its stick jutted halfway out the open door. Water hissed across a hot stovetop, endlessly, it seemed. 'Let me go!' the woman shrieked, and her breath wheezed out of her as though she'd held it far too long. Then she whimpered, and the godfather laughed at her insolently, straight into her whimpering which slowly changed to quick, laboured breathing, then to a smacking noise.

I stood there helplessly, witness to this millennia-old misdeed. Bloodlust woke within me; these were postman's secrets I wanted no part of.—Where was De Selby? I looked around. He caught my gaze and understood at once.—The dog bounced in his arms like something hot he wanted to get rid of, though there was no place for it in this world. I turned on him—it was his fault.

And then, as though resurrected, the second godfather was standing in the door again. Now he wore nothing but dirty white undershorts that stretched ludicrously over his stiffly projecting member.—Something within me, a feather, a grain of dust, a scale broke lightly loose and floated off as I saw him standing there.—And the godfather held tight to his member through the undershorts, as though to keep from losing his erection. He yelled at us to get lost.

—A piece of yourself is torn out of you, say the scriptures of the Bieresch, because you've got too much, because you've taken too much. You won't be stitched up—but look! There wait the scissors. Lie down, lie down on the bed. I'll hold you tight—shut your eyes. He'll hold you tight—shut your mouth. A grave is dug in your body, the coffin inside must come out now!—

I ran down the hill to De Selby, a laughing, leaping thing, a ball bouncing off to the side. A movement without rhyme or reason. It was as though a question I myself knew nothing of were suddenly swallowed up by its answer.

Friendship

And De Selby understood me.—From underneath the dog he held out his hand without a word and I took it gratefully. 'All forgotten?' I asked. 'All forgiven,' he replied.

I picked up my wheelbarrow again and off we went.—'You and your dog!' I said. I'd been just about to kill him, yet now he walked beside me again with his small, quick, resilient steps.

The road fell off steeper and steeper, my vehicle made larger and larger leaps and, in a sort of childish bliss, I tromped down the slope alongside the sexton.—There was no such grave!—Old Biereschek sat with their chins on their hands, hands propped on the bulbous ends of their sticks, hair flying, on the narrow benches outside their huts, which cut like ship's keels into the blue sky above them. 'Travel weather,' said De Selby.—I'd been just about to kill him.

And thus a strange friendship formed between me and the sexton, in which one talked while the other was silent.—With each word I spoke this friendship seemed to dig its way down into me, and each silence that followed seemed to reinforce its channels. I shovelled out earth from within me and he trod down the ground underneath with his feet.—There was an accord between us as between 'How do you do?' and 'How do *you* do?' And gradually this sense seemed to communicate itself to everything around us:

Outside one of the houses an old man had set up a little table with a green plastic washbasin. On a nail, below eye level, an old, broken mirror hung on the wall. The man stood before it with legs apart, bare-chested, bent crookedly forward to see. His suspenders hung loose at his sides, swaying to and fro with his vigorous movements when he took short steps to find better footing or, to the same end, spread his legs wide. He was so immersed in his activity that without any greeting, not wanting to interrupt him at his work, I placed his letters on the narrow bench next to the towel and the soap dish. I did it without his noticing me and returned to De Selby as proud as though I'd pulled off a minor masterpiece.

A breeze rose, mingled with the boisterous chirping of the hidden crickets. I felt as though all things had sprouted hair I could run my fingers through, and it seemed as I walked that the earth perfectly matched the rhythm of my steps now, rising to meet me when I stepped down and dipping beneath me when I raised my foot.

Friendship's End

The further we left the village behind, the greater the distance between each hut and the road, yet the greater it grew, the easier it was to cover. Near one of the last clusters of houses—De Selby was expanding upon his theory of the one-way system and claiming that it could easily be applied to our capacity for knowledge—I spotted Zerdahel by a shed, working on a stepladder whose rungs he reinforced by driving in wooden wedges with a heavy hammer.—*'Living consciously is like remembering,'* [32] said the sexton as I took the post from the wheelbarrow. 'Two inclinations war within me amid each experience. On the one hand, I want to abandon myself to it, light and carefree, as to a Way There. On the other, I turn around after each step to regard the road travelled. That makes everything snarl up within me. From the travelled paths I seek to reconstruct the future. The paths of our lives have crossed once before, back when Oslip nearly killed himself.—Do you remember?' I looked up at him questioningly. 'It doesn't matter,' he said, 'the important thing is that we should never have met again, because we and our lives are tied together. I live, and you slap me in the face for it, that's how it is.—The only form of knowledge we could really use, and use in the long run, too, would be a constructive disintegration analysis, as And Vice Versa calls it—the counterpart to his billiards technique, that is, the ability to calculate our life paths such that they never cross again once the first intersection has brought misfortune.—And that's what he always means when he says that mentally he's begun carving a new, unprecedented kind of billiard cue.—I'll explain it to you later.'

His words came like a blow. Again I dimly remembered the incident at the weir when Oslip had injured himself so severely. Standing next to my aunt, I had anxiously reached for her hand when I noticed how the beam laid on the stone began slowly to shift to the side as it see-sawed, making the accident inevitable. And then another hand slipped into mine, and when I looked, it was the hand of a fat little boy who was watching the spectacle intently. I looked at him and squeezed his hand. He squeezed back without taking his eyes from the scene. So that had been the sexton.—Without speaking, we had formed a sort of alliance back then, and that must have been what he alluded to.—When I got back from Zerdahel, I'd ask him whether he, too, had had that premonition of misfortune, followed by the sense of total liberation that you always feel when a punishment meant for you strikes someone else who happens to be in the way.

Zerdahel, busy tackling his ladder with all sorts of tools, gave no sign that he had long since spotted us. When I reached him, he finally looked up and said, 'You're doing quite a good job already!' As he spoke he straightened up, searching for something in his pocket. 'Wait, here's something for you!' he said, taking a small, hexagonal coin from the pocket of his trousers. He gave it to me. It wasn't one of our coins. The edge was filed away, a hole was punched in the middle. It was worthless but I liked it anyway.

I felt indecisive. Something in what De Selby had just said made me hold back. Trying to shake this uncomfortable feeling, I remained standing where I was. 'Where did you get the coin from?' I asked Zerdahel. 'Oh, they're from Lumiere,' he said. 'We play checkers with them. Some have a hole, some don't.'—'Aha!' I said. There was a brief pause, as Zerdahel said nothing and I made no move. Zerdahel looked at me sidelong, curious and expectant. 'Don't you need to be going?' he asked at last, but I still had that uncomfortable feeling. I couldn't go back to De Selby like that. 'What are you doing there?' I asked without responding to his question. 'The rungs have come loose,' said Zerdahel in a dry voice. 'Aha!' I said again, idiotically. 'At least fetch him over,' said Zerdahel, suddenly impatient, 'that's just not done, chattering away and making other people wait for you!' And at once he himself called for De Selby and invited him to join us.—The sexton shook his head and stood down on the road where he was, holding the dog as though it had grown onto his arms. 'Now he's offended,' said Zerdahel, 'no wonder!'—'I never did anything to him!' I said.—'Oh?' said Zerdahel facetiously, 'You're just stretching your legs here, is that it?'—'Sometimes his weepiness gets on my nerves, that's all,' I lied.—'What you do is your affair,' Zerdahel retorted, now acerbic, and turned back to his work. I didn't know what to do, but now I was even more reluctant to be alone with the sexton. So I called half-heartedly, 'Come on over, De Selby, don't be like that!'

But De Selby stood next to the wheelbarrow without budging.—'By the way, whatever became of Oslip?' I asked Zerdahel, more to break the uncomfortable silence than from genuine interest. 'Oh, leave me alone with your silly questions!' Zerdahel shot back. De Selby was still standing down on the road looking up at us, reproachfully, it seemed. 'Go on ahead!' I called to him, 'I'll be there shortly!' Again Zerdahel looked at me sidelong. 'What a liar you are!' he said, shaking his head, and the sexton must have felt something of the same, for now he cried, livid with pain, 'It's over between us, I tell you!' Then he shook himself and headed off. I stood there, somehow completely alone now. De Selby walked away down the road, Zerdahel hammered like mad at his ladder. 'Just as long as you leave the children in peace!' my aunt had warned me the night before as we lay down side by side in the enormous matrimonial bed of decoratively carved light wood. The words went through my head from the beginning, afresh, over and over again.—I walked slowly back to the wheelbarrow.

A thought was starting to form in my mind, I felt it but I didn't know yet what it wanted from me. 'Just as long as you leave the children in peace!'—I hadn't asked my aunt the meaning of this command and she seemed content to leave it at that. Somehow it had to do with how De Selby was acting.

In My Aunt's Bed

We had lain side by side in the marriage beds, arms folded under our heads. No one had spoken. Then she withdrew one arm from beneath her head and invited me in a gentle voice to come to her side of the bed.—I crawled over to her awkwardly and lay uneasy beneath the heavy blanket that barely warmed. And then she merely wrapped her arm round my chest and, snuffling a bit, went straight to sleep.

The dust in the bedroom, unaired for who knows how long, clogged my nose. The moon hung bright and deep in the opened window. Piercingly cold air, straining the skin to the splitting point, poured ceaselessly in from outside. The unaccustomed proximity to a woman I hardly knew, and disliked for her imperious manner, kept me from sleeping.—I thought of the night before. I recalled that book I'd once read in a single night, as though in anger at my mother. 'It's not true!' I said aloud. Behind me, my aunt stirred. How could she sleep? Wasn't she the least bit afraid?—I thought of Zerdahel and asked myself whether his drunkenness has been mere show. At certain points I'd had the impression he was lying.—I pictured his face, beginning with the long, curved nose, the small pursed mouth. He had a mole that bulged like a horn, seeming sewed between his eyebrows like a little round button. Was that the face of a liar? I didn't know.—And so I lay awake, while my aunt snored softly behind me, sometimes snuffling like a dog in her dreams.—When would the godfathers come? How late was it, anyway? One? Three? A little chime, seeming mounted just above my ear, gave the answer. It was half past one. Nothing stirred. So they wouldn't come. I gloated.—Just after half past three, when it was bright as day again, I fell asleep open-eyed.

—But in the morning six chairs were missing, a round table, a chest of drawers and my umbrella, which my aunt had hidden beneath the stairs. The contents of the chest of drawers—mainly photos, but also an old, cracked leather satchel and my uncle's rusty Wehrmacht pistol—had been dumped onto the floor. The kitchen scales had vanished, along with the top section of a white-painted credenza and a large, mended preserving pot. They must have been here twice—and I hadn't heard a thing!

Most of all we missed the table. It was there that my aunt had called me over to receive the last of her instructions just after all the guests had gone and we had straightened up the dance hall again.—From now on, my aunt noted this morning as we took our breakfast standing at the broad windowsill in the bare kitchen, we'd have to make do with the planks and sawhorses that had been set up in the hall last night for the godfathers.

'The Stalemate of the Bieresch'

'Come over here, Hans,' my aunt had begun the night before, pulling over a chair so that I sat across from her, our knees nearly bumping. 'It's time I told you something very important.'—Her voice was deep and raw, and something in her demeanour suggested that what was coming would be extremely unpleasant. She seemed to read my mind again, hastily adding: 'No fear, it's nothing for you to worry about!'—'Yes, aunt,' I said.—'Zerdahel,' she began, 'told you many things today that will be very, very crucial for you, but, as you can imagine, he's hardly told you everything. He knows the names quite well indeed, no one keeps them straight like he does, but he probably didn't say a word about the Monotomoi—And Vice Versa will tell you about that tomorrow—and you probably don't know anything about the mirrors. That's Jel Idézö's task, and I'll have to tell you a bit about them myself.' I nodded mutely, bewildered that my aunt was so familiar with the details of Zerdahel's speech, and that she so openly admitted something I hadn't yet guessed—that I was to be passed around from one person to the next like a child receiving lesson after lesson until he can be of use at last. 'You see,' my aunt began again, 'much of what you heard from the Jew today, and what I'm going to tell you now, will seem confused and unclear at first, for as we say, your eyes are still asleep. But soon you'll know the ropes better, and you'll stop hating us with such a vengeance.—You do hate us, Hans!' my aunt said reproachfully. I shook my head but it was true. More than once that evening, hatred, unaccustomed and vile as nausea, had risen within me.—'Look, Hans,' my aunt said, troubled, 'you must try to understand us, too. What on earth should we do? The curse has been upon us since the very first day! Each line, each word in our scriptures curses the Bieresch.—There's homesickness only at home, we say, because we can't go away from here, because we're cooped up for ever in the labyrinth of our hapless Bieresch history. We're homesick for ourselves, because no one can be as he is—everyone only mirrors the nature of his surroundings.—Our society has been compared with a honeycomb, and there's some truth to that. "Remove a single cell," says Zerdahel, "and you destroy the whole artful construction!"—Out where you come from, if someone asks himself who he is, he gets the answer he deserves, though it may not necessarily be flattering. You have more leeway. It's different here—we live closer together, historically speaking. The wall that forms your outer boundary, that's your neighbour's wall. Tear it down, and you're not out in the open, far from it—you're merely in the room next door.—There's a text on this in the scriptures. It's called: "He Who Asks Questions" or "Looking in the Mirror"—"*The change,*" it begins, "*in what did it consist? It is hard to say. Something slipped. There I was, warm and bright, smoking my tobacco-pipe, watching the warm bright wall, when suddenly somewhere some little thing slipped, some little tiny thing. Gliss—iss—iss—STOP! I trust I make myself clear."*[33]—There's no point in my reciting the whole text to you. But the upshot is that certain questions can never be asked because they would jeopardize the entire construction. Of course, it depends not on the questions but the questioner. And Vice Versa, for instance, may ask anything at all times. His questions are strictly harmless. Whereas some other persons can't be allowed to ask a single question, because their questions are so brutal that they destroy their own answers in advance. It's a delicate balance we're keeping here, and for that reason alone I must ask you not to do us an injustice. A single one of your mad, rash words can ruin us all—and you along with us, for after all you belong to us for a year. You're one of us, you always will be. Everyone realizes that all you can possibly want at the moment is to flee from here. But that's just how I feel, every single minute! That's just how Zerdahel and De Selby feel. And yet we all stay.—Maybe you can't understand that yet, but you, too, will fare much the same. For there's one thing that's quickly grasped, and you've long since grasped it, too, even if you don't know it yet—there is no hope. The clouds have closed over us Bieresch.—But there's one consolation—the life we live here has more humanity than any other life imaginable.—You're already a good bit more human than you were six hours ago. You're no longer so harsh and unrelenting!' My aunt leant forward on her chair and placed her hands on my shoulders, looked me squarely in the eyes and said, 'We're stuck fast in history. There's no going forward or back. There's no progress, there's no regress. No one can help us. So it is written, and it is true.—"*The mystery of your work,* one text states, *lies in the fact that it guiltlessly mirrors back that which you are guilty of!*"[34] Those are important words, though we may both find them hard to understand. At bottom they already contain what the Bulb calls "the stalemate of the Biereschek".—What does he mean by that?—I'm about to explain it to you,' my aunt said. 'Listen to the rest of the text first. It goes on to say, "*And so it produces you who have performed it.—Innately good, it turns evil because it allows that to become its nature which you pass off as your nature, yet which is nothing but your failure!*"—It might sound complicated, but it's the truth. In other words, put simply but not falsely, that means: what you do and how you do it, what we all do and how we do it, our works assimilate all that, it merges into them. It's like the feeling you have when someone gives you their hand and you sense that it's made you a different person.—And the Bulb, what does he say? The Bulb says that the handshake goes both ways. Surely you've noticed what an endless amount of work is hidden in the smallest and often homeliest things of ours—think of the handles of your wheelbarrow, take a closer look at And Vice Versa's billiard cue tomorrow! That shows that what the scriptures say is true. We put ourselves into things, we are a part of our work. And though sometimes we may seem to deal heedlessly with what our forebears have made, exactly the opposite is true. When you're delivering the post, pay close attention to how obliviously the Bieresch often sit holding a hand plane, a screw, how they stare at them. They hear the things speak. "He's hearing father's voice," as we call it. And suddenly the one who was sitting there engrossed leaps up, throws the thing away and runs off. "Father is angry," we say then.—"The reason why there's no progress for us," says the Bulb, "is that in contemplation of things, we ourselves become the things, and through them become their progenitors!" Life teaches us, step by step, to become our ancestors, and those who come after us will be as we were.—It is the moment when all people become brothers and sisters.—It is our good fortune.—Don't ask any questions yet, ask me afterwards!' my aunt interrupted herself as I shifted my chair to sit more comfortably.

'It's very hard then to grasp that such a thing as misfortune can even exist,' she went on. 'But there's no end of misfortune.—Because everything lies cheek by jowl in our minds, because it seems so obvious to us to link everything with everything else, because the feeling of brotherhood arouses the blasphemous desire for indivisible harmony!—"Work, then, is your mirror," the same text states further down, "and so you should break the mirror twice: once for its skewed image, and once again for its pallor!"—A contradiction? Not at all. But it has been interpreted that way. Minim and Malchim* have done so. The former proclaimed on the

* Meaning 'the apostates' and 'the denouncers of the scriptures'.

basis of these lines that salvation lies far behind us, that doom is inevitable, each sight of the evil world leads further into evil. They emphasize the first of the two parts. The latter concluded the opposite: all must be smashed to pieces, they believed, before the tiniest thing can be made better.—But nothing ever gets better, nothing ever gets worse—what was is, what is will be. History is an all-corrective injustice, the "stalemate of the Bieresch".—"Stays the Same" is quite a common name with us. It was supposed to be Oslip's. My Oslip!'—I pricked up my ears; the mention of this name seemed to bode no good, and indeed my aunt at once began to writhe on her chair as though in seizures. 'The difficult thing for everyone always was, and still is,' she said, and interrupted herself, 'Don't look at me like that!—The difficult thing is to see things and leave them as they are. How are you supposed to get a picture of life if you always plunge your hands right in?—To endure tensions that exist among all things is an art unto itself. And we Bieresch have taken it further than the others. "Your gaze is life's magnet. It attracts all that lies within reach", we say, and having realized the danger, we've learnt to bend the two poles together.—Our guilt is of a different kind: "Bake bread from the grain of my words," the scriptures ironically advise.—Our guilt, the guilt of people like Zerdahel, was and remains that of mingling the sacred and the impure.' My aunt was now speaking incoherently and indistinctly. She tilted her head back and forth as she spoke, and it looked as though some uncontrollable inner force were causing this motion, a large, heavy metal ball released to roll back and forth in her head. 'Just picture it: in Zagersdorf, which was once called "tükörszabó" (that is, "the mirror cutter"), and in Trausdorf—it's really called Tricksdorf,' my aunt exclaimed, 'a cloak of lies has been cast over the names!—the Bieresch have built enormous mirror-manufacturing operations. That's despicable, vile!' My aunt spat out the words, and spittle flew with them. She spoke with as much fervour as though this injustice were happening now, between us. 'We've carried out forbidden experiments. We produced mirrors that performed the most blasphemous tricks you can imagine. We've found ways to make mirrors that never fade, that reflect the identical image, not the reversed one. There were mirrors that winked when you looked in them. Mirrors that were black by day and painted pictures in the brightest of colours by night!—Biereschek mirrors!—Mirrors that let the image all the way through, showing it only on the back side. We've made the pure texts into filthy lucre. And why?—We sought consolation for the brows we'd beaten bloody on the walls of the texts.—"The texts are mazes," says Gikatilla, "a shallow, shimmering stream at first, with calm water, a calm current. But beware! Never go astray in their punctuation's swaying reeds! Beware the snare of the comma! Endless passages lead from period to period. Each dash is thin ice—*and through its glass you see darkly*!"—Words are mirrors, and a sentence is a room made of mirrors.—To truly grasp the world, we'd need skulls as large as it is!—And how large is that skull—it's a joke!' My aunt had risen to her feet, running furiously up and down as she spoke, as though caged. Gradually she began to calm down again. 'I suppose And Vice Versa is right!' she said then. 'Let's go to bed.'

Jel Idézö

The memory of the previous evening was strong and clear as a waking dream as I tried to overtake De Selby who had hurried on ahead of me to the knackerman. I moved in this memory at my pleasure. It was as though a different kind of window had been flung open within me, and not only could I see everything through this window, I could also pull things towards me at will to look at them more closely.

Ahead of me in the distance, as I daydreamed, a small, black, dancing dot appeared, but I couldn't decide if it really was the sexton. Because I kept stopping at the houses of the Bieresch, which used up the time I'd gained en route, it was impossible for me to overtake him. And I called the sexton's name, as often and as loudly as I could, but the wind must have snatched away my cries, for even in the houses where they ought to have heard my voice, no one stirred. Finally I dismissed the dark blotch as a trick of the eyes.—When at last I reached Jel Idézö's house, which lay apart from the village in a small depression, I saw his, De Selby's, head vanish into the hollow before me.

So it had been he, and he must have heard my cries, but he'd walked on defiantly like a sulky child as though to punish me.

Jel Idezö was both knackerman* and gravedigger for the Bieresch of Zick. His damp, squalid hut lived up in every way to the average person's expectations and prejudices about his profession. It was a tiny shack built of roughly cut planks, the outside perfunctorily daubed with clay.—In the door, which opened outward for lack of space, stood the knackerman's wife, who had already asked De Selby into the house. Just behind her, in the shadows, stood the knackerman himself. She herself was short; he was a head shorter than she and, in contrast to her, utterly decrepit. A reddish bullet scar slanted across his brow, ending at the bridge of his nose.—'Come in, come in!' he said, grabbing my right hand with both his own and not letting go until he had led me into his parlour-bedroom, where De Selby was already sitting at a little dining table that folded out of the wall.

The gravedigger had long, thin but powerful arms that gave the effect of prostheses. One of Jel Idézö's hobbies was making incense sticks, and their cloying smell hung in the room. On the table lay De Selby's *corpus delicti*, the dead dog.—After just a few moments I could hardly breathe and looked around for a window to open. But the only aperture was a small, nearly

* As the Bieresch call the knacker.

square rectangle holding a fixed, framed glass pane. The glass was thick and corrugated, meant to admit light from outside while making it impossible to look out. I'd noticed these tiny window openings in And Vice Versa's shop as well. No doubt they were meant to thwart the daydreaming stirred by obsessive glances outside.—Sitting with my hands between my legs on an uncomfortable, stool-like wooden chair, I kept looking around the room, whose four walls were covered from the low ceiling to the floor with photographs which the knackerman had affixed with pins. Each was like a window onto sombre surroundings and a sombre past.—'We've already heard about your mishap,' Jel Idézö interrupted my thoughts, and I noted at once how skilfully he defined the negotiating parties from the outset with this one single sentence. He went on talking quickly, tongue tripping, voice cracking, as though pressed for time, constantly reaching for the objects on the table.—We had barely any space in the tiny room, and so the knackerman's wife sat on a low kitchen stool in the narrow corridor that led alongside the room to the front door. 'Close quarters here,' said Jel Idézö, 'but it'll do, it'll do!'

Fourth Lengthy Conversation

As we conversed—and the entire time hardly anyone spoke but the gravedigger, De Selby said nothing at all, and I merely put in the occasional question—every now and then he burrowed his short, claw-like fingers, whose movements, due perhaps to the smooth skin, seemed gentle and sure, into the dog's fur and fondled it. And each time the sexton saw these absent-minded movements, his eyes filled with tears. The first time the knackerman noticed it, he said quickly, as though to avoid losing business, 'We'll be glad to get you another one, sir! If you like.'—At that De Selby merely shook his head, and he, too, placed his hand on the animal to stroke it. For the rest of the conversation this hand lay in the same place, immobile as a dead thing.—'I'll bury him today,' the knackerman said by way of introduction, 'sunset is a good time'.

Then he turned to me and me alone, though never addressing me directly, and for the next two and a half hours he didn't take his eyes off me for a second. This came as no surprise, following my aunt's explanations—he was simply a teacher performing his task with particular care—but this only increased my resistance against everything he said.

The knackerman launched on an excursus, first explaining that at one time the people of this region had erected special wooden scaffolds for dead domestic animals, resembling hunting stands. Human corpses, on the other hand, were buried in the ground, sitting or standing in specially constructed subterranean clay recesses equipped with a soul hole like a chimney that tapered towards an opening at the top. It bothered me that he spoke so blithely of ancient funerary rites in De Selby's presence, with no consideration whatsoever for the sexton's fate. And so whenever he paused for a moment, an awkward, sheepish silence prevailed, broken only by the cracking noise the sexton made by folding and stretching his hands.—'I imagine these were sensible measures,' Jel Idézö went on, unperturbed by such hints. 'They probably wanted to protect the animal corpses from carrion-feeding disease carriers, while sky burial was unfortunately never an option for human beings because they simply smell too strong as they decompose, unless you embalm them.'—He went on to explain that scriptural scholars had long ago interpreted these forms of burial using the legends' above-below model, a reading typical of the Bieresch, who, when encountering lacunae left by the loss of rational explanations, compulsively filled them with all sorts of nonsense. 'If you wish to reap a feast, bury not a man with a beast,' according to one of the well-known pieces of folk wisdom that jumbled things together without rhyme or reason. Here the rhyme took the place of the meaning that had been lost en route in the course of history.

'That was Zerdahel's father's name,' the grave-digger continued, standing up. Myopically he sought out one of the many photographs on the wall, laboriously detached it from its pin and brought it over. 'That's him,' he said, handing it to me. It was a picture of a fat little man in one of those fairground stalls that sell spun sugar and Turkish delight, talking to someone outside the picture frame. His mouth was slightly open, and on his head he wore the hat I'd seen yesterday on Zerdahel. There was a monyorókérek stuck in the hatband. 'He was Ashkenazi, his wife Sephardi,' said the knackerman. 'His name was "Lost En Route".'—By the way, do you know what your father's name was?—"A Stitch in Time"—saves nine,' Jel Idézö said, and laughed. 'That's also typical of the Bieresch,' he went on, serious once more, when he saw that I had no patience for his jokes. 'These names!—It must be how they remind themselves what they've done wrong; each name has its legend.—"Stand too close to the text and you see a blur: Beware! A chasm lurks behind the word!" goes one passage from the scriptures of the Bieresch. And so as not to forget the warning, they take one phrase from the text—"sees a blur", for instance—and make a name out of it.—Exactly the wrong thing to do!—If I ever desperately want to forget something, I repeat it silently to myself until I no longer feel a thing. And then I can be sure I've forgotten it.—"He runs around, / she's not hard to get,"' he started singing, ' "She squats right down / to dance a minuet!" That's a gravediggers' song. The dead *"dance a minuet"*, we say. Another saying no one understands!' he said pensively, back on his favourite subject.—'Why "a minuet"?—It was us gravediggers' duty to place a stone in the mouths of the dead.—Why? To invoke the beginning of decay? For the same reason people brought us photographs of the dead to choose from?—I have a photo of your father here, too,' he said, 'he was a friend to me.' The knackerman stood up and went to one of the two beds that stood head to head against the other wall. He lifted the bedspread, which like curtains in a nursery sported seals playing with balls, pointed sorcerer's hats, canes whirling through the air, elephants and chubby pickaninnies, and took out from under it a black wooden box painted with red flowers in which he rummaged for a while in vain. 'I don't know, I can't find it right now. So what does "dance a minuet" really mean?' he resumed. '"Minuet" comes from a Celtic word meaning "vein of ore".—Where is the connection? The stone wafer?—Is it an inversion of the Christian communion?—Typical of the Bieresch to twist the most vital of all rites into its opposite and reserve it for the festivities of the dead.—But how do we know what went on the minds of our forefathers? We know nothing, at any rate too little to have the right to meaninglessly echo their now-unmeaning formulae. That's why I bury the dead lying down, and the animals must also go into the ground. For that express purpose I have plastic bags sent from the capital.—We haven't been sufficiently informed!' he cried theatrically. 'We know in parts, we know in scraps! We no longer grasp the greater scheme of things because the lore has broken down.—They say our fathers embedded in the scriptures words that work like mirrors, making them untranslatable, so that they can't be bastardized.—I tell you, some of the sentences you read are so fragile, you feel they'd crack the moment you voiced them, and if you put your finger on certain sounds of certain words, they seem to fly away, and yet stay with you. At certain times these words and sentences are so incredibly sensitive that a single false emphasis destroys the entire meaning.—We have a children's counting rhyme that tells of that: *If words are mirrors / shadows become words.*[35] Put in different terms: if you divest the scriptures of their meaning, instead investing them with your own, the text twists into a phantasm, and the reader's shadow, falling upon it, becomes a peremptory, overpowering message.—As I said, the lore has broken down.—We've been left with the scriptures, but not the instructions for reading them. We have solutions, but the algorithm is missing.—If we had it too, we'd have a comfortable lead in every scientific field, believe me! As it is, we hold but a dumb piece of wood that tells nothing of the spinning top's magical motion.—Then it's best to follow Gikatilla, throw the dead thing away and go. That's what I've done, anyway—I bury the dead lying down, as I said, the way they do everywhere else in the world. Then at least they keep still.—And I've also managed to get the graveyard moved further away from the well!' said Jel Idézö smugly.

This scheme, he enthusiastically explained, had been anything but easy to enforce with a people as stiff-necked as the Bieresch—it had cost him massive efforts to make it a reality.—The legends referred to the wells on many different occasions as 'the eyes of Ahura', and because of its unusually high salinity the water was revered as tears wept by God. The dead were brought as close as possible to God's eyes in order to commend them to his protection.—And despite these various superstitions rooted deep in the Bieresch soul, he had pulled it off by beating his fellows at their very own game.

'You know the legend of Yglemech and Tam,' he went on. 'Yglemech —actually Yglemeech—is a place name, Ilmücz, as is Tam, a corruption of Strem, a town further to the south.—The legend of the meeting between the two is based on an actual event that took place in the 1460s. At that time the inhabitants of Ilmücz left their village on the advice of one of the Bieresch. The wells were tainted. The entire area was one great swamp of corpse-water and toxic gases!'—The handful of earth that burst into flames when Yglemech picked it up stood for the swampy ground which at that time was extremely gaseous, the knackerman went on to explain. The well water congealing to a crust of blood on the Anochi's hand was a reference to the extensive mingling of groundwater and graveyard run-off. The legend was thus to be seen as an urgent warning by the Anochi of Ilmücz against the consequences of the ordinary burial procedure, directed at the Anochi of Strem and his fellow townsmen. They had not followed this advice, however, and that was why they had been wiped out.—The repeated statement that time had come to a stop for Yglemech was meant as a drastic warning of death's menacing proximity, and the phrase 'This place is Monday. A crack echoes through its eternity!' was a symbol of the graves opening, their toxic efflux threatening to destroy all life.—'And the warning came in time!' Jel Idézö cried. Again it struck me how a person spoke of something long past as though it were happening right now.—'If only the Stremers had understood how to interpret the message!' he wailed. 'But in their blindness the Bieresch struck the *e* from "emeth" and summoned "meth" (death)!'

Giving way to an impulse, I glanced warningly at the knackerman, signalling him to be mindful of De Selby's presence, for during this story the tears kept rolling down his cheeks. But either the gravedigger didn't notice my signals, or for some reason he simply refused to acknowledge them, for once when it happened again he snapped at the sexton almost uncontrollably, in a tone of rebuke, 'You don't have to take it so awfully hard. After all, he was just an animal, and you've got the worst of it behind you now!'

'You know,' he said, turning back to me as if to justify his annoyance, 'it's an old superstition in these parts that after people die and the grace period is over, their souls enter animals.—So many proverbs here ascribe to domestic animals what's actually true of humans.—That's especially striking in the references to dogs—and of course turkeys!'—Trying again to get him off this subject somehow, I kicked him under the table. The attempt angered him, and now he raised his voice and snapped at me, 'It's not often you have the chance to hear these things, young man! Your attempts to protect De Selby are really nothing but deceptive manoeuvres. You just want to save your own skin!' I had no idea what he meant but his strident, assertive tone brooked neither questions nor contradictions. '"To make someone carry a dog outside the village" is an expression of ours, meaning to let others atone for your foolishness and faults.—Yes indeed, why do you think De Selby has come here with you today? For his own pleasure?—He's the victim of a superstition and that makes him your victim!—You see, an addendum to the legend you're familiar with convincingly asserts that Yglemech, from whom the village ultimately got its name, was deemed mad by his own townspeople and that one day, "to the ridicule of the crowd", he carried his dead dog out of the village and buried him there, far from the well. He had come to Ilmücz not long before, and the Bieresch treated him as a stranger. And on the day of this symbolic burial another stranger came to town, and since then we've had the custom that when the new proxy comes, the latest arrival must carry a dead dog out of the village. If you like—and believe me, everyone likes it!—none other than you is guilty of De Selby's dog's death, and for that reason alone I ask you whether it isn't high time to be rid of this superstition.—But it seems you Biereschek are all the same there—like dogs you return to your puke, and you mark the way with your urine!'

His voice was completely altered as he said that. It was deep and seemed to come from far away. It was not his voice, but the voice of a hundred humiliated De Selbys melded into one, and somehow my voice was a part of it too. I cringed, glancing over at the sexton. Had he been toyed with like this once as well? I believed he had. For as lightly as though an ancient vengeance had been fulfilled, he said, 'See, even Master Knackerman says so: You're to blame!'—I looked at him and burst out laughing. What was happening here, and here with me, surpassed my capacities, and for the first time I realized it. In the silence left by my ugly laughter I heard my mother wailing: 'They're robbing him of his future and me of my life!' It was the other way around.—Jel Idézö gave me another inquisitive sidelong glance and decided: 'You're not feeling well.'—I nodded. He stood up and went through a curtained glass door into the kitchen to rinse out a glass and bring me some water.

'You know,' he said, his head turned towards me as he rotated the glass in the stream of water, 'at one point I made it my policy not to take my life personally, yet I've never let myself become cynical.—We live under the sign of Pisces,' he said, coming back with the full glass. 'Ég, Hal, Jár and Szél,' he listed as he placed the glass on a small crocheted coaster on the table in front of me. 'Ég, we're burnt out; Hal, we're as mute as the fishes; Jár, everything goes on, Szél, wind carries ashes.—The second lesson has almost been mastered: we've learnt to stay mute and show no feelings.—How does Urs put it: "*Feelings are for your free time*!"[36] And so we hardly have any. Free time is when someone has died. Then for a moment the world is out of joint, and that does us good. But even these feelings are none—they're memories of early feelings, primeval feelings, the fleeting excitement that elsewhere great things are happening. And the surge passes, leaving but the stale taste of the tasteless void. The legend rightly says, "The community closes over the gap like water under the dipper!"—"I don't feel anything, do you feel anything?" we ask. The Biereschek feel nothing any more, believe me, and in this state the longing for pain is painful.—Naghy-Vág, for instance—he curses his hump five times a minute, but he wouldn't trade it for anything in the world. Or look at this scar,' said the knackerman, tapping his brow without touching the red mark. 'Or think of my peculiar name: "Idézöjel" is a quotation mark.—You wouldn't believe the teasing I suffered as a schoolboy for my father's little joke! Even Zerdahel is no exception. He calls me "the quotation mark that ends direct speech" because the scriptures like to compare direct speech with life. Everyone has epithets here, it's just that I've had mine from birth.—I've paid for it a thousand times over, and I'll go on paying for it like another man's debt that can never be covered. All the same—if the Biereschek forced me today to cast off this name of mine, I believe I'd do myself harm. And yet there's nothing to this attachment but a cowering self-pity that can't look away from itself.—This scar here,' Jel Idézö went on, looking at me and De Selby by turns, 'is from the last war—Germany against Russia.' He spoke of a prize fight between nations. 'A splendid April day, the heavens smile above the swampy forests, you're strong and unbending, thirty years and three days old. You sit outside the bunker playing pinochle with your comrades, the mortars rumbling around you, and if you don't look too closely, you think the corpses flung over the mounds of earth are summer clothes brought out to air. The sun emits a hum, like today. Fragrant cigarette smoke curls up from the trenches, and the guns, stacked in pyramids, gleam so brightly in the light, you'd like to turn cartwheels for joy.—Any moment now someone will crack a joke! And then it happens: a shell lands beside you and rips your stomach open—feel!' said the knackerman and guided my powerless hand to his side, where I felt the round, metal-hard closure of a stoma beneath the cloth. I jerked my hand back. Overcome by a violent wave of disgust, I stood up and sat back down. 'You see,' said Jel Idézö, 'all were dead but me.—And to this day I catch myself imagining that for no reason at all someone I'm sitting and talking to suddenly rises into the air before my eyes and sails away. That's how deep a mark it left.—I'd just been telling my comrades stories from home. I began a sentence, and when I looked up again, I was lying on the ground, feeling how easily life flowed out through a hole in me. I simply went on talking. The sky arched so blue above me, wrinkling now and then like a brow. Beneath it all was quiet, even the strong wind which swept through the trees and shook them, silent and ruthless. I talked, and no one listened to me. I think that saved my life, strange though it may sound.—A Russian officer who looked like a primary-school teacher in some memory went around among the corpses turning them over with his walking stick, body by body. Then he was standing over me. I begged him for the *coup de grâce*. He shot, missed and ran away. For the first time in my life I was alone, and I felt a stinging in my nose, growing stronger and stronger, like a thought cutting its way to freedom with a knife.—At the time I was so angry I could have killed the Russian. Today I'd like to chat with him over a large glass of beer.—*Mawkishness is the flip side of machismo,* as they say. The real feelings, at any rate, are absent.—I picture him sitting across from me in the "London", joking and falling silent with me. I tell him the crazy doings of the Biereschek in Hungarian, and he laughs at me in his mother tongue.—Run-of-the-mill reconciliation!' The grave-digger laughed like someone who knows he's lying. I sat there rigid, unable to come up with a word in reply. When I looked at him, he met my gaze calmly. I no longer counted for him. 'The Russian and I,' he said, 'we aren't actually real. Both of us existed only for a moment. In one moment we lost everything; then the world returned to its original state.—Do you know what the Biereschek call the noise made by a stable full of ruminating cows?—"Standing with the motor running!" That's it. It's the same noise you hear when you bend way down and the engines pound and whisper in the earth's interior.—Since that time it's as though there's a disconnect—the Russian is vegetating in the country as a village police chief, somewhere between Irkutsk and Omsk, or wherever. At night he fucks the woman he clobbers half-dead by day when he's drunk. He fucks and clobbers. He wants to beat it out of her, the reason why he missed me back then. That's all he wants to know, and she can't tell him.—Whereas I know it and it does me no good.—Sometimes I lay awake in bed nights and can't fall asleep. Something grows in me and out of me, gigantically large. It grows and grows, on and on, until it reaches the sky, all the way to Russia and China. It grows from the need to call out, to tell him the only real reason there was. But something in me holds its mouth shut. It can't call out. Then it collapses again, turns back to nothingness, to what it was before, and all is quiet.—Do you know the feeling of having to blow up a balloon with your navel? Just picture it!—I had a dream once: I felt that I was pregnant with a baby and soon I would give birth. Two doctors stood to my right and my left, with surgical shears in their hands. "He'll have to decide soon. But there won't be any stitches!" said one of the two, and I know that I was supposed to choose the orifice through which to deliver the baby.—Sometimes I have the definite feeling that our orifices were created solely for the doctors' curiosity!' the knackerman interrupted himself.—'But somehow I couldn't decide, even for the baby's sake, and as though everything depended on it I asked anxiously, "What will it be?"—"A girl," said one. "A boy," the other countered firmly.—"I can't!" I cried, and the doctors yelled, "You must!" And in extremis I felt my long-healed navel open, reluctantly and in endless agony, and through it I pushed the child into the light.—It was a boy, hanging in a transparent pig's bladder on a long, tough umbilical cord, one thumb in his mouth, eyes closed. Cutting together, the two doctors severed the cord. I fainted and woke up.—I had a terrible bellyache because I'd forgotten to evacuate my bowels the night before.'

I got up to run outside, but crouched down again, weak as one who drags himself out of his hospital bed to sink on the nearest chair. My ears buzzed, my gaze fell on De Selby's dead dog, lying on the table. A foul smell as of intestinal gas rose from him, but it wasn't meant for me. I belched softly behind my hand.

The knackerman had gotten up again, rummaging about the kitchen. 'Drink this,' he said, his mouth right next to my ear, and waved a glass of brandy under my nose. 'You've got something for every occasion,' I heard myself whisper. I bit gently into the rim of the glass, breaking out a piece. Then I vomited suddenly on the dog's corpse. 'Like with Mother on the bus,' I said.—The knackerman's wife took me by the arm and guided me to one of the two beds. She wiped my mouth with a damp cloth.

The two men turned towards us and almost simultaneously, as though they'd spent months rehearsing for this moment, they propped their elbows on the tabletop.

Funerals and Mirrors

I'd fallen asleep and woken up again. One of the knackerman's long explanations murmured along smoothly. The words seemed to sway so in the sentences that I shut my eyes again. I slept a little more. Then I was woken by Jel Idézö noisily pushing aside the chest next to my bed and taking out a strange instrument like a washboard with a row of catgut strings stretched across its back. As before, his wife sat watching him from the little footstool by the door.—Jel Idézö looked over and saw that I'd woken up. 'Ah, Hans is awake again!' he said.—'Every Bieresch, they say'—he was evidently continuing some previous conversation, but acted as though he were addressing me—'every Bieresch has a roomy armchair awaiting him.—Me, I've been forced by life into the narrowest nook to be found. And probably I'm not even a real Bieresch, I just sell them dogs for their souls.—"Halfway" was one of them!' he said, patting the dead animal. 'You sell dogs to the living, you write poems to the dead.—Too bad you weren't at the funeral!' he said, turning towards De Selby. I knew he meant my deceased uncle's funeral, and I turned my face to the wall. But as soon as I turned away, I was wrenched back. 'Shekhinah!' the knackerman cried. It sounded like an invocation, so powerful were the guttural sounds he forced out. Then, seeing how he had startled me, he said with a laugh, 'That was your uncle's name. You mustn't fall asleep!' He reached for his instrument and struck a few notes, and then, chiming in with his music, he sang a Hungarian song with a most peculiar sound, for all the vowels seemed to have been stricken from each word, and he made the consonants hum on in such a way that their tone diverged more and more from the reverberating notes of the instrument. It was somehow quite an impossible song, an edifice of infinitely many stanzas, building up quickly and collapsing again, and sometimes the knackerman himself seemed to cower beneath the notes. Twice he leant so far back I thought he'd fall off his footstool, and the woman out in the vestibule spasmodically covered her face with her apron, moaning, 'Oh God, make him stop, please, make him stop!' When his song was finished he rose heavily from his footstool and went over to the sink to take a gulp of water straight from the faucet. Then he asked me, 'How do you like my song?'—'Well, I don't understand it!' I said.—'Except for the title, it's written in the gypsy tongue. The title is Yiddish, meaning "the lesser light"—this refers to the moon, actually the half-moon.' Then he sat on the bed next to me and began to sing again, this time without the previous acrobatics and in German. It also seemed to be a different tune, but that might have been because he sang unaccompanied. 'Shekhinah,' it went, 'look, look there: the other verdict! / The milksop / halfway / out of flowing water / laughs without rhyme or reason: your mirror!'—Over the past two days I'd heard all these words as names.—Hadn't Zerdahel said that the first godfather would be called 'the Lesser Light' once his time was up?—I had no time to ponder any further, for the knackerman turned back to me to call my attention to various details of the text.

First he pointed out that in the legends of the Biereschek the relation between sun and moon is compared to the relation between image and mirror image. Then he called to mind what Zerdahel had told me the evening before about the relation between the heavenly and earthly self. Finally he explained that the poem was a description of my uncle's life, the first half marking his life's beginning and end, while the second part stood for the middle of his life and the vanity of all his hopes.

'But the most important thing,' he went on, 'is the notion of the mirror. It is essential to every funeral poem, and, equally essential, no one may keep a mirror belonging to the deceased—they must pass it on at once to the knackerman.—Mirrors are sacred to the Bieresch. They do not merely reflect the light, like the moon, themselves soulless, they also observe everything, without comment, as it were, and without letting it touch them. As a symbol, they pervade all the tales and myths of our people.—One of our oldest accounts assigns them a central, I should say *the* central role in the life of the Biereschek. It claims that in ancient times the four founding clans of the Bieresch people gathered at one of the salty waterholes in the area, the "Eye of God", no longer to be found, after which an inn is named in Szil, on the other shore of the lake.—The four clans signify the four tribes of the Magyars, Croats, Gypsies and Vandals as well as the four points of the compass, the four ages and the four elements, which the names of our forefathers clearly reflect—"Ég" means "to burn", "Hal" means "fish", "jár" means "to go" and "Szél" means "wind".—The story tells us that they stood around the waterhole and from that starting point divided up the land. "Burn" was given the forested north or north-east, "Wind" the plain to the south-east, "Fish" the lake region in the south-west and "Go" the wine country in the north-west. After this partition, the story goes, the realm's founding fathers reached their hands across the water to form a wheel and then let go again. As they did, one of them—the legend claims it was Ég—stepped into the water which they had just declared to be sacred. Ég cried, "I've kicked God in the face!" And when the three others looked into the water, they saw the surface ripple calmly into little waves, and there was no end to this rippling, and the four faces reflected in the water mingled and merged into a monstrous new visage.—Ég is said to have immolated himself soon after in his woods. Hal, who in penance built his house in the big lake, lost his life to a local underwater quake. They say Jár never returned from the first inspection of his lands, and Szél lost his mind from the mad whooshing of his windmills, so ill-built that they created contrary air currents which offset one another and made an eerie music of ceaseless clattering and laughter. In a fit of madness, it's said, he tried to wipe out his entire family, but he began at the wrong end, with the unborn child in his wife's womb.—Fortunately—or unfortunately—Szél's oldest son Oda Vissza managed to intervene in time to prevent the worst. Oda killed his father just as he was slitting his wife's belly, but he himself was beset by madness in old age. He, too, tried to kill his wife and was stopped and killed by his eldest son. And so on.—That, more or less, is the legend of the origin of the Bieresch people. It forms the basis for the later legends and ends by proclaiming the curse that the fate of the four founding fathers will repeat itself until the end of days, for Ég's sacrilege occurred at precisely the tragic moment when the hands of the four men touched in an oath above the eye of God. For individuals, the curse is lifted by giving their mirror to the knackerman for safekeeping.'—As the knackerman mentioned this custom, I recalled the pale patch I had seen on the wall of the wardrobe at the entrance to the dance hall. Had my uncle's mirror hung here? Convinced that it was so, I laid my head on my arms.

'Later on,' the knackerman went on after a brief pause, more loudly, no doubt for fear I might fall asleep again, 'the four tribes of the Bieresch that once dominated the entire Tortonian region became mingled. And whereas previously it was clear to each individual what fate ultimately awaited him, we live today in nearly the same uncertainty as you people do out there. And genealogy is no help here either, simply because too much mixed blood runs through our veins. And in the desperate hope of finally finding out who people are, the "Year of Our Dead" was introduced. And that's why you're here. It's supposed to become clear who you are.—By the way, do you know what the godfathers were doing in the station pub while you and your aunt were on your way to the dance hall?—They were placing bets on whether you're "Talks-Inward", "The Wrong Explanation", "Heads or Tails" or "Firedamp".—The latter would fit best into their story,' Jel Idézö said, and added maliciously, 'and that's why no one bet on it.—"Heads or Tails" got the most votes.—A fine name!' he said with a laugh.

I was half-sitting on the bed. I had to get away from here. 'Stop,' I said, and my teeth chattered rapidly.—'I'm done anyway!—You've heard everything,' said the knackerman, and now he picked up De Selby's dog. 'Please—be patient one more moment, there's something I have to give you,' he interrupted me as I headed towards the door; then he went outside and left me alone with De Selby. We looked at each other. He was a stranger. Formally, as though the entire past had been wiped out, I asked him if he would accompany me. I wasn't surprised when he explained in a cold voice that he had to help Jel Idézö bury the dog now. 'Well, goodbye then!' I said weakly and went to the door.

It opened as I reached it, and I nearly collided with the knackerman, who held the compensation promised for the sexton—a little spaniel, still blind and almost hairless. 'Here!' he said ambiguously. 'Keep it warm!' He handed me the animal. I picked it up and petted it. It shivered a little, perhaps because it didn't know me. And what had Jel Idézö wanted to give me? I looked at him, waiting, but he did nothing. Then I understood. Again I screamed and heard myself screaming, 'No, I won't take it, I don't want a dog. You can't do this to me!'—Through the haze that filled the room I saw Jel Idézö's hand twitch as though he wanted to slap me. But then he merely laid it firmly on my shoulder and pushed me through the open door. 'Don't play the fool,' I heard him say before slamming the door behind me.

I don't know how I got home. Evidently I'd put the dog in my wheelbarrow and covered it with my uniform cap, as it was already cold outside.—Who, I wondered, would end up killing it? Would the knackerman tell me the same thing when my dog was dead?—Once I must have stopped and crumpled up the rest of the advertising flyers and spread them out to make a cushion so the dog would be more comfortable. At home, outside the dance hall, where the two lamps at the front door were already lit, I found that the animal had chewed the paper to bits.—My aunt, who must have been watching for me a long while, waited shivering in a capacious overcoat. 'Come in quick, my boy!' she whispered. They were the first warm, human words since I'd arrived in Zick the day before. 'How you're shivering! How cold you are!' she said in alarm when I finally reached her. I was trembling but I wasn't cold. Something in me had died and something else had taken the place it left. That was what made me tremble so.

At some point on the way I'd stopped in the middle of the road. My experiences at Jel Idézö's passed before my eyes once more. It was all over!—I recalled that I'd squatted on a moonlit path to relieve myself. But I was too late. My undershorts were filthy, the uniform trousers completely soaked. I'd taken off both, thrown away the shorts and washed myself in the stream at the first opportunity. I'd continued on my way half-naked. The trousers lay in the wheelbarrow next to the dog.

Before that I must have stopped by the 'London', because I distinctly remembered a conversation between Zerdahel and And Vice Versa, who sat drunk at the table where I'd sat with De Selby that morning. 'Memory lies,' say the Bieresch.—Perhaps that's true—for what I recalled of the two men's conversation seems impossible to me, unreal even today, though later I often heard the children singing a song which I'd known by heart ever since that evening, and I fancy I'd heard Zerdahel singing it:

He shows other children his smiling face,
and plays 'back and forth' with them.
And ah! Without the Bieresch child,
They wouldn't know what to do.[37]

'Back and Forth,' I later learnt, was once quite a common name in this region. Later it was replaced by a different name which seemed more apt—'félúton', a Hungarian word with a similar meaning.

As, cradling my dog, I entered the pub where And Vice Versa had played his game with the billiard balls that morning on the table now covered with a dark cloth, I witnessed the following conversation.—First, Inga invited me to join him and the Jew at their table but I politely declined. Zerdahel had agreed with me. I hadn't taken this agreement as a proof of sympathy, however; in my short time in Zick I'd seen much too much to see such conduct as a reliable sign of friendship.—If I had joined them, Zerdahel probably would have acted delighted. All the same, silence fell after this exchange of words, and there was a long pause before the two resumed their conversation.

'Where were we?' And Vice Versa began.

'I was saying you'd be amazed,' said Zerdahel, 'if we ever tried to plot our families' trajectories, for instance, a decline like that of Rák's.—The curves would cross in space all askew. There are no formulae to calculate those, not even your little electron brain would help us there!'

'Don't exaggerate,' And Vice Versa said.

'I'm not exaggerating,' Zerdahel replied calmly. 'I know it's so!'

'What do you know?'

'You have a son,' the Jew declared, as though prophesying.

'And to what would I owe this honour?' And Vice Versa asked facetiously.

'To the constellation,' said Zerdahel with great significance.

'You know that's completely impossible.' And Vice Versa was suddenly serious, too. Now Zerdahel laughed.

'Please don't make fun,' And Vice Versa said.

'I'm not making fun—I swear by your balls,' Zerdahel said solemnly, rising from his seat to make a bow.

'I have no balls!' And Vice Versa cried angrily. 'You know that perfectly well!'

'I'll say it again,' Zerdahel said in the same tone, 'I swear: You have a son!'—I turned away, finding it all so infinitely vulgar, but Zerdahel went on speaking, unperturbed by my behaviour, 'All you need to do is look around—there he stands!'

I wheeled about and met Inga's gaze—he was utterly baffled.

'Who's standing there?' he asked incredulously.

'"Félúton" is. He's your son!' said Zerdahel, pointing at me.

'You're mad!' And Vice Versa screamed, but like me he suddenly realized that Zerdahel had told the truth.

'Félúton,' I learnt later, was the Hungarian word for 'halfway'.—It had been the name of De Selby's dog. It was my name, then.

—'Somehow,' De Selby had said to me at some point morning, 'none of us manage to cope with this life.—Not you and not I!'

—'Try it with a different one!' say the Bieresch.

PART TWO

The Great Potlatch

'Our history is the knot that ties itself when loosened,' say the Bieresch.

ONE
Typhoid

During the first phase of my illness, which had broken out so suddenly in the knackerman's house and then lasted several weeks, it was as though I'd already died.

I lay doubled up, legs drawn to my chest, under the duvet which bulged over me like the crust of a loaf, my right foot shooting out from under it erratically like an animal in ambush.—My eyes ached in their sockets, and I felt that my entire body was covered by a thin sausage skin taut to the point of splitting. Time's beat was given in silence by my lids, apparently the only body parts that were subject to my will and still belonged to me. They admitted the image of the bright little window apertures in the dance hall, where my aunt had had my bed moved, believing I would recover more quickly there; and they caught the images that came from within me, and under my lids these images drifted slowly upwards over my eyeballs. Both my hands were clenched in firm fists, the thumbs stuck inside them like two little wooden pins.

My mouth was always open a crack. From it flowed a thin, unbroken thread of saliva which left an unappetizing coating on my teeth and a sort of quickly drying, yellow scab on my cheek which my aunt wiped away with a moist cloth when she came into the sick room to straighten up my bed.—Part of my life seemed to flow from me with this saliva, but it was a life I no longer cared much about anyway.

Due to the risk of contagion I slept separately from her, all alone in the vast, nearly empty room, often lying still on my side to listen to the rushing in my covered left ear and the chirping noise in my open right ear, which projected up stiffly, growing shovel-sized from my head.—The low-pitched rushing indicated the shift in the movements of my blood, as I'd been told, while the high, almost singing chirp signalled the activity of my overstimulated nervous system.

Sometimes these two noises mingled within me to a kind of noise commentary on the happenings in my body, where in my imagination a gentle soft animal, a quietly peeping mole, burrowed its scratching, rustling way through crumpled paper and crackling wood shavings. And amid this rustle, or so it seemed, incomprehensible sentences and sentence fragments were intoned in Asiatic languages, rapidly shifting between high and low, from one end of my body to the other.—They were snippets of negotiations evidently conducted at incredible speed, and often the parties seemed, in a flash, to have agreed on controversial points and then fallen out again.—Then once more I listened intently to the blowing of my breath, detached from me, sounding like my aunt's breathing that first night in Zick; as though roused by my listening, it retreated deeper and deeper within me until it lay at last in the very depths, at the bottom of my lungs like a dead thing.

At such moments mad fear as of a whip's lash shot through my body and, with a cry meant to end this endless horror, I threw myself weeping from my bed and collapsed with a whimper at its foot.

After each of these cries my aunt almost violently forced open the door of the room—she always seemed quite close by, as though waiting for me to cry out again—looked around, as though there were intruders to drive away, and hoisted me, already quite weak, having lost much of my former weight and now down to barely sixty kilos, in her strong arms to carry me back into bed.

There I lay still, having cast off cares, fear, life and death, and often gazed for hours, thinking of nothing and remembering nothing, at the ceiling of the room, which gleamed down at me white and provoking and on which, through the tears that seeped away beneath my eyelids, the little cracks in the plaster joined of their own accord to form river courses, country roads and mountain chains, maps of unexplored regions. And on these maps—like a schoolboy faced with a geography test—in my imagination I marked smaller towns with a dot, larger ones with a dot in a circle, and capitals and cities with a grey-shaded field.

I was always delighted when, by way of variety, this sky showed me a new, as-yet-undiscovered section of the world map, and in the sprawling network of arteries I identified a river course I did know, picking up its trail like a clew, unspooling it and following it without difficulties to its end, to its confluence with another, wider river.

Such imaginative exercises could last an hour or longer. They reminded me of De Selby's theory of the one way system; I never managed, not a single time, to follow a river from its confluence back to its source, because I always halted, baffled, at the junctions where the tributaries branched off.—Whereas if I followed it downstream, I rushed along, reeling down the meanders from river bend to river bend, falling from one basin to the next deeper one.

'And so,' I though sleepily, 'one may move from the pool of illness to the pool of sleep, and from this finally to the pool of total dreamlessness, which for you shall one day become the pool of total recovery. —These are exercises,' I said to myself. 'You'll see, they hasten your convalescence, and you're sure to regain your full health.'

Turnip

At the beginning of the illness—which the doctor, reachable even in this region that seemed cut off from all natural, vital growth, immediately recognized as a rare combination of special types of nervous fever—my eyes had tolerated only smooth, motionless things. The very wrinkles in my bedclothes had caused me extreme nausea, likewise my hair, which had fallen out in tufts and lay on the pillows like someone else's rubbish, and once the mere sight of a daddy longlegs sailing up the wall in a draft had made me vomit into the china washbasin by my bed in which my aunt rinsed out the washcloths when she'd cleaned my mouth and face.

Even later on I was completely exhausted at times. My head was too heavy, full of woozy chaos, my limbs ached as though they'd gone through brutal contortions, and above all my hands often trembled at the slightest movement.—Bouts of ague coursed through my seething body and, as on my first visit to the knackerman, my teeth knocked together, clattering helplessly. To relieve these agitations, all I ever wanted was to quickly leave my bed, but, barely strong enough to grasp the edge of the mattress, I fell, beaten back by fists, into the rustling cushions, for suddenly cracks appeared all over the dance hall walls as though in an earthquake, sand and lime seemed to sift down upon me from invisible openings in the ceiling and toilets began to flush of their own accord on floors that didn't exist.

After about three and a half weeks I was more or less—'halfway,' as the unsuspecting doctor put it—recovered, but the very mention of this name set me back another ten days. The skin of my face tautened again and my body was distended by intestinal gases.—At last, however, I was allowed my first meal, albeit only thin soup and porridge, and sometimes my aunt—her behaviour towards me had changed fundamentally since the night of my naming, now overly solicitous—brought me a little lukewarm brandy in a cup. 'To strengthen your poor, weakened heart, and make you better again quite soon.'—Later I was allowed to sit up by myself for the first time (not counting the involuntary, but unavoidable, horrified leaps out of bed) and also received permission to read three books my uncle had left behind.

One of these books was a ten-year-old illustrated catalogue for stamp collectors; the second was on horticulture, proclaimed by the dust jacket as Collin's famous work *Planting the Best French Fruit Trees: A Thorough Guide*; the third bore the title *Almanac for the German Family*, and below it *Vade Mecum for Young Ladies*.—Once again I found the former owners' names in long rows on the inside covers, once again all the names, down to the last, that of my uncle, were crossed out, and I felt confirmed in my fear that these books, too, were moveable goods that could be stolen from my bedside at night along with my washbasin and my nightstand.

An enthusiastic reader, I soon finished the books and read them a second time. I searched the stamp catalogue for depictions of young African nations' sacred heraldic animals and pictures of strange tropical birds, as I'd always been interested in zoology and had planned to become a naturalist some day. Collin's book interested me mainly for the section on the grafting and pruning of espalier fruit, which contained a history of fruit tree grafting in ancient Mesopotamia, the Persian Empire, and among the Egyptians, sophisticated cultures that had all held to the notion that trees had inherent sex-specific characteristics that predisposed them for the grafting of certain scions, while the fixed sex role precluded the grafting of other ones from the outset, unless such an '*unnatural transplantation of incompatible and hostile races of wood*'[38] was desired for the manufacture of divining rods and other magical instruments.

And over and over I leafed through the *Almanac*, in which alongside recipes and housekeeping and child care instructions I found the symptoms of typhoid, my affliction, presented in detail.

'*He's been struck by the hoof of a mule*,' they say here when someone raves with fever.—This illness had dealt me a deep, gaping wound, and in the beginning I often felt I had a small hole in my chest through which the air escaped as through a side exit. The wound fever still racked me, but gradually a scab was forming around and over this opening. It was a great star-shaped medal conferred on me to cover the scar that would remain.—Filled with pride, I wanted to show this decoration to all and sundry—'Here, look here, my Cross of Valour, the bar, the ribbon!'—above all to Turnip, my little dog, whom my aunt, after consulting the doctor, had reluctantly admitted to me in the dance hall.

I also read to the dog at random from my three books.—She lay blinking, her short legs stretched out in front of her, on several tattered floor-cloths which my aunt had spread out for her by the door across from me.—When I looked at the animal, lying there and gazing up at me mutely, I had the strange feeling that the first two days of my stay in Zick had, so to speak, become flesh in her; that she was a living memorial to my self, or an early stage of it turned memorial, which I had forced out from me as though giving birth and which, perhaps quite soon, would take my entire illness upon itself; indeed that it would bear in my place what had been ordained for me.—'Egynek—egyeb,' I said to her. This, as I had learnt, was the refrain of a counting rhyme, meaning 'one for the other'.

'*One person's illness,*' I read to this body that was a piece of myself, '*has a harmful effect on the other, adding to his work, taking away his joy in life, bringing care and sorrow to the house.*'[39]—Regarding the word 'typhoid', I learnt from the *Almanac* that it means 'smoke', 'haze', 'stupor', perhaps even 'stupidity', and that it belonged to the same family of words as 'dust', 'dull', 'dark' and 'dumb'.

'At one time it was generally known as nerve fever,' I said out loud to my dog. 'This is the term for various severe medical conditions associated with high fever, in which the nervous system persists in a prolonged state of torpidity.—The intensity of the fever, which poses the greatest risk at the outset of the illness, is combated with full baths cooled by pouring in cold water at the foot end while the invalid sits in the tub. Apart from lowering the fever, these baths achieve bodily cleansing and overall stimulation, especially with insensible patients. This transforms severe cases of typhoid into simple ones and reduces mortality to a minimum.—To avoid the risk of intestinal laceration, the patient is initially given only liquid or semiliquid nourishment, and that in small portions. Though the symptoms are life-threatening at first, the illness often ends with the patient's recovery. As for the treatment of typhoid, the patient must first be quarantined. The sick room must be large and frequently and thoroughly ventilated. The mouth must be cleansed regularly with a damp linen rag.'

'*Typhoid*,' I read on, giving Turnip a warning look, '*is an extraordinarily contagious disease. The contagion is contained in the air and in insufficiently ventilated rooms can persist for a long time without losing its effect.*'

TWO

The Prehistory of Invention

My aunt had scrupulously followed all the recommendations of the *Almanac* I read to my dog and, in compliance with further instructions, had often dragged me out of bed in the middle of the night for a bath, a dose of quinine pills, a cup of iodized water or a bowl of porridge. Each ministration ended with a spoonful of honey, for, as my aunt explained to me, death hates the smell of bees.—Nonetheless I suffered repeated setbacks when—still in her arms, being carried through the house—I suddenly saw a white patch on the wall where the coat rack had once hung, or the vacant spot on the kitchen floor where the big, scratched dining table had stood.—Then another paroxysm of fever or nausea would rack me, the walls parted, the floor quaked, my bed flew through the air with me in the middle, a small battered thing emitting the foul smell of unhealthy inner winds.—*'He's been given burnt fur,'*[40] they say here. That was how I smelt, and this smell, it seemed, departed my body like a stranger who shook his head over the degree of squalor I tolerated in this body's household affairs.

The illness refused to release me. I was unware of my aunt when, as she later reported, she rushed into the dance hall at the renewed bursts of terrified screams which now sounded shrill as birds' cries.—I sat in bed immersed in myself, back rigid as though braced from behind, febrile, fantasizing speeches to the bedclothes' mountain ranges.—'It's Monday,' I said, my aunt told me, 'in it the minutes break asunder.' I addressed everything despairingly in the second person; for myself I used the third. 'You mountain, you mountainous bed,' I said, but also 'You breath of air!' when the door opened and 'You bird of the air!' when my aunt came in.

There was no more difference between sleeping and waking. In my twilight dream, all things were as one, unfolding along- and inside one another, doubled and multiplied, as though space and time had somehow been concertinaed the wrong way around.—If my aunt wiped my mouth with the washcloth, I begged her once she was done to do it at long last; if the door opened, it had been open already anyway.

The identical visions haunted me, often repeating over and over before unfolding fully.—Whenever I looked out the window, a little mule ('Szent-Mihaly öszver!' my aunt cried when I told her about it afterwards) stood out in the garden by an apple tree, always in the same place, grazing tranquilly even as it stretched out in spasms and brayed wildly, though there was nothing in the window, and in the tree behind it the linens for my poultices hung motionless.

Once I was startled from my daydream by excitedly whispering, probably imaginary voices beneath the window. I sat up in bed and yelled, 'What's going on?' without receiving a reply. Then one time I imagined someone whispering outside my door. *'Már menöfélben van!'* I thought I understood. *'Még nem* menöfélben van!' I called back, meaning 'He *still can't* walk yet!' but there was no one there to hear. A third time I started up because I was convinced I'd seen six men armed with sticks trying to drive the mule from the garden into the dance hall. But the mule had stood its ground, and I took that to mean that I wouldn't die yet.—So I called out to the door, and a moment later the six godfathers were really there, all lined up against the wall of my room. Holding little round hats, they looked like prematurely aged pupils in an old class photo—and in fact such a photo, from my grandfather, hung just above them in a broad frame on the wall.

On certain days, towards the end of the illness, I was kept awake by an incessant, sizzling whisper outside my door, interrupted now and then by the trumpeting sound of my aunt blowing her nose.—On the last day, as I still lay motionless in bed though paralysed by the noises of the earth that turned swifter than usual beneath me, I quite clearly heard my aunt scolding a visitor, stifling her voice so that I wouldn't understand.

I pricked up my ears when she hissed the words 'kitchen table', then 'toolbox' and 'credenza', for these were things that had been stolen from us.

I crept to the door and peered through the keyhole, but didn't recognize the man who stood outside with his broad back turned towards me.—On and on, as though by rote, my aunt reeled off her list: 'wardrobe,' she whimpered, 'sewing kit', 'preserving pot', 'his suitcase with everything in it', and, almost triumphant with despair, she added, 'So now you've taken my washtub too!—And how, pray tell, should I cope with all the bedclothes without a washtub?' She pronounced the word 'washtub' as though the thief had split her tongue with an axe.

Fifth Lengthy Conversation

I had soon gathered, from her manner of address, that this man she was speaking to, and did not want to let in to see me, was a godfather. It enraged me all the more that her tirade insulted *me* instead of him, though no doubt she fancied it was for my sake that she demeaned herself to the point of indignity. And when her wailing finally became intolerable—she'd thrust out her lower jaw in despair and, as it were, heaved her reproaches out over it—I pounded my fist on the door panel and cried as loud as I could, 'Let him take everything, let him set our house on fire, so we'll finally have peace and quiet for once!'—Then I went back to bed and lay down, still trembling all over with fury and weakness.

The door was flung open.—'Come in!' I cried, and in came the sixth godfather, a youngish fellow, clearly somewhat short-sighted, bent forward slightly because of his height. Behind him, hunched and teary-eyed, my aunt.—'Get out!' I snarled at her, and she actually backed out through the door again, closing it behind her.—The godfather stood there frozen, gaping after her foolishly, then came closer to my bed, his gaze still riveted on the miracle of the closed door, and reached abstractedly for the only chair. He sat down on it and looked at me.

'I'm Lumiere,' he said, softly at first, as though not even sure of his name, but immediately collected himself and went on, his voice increasing in firmness and conviction.—'You may ask yourself,' he said, 'to what you owe the honour—clearly, for you, a dubious one—of my visit to your sickbed.'—The sentence seemed to unwind its way out of him, but when it finally stood, it seemed produced in advance, cast in a mould and then cooled. He had himself well in hand.

He stood up, glanced back at me and began a long peregrination from one end of the room to the other, turning back to me often as he spoke and swinging his left arm like a pendulum in time with his strides. The tone in which he spoke rarely changed, but his turns of phrase seemed choicer and choicer, his words more and more precise, emphatically punctuated at times by gestures that had clearly been rehearsed. But I felt less and less as though *he* were speaking to me—it was someone else, a teacher perhaps, who had taught him all these statements and phrases in week-long drills, and sometimes it seemed that these gestures and words pressed into my hand, by turn, cold metal door latches, gleaming brass handles and smooth-polished walking-stick knobs which I was helpless to fend off, and I was just as defenceless when he took them away again.

'It's not all that difficult,' the godfather explained at last, lowering his voice.—'Five komakok* were here. I am the sixth and last.'—Doorknob.—'The last one is more persistent,' he paused, 'and practically immune to well-meant auntly subterfuges.'—Brass latch.—'He's simply too shrewd.'—Handle.—Lumiere interrupted his journey and looked at me, crossing his arms over his chest.

'With him—' He smiled, flashing two silver crowns in his mouth. They looked like the heads of rivets.—'With him transparent excuses about the sorry state of the invalid—who's actually haler and heartier than all the rest of us put together—won't take, by virtue of his position alone!' He winked at me. For him I was an old friend who was trying to pull the wool over everyone's eyes and whom he'd seen through but, as though from the kindness of his heart, would allow to go on shamming.—I closed my eyes. A book I'd read years ago came to my mind.

'He'd been drinking, and felt mysterious,'[41] one passage went.

'Well, let's get to the point,' Lumiere went on.—'I come to you (what do the fish in the fable say to the

* As the Bieresch call the godfathers.

fox?) as a friend—' he cleared his throat, sat down beside me again and went on in a business-like tone, '—without ulterior motives or reservations.'

Lumiere's breath smelt. I turned away, breathing heavily beneath the heavy, damp bedclothes.

'That may seem implausible to you,' the godfather went on, raising his voice, 'in view of our apparently divergent interests . . . '—'Divergent interests,' I thought.—He might have been a razor salesman.[42]

' . . . but,' he added grandly, 'believe me—it is the case.' He was lying.—I raised myself up in my cushions a bit to laugh at him but collapsed back in them at once for sheer weakness.

'It's not easy, I know!' cried Lumiere, misunderstanding my reaction, and rocked his head thoughtfully from side to side.—'Your standing with us is not ideal. You've forfeited much of our initial sympathy.—Now you'll have to redouble your efforts!'

As though his appeals were meant to give me courage, he laid his left hand on my knee. A shudder ran through me, and when I reflexively stretched out my leg, he withdrew his hand at once. All the same I trembled at the revolting notion that with this brief touch he had discharged a toxic liquid which was now corroding its way through the duvet to me. I pulled the coverlet up over my nose, still racked by revulsion.

'But in all seriousness,' the godfather began again, and studied his fingernails. He looked about for something. Then he spotted it—a saucer on the windowsill in which my aunt had laid out my medications for the night. He rose—it almost looked as though someone else were lifting him and carrying him swiftly to the window—and fetched the saucer, placing its contents neatly on the windowsill. A vial fell to the floor and rolled a short way. He hurried after it and picked it up. Back at my side, he took out a cigarette and used the dish as an ashtray.

'I have come on behalf of the interim aid society,' he said. 'Now, what is that?' He paused and then answered his own question. 'The interim aid society is a relatively young organization, initiated in the first third of the last century during the first great exodus of the Biereschek from their ancestral communities.'—He breathed in sharply through his nose and stared at me through the lenses of his glasses like a blind man.—It was all learnt by rote; from the monotonous ups and downs of his speech occasional words, as though wrongly stressed, loomed in increasingly unexpected places, like the arm of a drowning man.—'It's a sort of reintegration aid, then,' I heard the godfather say. 'And it's aimed at recent immigrants, inexperienced Biereschek folk such as you . . . '

'Biereschek!' I repeated, as if to point out this word.

' . . . or such as I once was,' Lumiere went on undeterred. Now he raised his voice again. 'Yes,' he cried, 'believe it or not, I too was once in your position!'

'I too,' I said, burrowing my head into the pillow.

'I too,' the godfather repeated, 'tossed in my bed once night after night and, trembling, asked myself "Will they come back tomorrow?"—"What will they take this time?"'

I raised my hand defensively. The walls of the room seemed to bend apart, the ceiling curled up. Through a crack in the roof I saw out into the open, into a hot, leaden, windless sky which had sunk closer to the earth as though beneath its own weight.

'I too,' Lumiere went on, 'plagued by responsibility for the fate of those entrusted to my care . . . '

'Those entrusted to me . . . ' I heard myself repeat.

' . . . spent many a sleepless night.—I too . . . '

'I too!' I cried.

' . . . finally despaired in it all and asked myself despairingly, "Can I persevere?"'

I started up.—'And did you persevere?' I snarled at him.

'No,' replied the godfather calmly. He gazed at me. Then he looked thoughtfully at his cigarette, smoking away in his fingers.—'But at least I gratefully grasped the hand that reached out for me!' he said firmly.

'This hand?' I cried. 'Your hand?'—I fell back in my bed.—'First you people kill me,' I said weakly, 'and then you want to save me?'

'Halfway!' said Lumiere, as though I horrified him.

'What is it?' I asked.

'You mustn't talk like that, Halfway!' the godfather said urgently. He sat on the edge of the bed beside me and placed his hands on my shoulders.—'Look, Halfway—you'll permit me to call you that, won't you?'—Another shudder ran through me, and he removed his hands at once.—'Believe me,' he said, folding his hands, 'a young person needs help, he seeks help! And to provide help where it's really needed—that's what our organization is for, after all!'

'I don't want your help,' I said, turning away again.

Lumiere leant back and sat for a while, no doubt waiting out the effect my words had upon him, motionless, hunched.—'We all make mistakes,' he said at last.

I looked at him. Sitting there pressed down upon this last ill-used chair, his eyes darting restlessly, his body seeming tensed in spasms, screwed together and nailed to the seat, he looked as pathetic as the chair itself. A drop of sweat emerged from the hair at his left temple and made a thin trail past his ear and down his cheek. It was followed by a second, quicker drop.

The godfather extracted a handkerchief from his trousers and wiped his face and the back of his neck.—Then he began again. This time he sang, his high voice veritably chirping the words of his song:

A leaf breaks from the tree of life,
Another takes its place.
It brings you luck—
and as for me?

For me it brings disgrace.

'That's one of our oldest folk songs,' Lumiere explained, 'called "Unfair Comparison".—It's my favourite song,' he added.

'I don't want your help,' I said once again.

'I know,' said the godfather. He took another cigarette from the pack. 'I know,' he said. He went on humming his song even as he stuck the cigarette in his mouth. He lit it, took a deep drag and held the smoke overly long in his lungs. Then he breathed it out, and coughed.—'Smoking hurts my young voice, says the doctor,' he interrupted himself hoarsely.—'It's like they say: "The hounds of death are barking from within me".'

And apropos of nothing he asked quickly, 'Do you play chess?'

The History of Chess

From the inside pocket of his jacket the godfather produced a small, folding travel chess set.

'I always have this with me,' he explained, holding it out to me. Then he opened it, took out some of the figures, put the rest in his trouser pocket and set the board on his knees.

Continuing to whistle his silent tune, as chess players do, he began to insert the figures in the little round holes according to a certain plan. At last he had created the desired arrangement.—The problem was a laughable one: Black, whose move it was, was at a severe disadvantage; moving first, he foolishly exposed his knight, enabling White to capture it with impunity.—Paying me no mind, Lumiere went through the game, and the rapidity of his moves showed that he had played it hundreds of time before.

'Zerdahel claims that I invented chess,' he said casually, capturing the black knight.—'He's much too kind!'—Now Black was forced to exchange bishops.—'I've helped popularize the game among the Biereschek—' he waved his hand dismissively, his gaze never straying from the board. 'But I didn't invent chess.—White wins,' he interrupted himself. He rose from his seat slightly to slip the rest of the figures into his pocket, and looked at me.—'I don't play it any more, either,' he said finally, 'all I play now is draughts.' He laughed sheepishly, as though he'd made a joke that embarrassed even him, folded up the board and weighed it in his hand.

'It wasn't I who invented the game of chess,' he went on, 'but an ivory merchant on the Indian peninsula more than four thousand years ago.—From there it later made its way to the Persians, who in a sense achieved a never-equalled mastery in this discipline, though it must be said that they regrettably departed from the original form, which we play here. You're probably no expert on the subject, but I can assure you that Indian chess is the more intriguing and more just of the two. As I always say, Persian chess is sharper but lonelier.—No matter.—On the whole, the rules of the Indian game match the Persian version: pawns move forward one square, and on their first move can also proceed two squares at once. The rooks traverse any number of vacant squares vertically or horizontally, but the bishops always move diagonally, on squares of the same colour, while the knights always jump three squares (starting square included) to a square of a different colour than the starting square. And the king, on whose preservation the outcome of the game depends—for if he can no longer move,' Lumiere expelled these words sharply, as though furious at having to sit here explaining the rules to me while outside his king might be in danger, 'he is "checkmated" or "meth", meaning "He is dead!"—while the king, then, can always move one square in any direction, forward or backward, to the side or diagonally, our game, the original Indian game of chess, does not have a queen who, in the conventional manner of play, combines the movement of the bishop and the rook.—And thus it is impossible for us to trade a pawn for a queen.—We're not at the marketplace here!' the godfather cried. 'What do you want?' he asked irritably. 'Truth is dear, as we say in these parts.—If you want chewing gum, you'll have to ask over at the Jew's, he'll be happy to trade!'

Lumiere broke off. He had talked himself into a fever. His mission, the interim aid society, was forgotten. All that counted now was chess.—And where did he think that would get him with me? What did I care about chess games?—I rolled onto my back and gazed at the ceiling.

'So if it were up to Zerdahel,' he resumed, 'I'd have invented chess. If it were up to him, you'd be "Cries from the Fire!"—Nonsense.—Nothing repeats itself, nothing gets invented. "The wheel," we say here, "had a long way to roll before it found Man."—Isn't that clear enough? Doesn't that say everything?—Just imagine!' Lumiere leant so far towards me from his chair that he almost lost his balance. He propped both his hands on the edge of my bed. 'Zerdahel believes we're reborn. You and I, he says, are repetitions, rebirths, creation's manufacturing errors in serial production.—"We regret" he mocks when someone dies, "that this model is no longer available at this time." Or "'Walks Between Two Windows'? We don't carry that here at the moment, but we've got 'Laughs Without Rhyme or Reason'. Will that suit your needs?"—That's how he talks. Awfully funny, isn't it?—But ultimately rather petty.'

Lumiere broke off once again.—'Laughs without rhyme or reason,' he said, tossing back his head as he took out and lit another cigarette. 'Our entire life is one great laugh with no reason!'

He spoke as though to himself, the cigarette in his mouth, then got up abruptly, walked over to the window and stood for a while gazing out into the little front garden where the trees swayed rustling in the wind.—'Maybe it'll rain!' he said, pointing his cigarette at the sky.

Smoke curled up between his fingers and vanished out into the open. The stunted little apple tree where my aunt always hung the laundered cloths after changing the poultices tossed back and forth in the fierce gusts of wind; someone seemed to grab its crown now and then like a hank of hair and shake it. The leaves shivered and showed the whitish sheen of their storm sides. Birds rose from its branches as though catapulted by springs.—The entire tree seemed to shudder, and the flailing of the branches behind the silent form of the godfather, who stood right between me and the tree trunk, reminded me how I had once followed a man up a steep slope on one summer stay in the mountains.

On his back, the man, a childhood friend of my mother, had carried a milk can which gurgled continually, as with laughter.—I recalled the driver who had brought me and my mother to Vienna. Where was my mother now? What were my sisters doing? How did my brother fare?—While I was dying here, they lived on.

Hatred rose up again within me, hatred of everything, above all of Lumiere, who stood at the window quietly smoking, his back turned towards me—like that man back then on the mountain, who suddenly, while walking, as though I weren't there, had raised his arms and wheeled them. At the same time his mouth made a strange noise, like a flutter. Then he took a few mighty strides and uttered a high, jubilant cry, whirling his arms more and more wildly. As abruptly as he'd begun, he broke off.—'What are you gaping at?'

he asked angrily. Tears rose to my eyes, but he didn't care.—'Don't go blubbering again!' he snarled and strode still faster.

Cowering from his threat, I'd followed him in silence, but the feeling that he'd abandoned his attempt to fly only because he'd suddenly remembered that *I* was following him, and I, son of the woman who'd forsaken him, was unworthy of witnessing his exuberance, had made me keep crying quietly. And suddenly I remembered that for some time his shoulders had gone on twitching, as though struck by my sobs, and that I, sobbing on, had imagined other unknown, perhaps still more untameable forces dwelling within him which I would not see because he refused to release them in my presence.

And, as though he were mysteriously in league with him, Lumiere cut off my memories, abruptly starting to speak again.

The Prehistory of Inventions

'For Zerdahel,' the godfather began without turning around, 'the riddle of life is solved.' Now he turned and looked at me. 'Because for him there is no death.'

'Last week over in Pamagh I listened to him in a pub without his noticing. Enemies rarely offer such opportunities. They must be seized. So I listened, though that's not my nature otherwise. And indeed what I heard was most remarkable.—"When he speaks," De

Selby always says, "I'm afraid he's about to strike out at me." The fat man's right. Zerdahel has claws—he talks with a pickaxe!—As I came into the pub, he was just saying: "When I talk to you like this"—It was clear to me,' the godfather interrupted himself, 'that he was talking to Inga, though I couldn't see him and I'd thought he was at home—"when I talk to you always feel I ought to apologize a thousand times over for using words. I'm serious.—De Selby," he went on, "once said to me: My thoughts move so fast. They're like streams leaping wildly through my head, and I always feel I need only open the sluices to my mouth and it would all come gushing towards you, the water would clear and all would be clarified. But when I do, it's as though the water freezes over within me, I fear I'll bite my tongue at any moment, and my mouth is filled with mouldy driftwood!'

'"It's true—images would be much better", said Zerdahel,' recounted the godfather. '"Words are bad. Our mouths are remorseless as quarries.—I myself," said Zerdahel, "sometimes imagine I could suffocate when speaking, because it's not air that wafts my words, but a stagnant, century-old stench, wads of smoke piling up within me to form impenetrable darkness.—An ablakok phenomenon, in other words. Only it's no refreshing breeze the flung-open windows let in—it's the bad breath of the ancestors peering curiously into our parlour.—My father once summed it up quite aptly: 'Do you know why the Bieresch read so little?' he asked me once, bringing me a book as a present from one of his journeys. 'Because even the truth stinks of garlic!'—It's true. And his words smelt accordingly.—No matter. The important thing is his message: *'What lies in language was put there by the ancestors,'*[43] as the saying goes.—Prehistoric experiences, knowledge reaching back into our pre-human past freely usurps the expressions of our feelings. Your disgust at the caterpillar is the greed of the rooster in you that would peck at it and the ebbing tremor of the leaf in you that feels gnawed by it.—We fall flat on the open field because the clear, cloudless spring sky above us is filled by the rush of vast wings in the past before our past, when we were small furry animals innocently scampering about.—What was it that old Bruno always said?" asked Zerdahel.—Bruno was like a grandfather to me,' Lumiere explained proudly.—' "He said," he went on, *"It is not Man who has broken into the laboratory of nature, but nature that has drawn him into its machinations, achieving through his experiments its own obscure aims."* '[44]

'Zerdahel paused,' the godfather went on. 'He looked over at Inga, but Inga made no response.—" 'It's not *me* speaking,' De Selby said," Zerdahel resumed, "it's someone else sighing with my voice.—And it's true: every single word—and thus, of course, the circumstance which it describes!" the Jew cried,' said Lumiere, ' "every conceivable combination of sounds and statements has been run a thousand times through the filter systems of other brains, through the mines of other hearts.—It's insane! You yourself feel you've been wrenched out of context!—You say something, you've barely begun to speak, and already an unmistakeable feeling sets in—you're playing with an old set of children's building blocks in which the most important pieces are missing and the rest are already so worn that you could stick your hand flat into the cracks between the words.—And you'd like nothing more than to destroy the whole wretched pattern of blocks you've been building and tinkering at hour after hour with one blow from the side of your hand.—And we could say the same thing of ourselves. *'Each person,'* they say, *'is like a living word with its own meaning.'*[45]—But not even that's true! We're dead words without a context. Our lives are nothing but scraps of sound flitting through the broken-down thought-machine of the Holy Ancient One.—If De Selby really could open the sluices of his words," continued Zerdahel,' said Lumiere, '"he'd be in for a surprise! What's the riddle within him?—The hurdy-gurdy of history.—But though he concedes, like any rational person, that the most brilliant artistic achievements of our language, all that ever was or has yet to be said and written, has since the very beginnings of our ill-fated race been anticipated and stored in dictionaries and grammars—enchanted, transformed into a different word sequence, a different order, but present all the same—he persists stubbornly in the notion that he himself is something fundamentally different and new: an oven-fresh, crispy cake whose soft insides hold as-yet-untasted pleasures. Rot! What's inside is chewing gum."'

'"You know," Zerdahel said then, rising to his feet,' the godfather recounted, '"what we think, what we speak and what we are—these aren't our inventions, inspirations and discoveries, these are the pre-engineered vicissitudes of nature's incalculable system."—The Jew stood up and went outside for a moment; I began to think he wouldn't return. But he came back at once and resumed his seat. Inga remained silent.—"Maybe he wants to hear him out first?" I thought.—And then Zerdahel began again. "Not long ago I was talking to Naghy-Vág in the 'London'," he said.—"The Unicorn was in the best of spirits, describing his altercation with De Selby. It was about the dog. His forgotten cigar smouldered in the ashtray even as he took out another one, and I, just as unthinking, lit it for him.—And suddenly—as I realized this twofold inattention, and as he leapt up in the middle of his speech, twisting back and forth, stretching out his arms and and crying 'You are the murderer!' in imitation of the fat man—I felt the flame spring once more from my extinguished match.—This invisible rekindling," Zerdahel cried, "ignited in me the memory—and I do mean *memory*, not *feeling*!—the memory of how the fire ate its way up the match, burnt its way down my hand, my arm and my body, how I crackled and sang in this fire that crept onward inexorably, how I melted to a little lump of rubber hissing in the heat, how my flesh, turned to ash, fell from me piece by piece."'

'"At that moment," Zerdahel cried again,' said Lumiere, '"at that moment I realized, 'That was you!'—that was what I myself had been in one of my previous lives. And if Nagh had so much as glanced at me, I know I would have died on the spot.—Something in me had suddenly been ready to revert to something else that had been there before—to a scorpion leaping on forever betwixt fires, to a burning bush."'

'Zerdahel stopped speaking for a moment,' the godfather related. 'He took wild drags from his cigarette and flapped his hand at the smoke as though to beat back his memories, and I had to struggle not to laugh out loud, for at that moment he looked like the burning bush in person. "Thank God!" the Jew sighed then, "Nagh didn't look.—He sensed something too, because apropos of nothing he clapped his hands and cried, 'Jesus, I forgot to give the chickens their water!'—but he didn't understand me, I'm quite sure of that.—Now, of course, it's easy for me to laugh it off, it's over, after all, but back then, I know, the water in his remark extinguished the fire in me and saved my life. I'll never forget that!—I treated him to a pitcher of wine.—No matter.—What I mean, once again, is: forgotten, buried, blinking up at us, our earlier lives live on within.—Fetch a shovel, shovel them out! If only! It can't be done, you see.—What is it you always say? 'We don't live, we explain life!'—Quite right.—So many vegetable questions amassed within us in our previous lives, and so many animal riddles, that at last all this had to crystallize into human wisdom. And that's where we stopped.—The animals ask within us, and it's as humans that we answer. The simian sorrows in our breast elicit our cities' resounding stone forests. We dig for treasures and find the bones our canine forbears buried.—Behind us lies Egypt, before us the Promised Land. The walls of the sea loom right and left. The sun stands still. Yesterday is today. A crack echoes through eternity.—We are the asses of the proverb who set out to seek horns, we come home without ears!"'

Now Lumiere lit a cigarette, took a few drags, got up and walked over to the window, swaying slightly as though he'd been drinking. There he stopped, his back to the window, and frowned.

'Had Inga been present,' he said firmly, emphasizing each word, 'he would never have let it come to that.—I say, Had he been present!' the godfather repeated. 'But he *wasn't* present.—Zerdahel had merely been rehearsing the next quarrel he'd have with him.—Crazy, isn't it!' He paused again.

'But what is the implication of all the Jew's claims?' he asked. 'Surely that we are reincarnated beings, victims forced to return to the place of their deed.—But the scriptures teach us that this place does not exist. *"I've never seen this place before,"* a legend says of it. *"Brighter than the sun is the star that shines beside it.—Turn back! Be gone! You are not who you once were."*[46]—What, then, does Zerdahel mean when, bastardizing the scriptures, he insists that all we think and do has long since been thought and done? He holds that each deed is the dog's return to its vomit, the repetition of each deed ever done, forced to repeat itself over and over on into the distant future. But if that were so, our scriptures could not be what he himself always lauds them as: the ever-new, never-ebbing source of our knowledge.—No,' Lumiere said firmly. 'Invention as repetition, which Zerdahel would like to persuade us of, is a lie. It's as old as the Histrions themselves!—"*And if you made candles,*" promises one of our myths, "*the sun would shine on you day and night.*"[47] That doesn't mean that what we do is in vain. It says that *as well,* but first of all—and surely this is the crucial thing—it promises that Ahura's light will shine eternally upon our deeds. "*And if you wove shrouds,*" that myth goes on, "*no one would die any more.*"—The same promise!' cried Lumiere. 'The myth commands us to make candles and weave shrouds!—And it was Inga who first solved the mystery of this contradiction.'

The godfather looked at me.—'"Inventions," or so Inga began the famous explanation which he wrote down after solving this riddle, "inventions are components in the self-regulating process of our history."—Did you notice that?' Lumiere interrupted himself, 'he said "process", not "cycle"!—"Each invention, each discovery," this explanation states, "negates itself by thoroughly and finally spoiling its own preconditions." And here he uses a highly illuminating simile. "A tree gives you its shade as long as it stands," he later explained his insights. "If it falls, so does the shadow in which you sit. And a ladder you've made from its planks can no longer be leant against it." He uses this image of the ladder yet a second time, saying: "The strength of the ladder you ascend to knowledge is used up in climbing. Once you reach the top, the ladder is gone." [48]—And another passage in his explanation goes: "The clock hand of the world clicks forward. You've changed one single piece, and with this piece all other pieces, yourself included!—Everything touches, and all the cogs begin to spin when you move a single one of them!"—I rank these words among the finest statements by our generation,' said Lumiere.—'No wonder! I'm living proof of them.'

At the Inn

'Listen,' he went on, wiping his mouth with the back of his hand.—'This happened three years ago over in Tadten, at the Sign of the Cow. Stitz and the others had been at the fair in Varbalog, I'd come from visiting a distant uncle in Bala. We'd arranged to meet at the turning for Zick, and it was still early, so we sat at the inn a while longer. Those crossroads!' the godfather cried exaggeratedly.

'We were already quite drunk when Stitz suddenly came over to me and said he'd like to play a game of chess.—It was such a bright afternoon! We sat together, the innkeeper made us carp soup. Rák borrowed a saw from him and played music on it, and his wife sang along.—What a voice that Anna has!' Lumiere cried again. 'A song to drive you mad.—No matter. Inga played a slot machine, and the Jew, throwing dice with Naghy-Vág, told him he'd once seen a man sitting all by himself at a pub table, throwing dice, and he'd been able to change the number of dots on a die on the table before him at his pleasure, without even touching it.—That angry clatter of the dice!' Lumiere shook his head.

'Maybe that was it,' he said.—'At any rate, Stitz suddenly sat down beside us. Your esteemed aunt was there, and Oslip, of course, who even then was barely able to sit upright in his chair.—So, Stitz sat next to us and stared at me without a word. There was something eerie and malevolent about that, and all at once I couldn't stand it any more—I knew what he wanted from me!—and I asked him: "So you want to play with me?"—He nodded. He'd asked me a hundred times before, a hundred times I'd turned him down, and now I offered it of my own accord! Why?—I don't know.—At any rate, we set up our phalanxes, the queens next to the board where they belong, and only eight moves later the horse was already sweating over an idea to ward off the impending checkmate.—That noise in the pub room! All the light!—It went to my head, and while Stitz was still thinking I absently began arranging the captured pieces in the sequence and order of their capture around the two excluded queens. And by taking the queens for kings—How was that even possible?' the godfather interrupted himself, shaking his head again—'by taking them for kings, I began playing a second simultaneous game on the chessboard pattern of the gaming table on which our chessboard stood. Naturally my position here on the tabletop was highly unfavourable, because on the game board I already had an insurmountable lead. You had occasion to verify that just now.—Whatever the case may be: I made three crucial errors back then,' he went on resolutely. 'First, it's forbidden to play with a weaker player. Second, you don't play in the presence of ladies. And Third—and that was naturally the crucial, unforgivable thing—I willingly gave the queens what is denied them by nature: the power of kings!'

Lumiere took out a handkerchief and blew his nose. He thought for a moment, then went on.

'I was toying with the thought of how to win this second game as well—out of competition, so to speak, and without the horse noticing—and quite crazed by this crazy plan I weighed the next six to eight combinations of double moves.—Beside myself, I slid the figures back and forth on the table, while Stitz was still ruminating, and then everything on the upper and lower boards came to life before me. The rooks swayed their hips weirdly, a pawn dropped his trousers to openly shit on his square, a bishop who'd been waiting in one place the whole time took off his shoe and inspected the sole of his foot, and a few squares away one of my knights had turned his back to the centre of the board and was chatting with an opponent.—I picked the figures up, examined them, set them back down again. Now the others noticed that something was wrong over here and came over from their tables to join us. Oslip writhed back and forth beside me, twisting his hands, and then—boom!—it was as if someone had clubbed me on the head from behind—Stitz reached for his glass, took a swig, rolled his eyes and moved. It was a completely idiotic move, sacrificing his knight for no reason.—I leapt up. Stitz never played *that* badly! Of course Oslip understood none of this but he laughed as though he did, his body twitched as though he were about to puke, the tables around me revolved as the figures had on the board, and, not knowing what I was doing, I went over to the window, pulled out my cock—in the middle of the pub!—and pissed into the köpócsésze!'* He spat as he pronounced the word.—'Don't laugh!' the godfather cried out. 'You have no right!—I was so caught up in this double chess madness and thoughts of how I could make this game playable, and then came this move that wreaked havoc with all my calculations. Only one move would have made sense, and it was obvious.—And now I stood there at the window, oblivious to everything, seeing and seeing not—the water that spurted from me in an arc, my wetted trouser legs, the others, laughing and hooting and spurring me on, and again those two boards, double chess. And as I saw all that before me

* The Bieresch word for a wooden crate filled with sawdust set out in pubs in place of a spittoon.

in the sawdust, as clear as a fire I doused with my water, I suddenly realized that I had irrevocably lost the game on the table's peripheral board, because Stitz had left his knight exposed on the main board and I would have to capture it.'

The godfather's face twitched. He heaved a deep sigh.—Then he said sadly, 'I saw this knight, this horse figurine, rear up before me and collapse. A crack ran through the bishop on the board. My queen clutched at her heart while her opponent brazenly lifted her dress and turned her bare behind in all directions.—Éducation sentimentale!' Lumiere suddenly said in French.

He blew his nose again. Then he went on calmly, looking me straight in the eyes again.

'I hurried to our table to warn Stitz, but it was no use.—As though he'd seen through my plan before I did, he sat there calmly with folded arms, looking at me mockingly. Impotent with rage, I overturned the table, board, figures and all, and walked away.—I haven't touched a chessboard since, though my fingers twitch at the mere thought.—But each thought of this game evokes the memory of my invention, complementary chess, the image of the secondary board slowly filling with life as the primary board empties, and the image of that firm, pale, female behind I saw flash out for the fraction of a second.—Lost and not found. The Trojan Horse. "Mulch for the next year!"'

Lumiere leant back and spread out his arms. Then he

clapped his hands and set out anew on his long journey through the room.

'So chess no longer exists for me,' he said with an all-concluding motion of his hand.—'So there's an end, for good, to primary and to secondary chess. Over and done with.—And what have I learnt from that?—That women also have behinds?—Exactly. *"He seeks something he lost in another life,"*[49] say the Histrions. Since then *I* have sought in women's arses what I once found without seeking in chess. The women drive me mad! Your esteemed aunt, for instance. I have a photo of her—would you like to see it?'

He came over to my bed again, sat down on the chair and leant over me confidentially. I shrank back. Lumiere shook his head and breathed in sharply through his nose, as though disappointed.

'Inga, at any rate,' he said, serious again, 'holds that the clicking forward of the clock-hand clicks the world's whole clockwork forward. That the smallest shift shifts everything.—And it is true. "Nothing repeats itself," says Inga, and Zerdahel says, "It is as it was."—He even wrote a story about that once. Zerdahel thinks *he* can write stories too. He *can't*!'

THREE

Two Legends

From the breast pocket of his jacket Lumiere now pulled out three multiply folded pieces of paper. I opened them. All three sheets had been typed with the same typewriter. On each text the godfather had made notes in shorthand, which I could not read. The first text I read was signed.

Its title was:

The Presence of Memory[50]

'He pushes a lever,' I read, 'the backdrops sink down from the fly loft. The curtain swishes up. The actors assume their attitudes. Now the beautiful singer comes and starts to sing bewitchingly. Everyone listens, rapt. The fettered king is carried onstage from the back. The light grows dimmer. Now the beautiful singer begs for the king's life with plaintive words. But the cruel ruler must die. The audience holds its breath. New backdrops lurch down from the fly loft. The angel of death beats its wings, and the guards take up their posts by the tomb. That is the end.—Everyone applauds, perplexed.

'What follows from that?—You shake your head, straighten your trousers. What to do now?—You can't go home—the evening has barely begun. Yet the auditorium is already half-empty and soon someone will come to lock the door.—"Maybe I can hide from the usher by lying flat on the floor between the rows?" you think. Maybe the cleaning lady—you've known her for years—can be swayed by a small sum of money, and you'll manage to go undetected until tomorrow evening. Tomorrow evening!—Tomorrow evening they'll show the same play again. The same play, the same cast. And so you stand—one hand forgotten in the other from the last of the applause.

'Then a hook is released, someone pushes a lever.

'And the curtain rises with a swish.—The beautiful singer wafts up from her bed and starts to sing beguilingly. The audience is quite taken with the song. The reddened eyes show it, the cries of approval.—With a sigh the dying king surrenders to his cruel fate. The angel of death sinks slowly from the fly loft. The singer interrupts her plaintive lament. The tomb guards enter.—All assume stricken attitudes. Now comes the end.

'The spectator applauds, perplexed.'

The Celldömölk Manuscript

I turned the sheet over to see whether there was writing on the back, but it was blank. And so, without looking up, since I felt the godfather watching me from the corner of his eye, I began to read the second sheet of paper.

'What a strange life we live,' it began.—The legend had no heading.

'What a strange life we live!

'Of Anochi Jóték, or "the benevolent", we are told that the guests he invited to a feast actually succeeded in writing down the history of their community in the manner demanded by the scriptures, stringing together the names of the community's members in a common order without forgetting a single name.

'This event is without parallel in the history of our people. And so it must have been all the more terrible for the Biereschek of Celldömölk, and all the more terrible for us, who grow straight from their rootstock, that this narrative vanished from the earth the moment it was written down.

'—It was extinguished before Ahura's eyes, they say. Alas! For even this community, a once-flourishing town, is sinking further and further into squalor, as shall be told.—

'A year after this noteworthy episode, it's said, the guests of yore (who from the day of the calamity had given themselves up to idleness, neither tilling their fields nor breeding their cattle), through a mysterious twist of non-existent fate, all without exception arrived at Jóték's house at the very same hour—this time, we are told, because each wished to tell his host how all his endeavours had failed. For in that year all of them had pursued the duties and tasks assumed by anochis.

'The meeting took place without prior consultation.—But before giving their accounts, the guests, in view of the strange repetition of circumstances, which they saw as a sign, undertook once again to solve the task, all in high spirits and certain of imminent success.—Indeed, this time, too, the ordering of the names was successful. But only half-successful, to the misfortune of those assembled, and of us all, for due to an inexplicable darkness that suddenly descended on their senses, it was never written down.

'—Ahura's ears closed themselves to the Biereschek when he received their message.—

'A year later, the same thing happened one last time—the same guests, the same feast.—However, from the outset the unlucky star of anticipated disappointment shone upon their endeavour. The men were distracted, plagued by the premonition of now-ultimate failure, the atmosphere gloomy in the extreme.

'Several of those present, as they later averred, sobbing with emotion, had found themselves unable despite strenuous efforts to produce the seamlessly joined names.—Their deafening stammer had sounded from nearby like resentful rustling among leaves, and had been audible from a considerable distance as splintering glass, or better, as the cracking of an ice sheet on a vast lake.

'—Ahura's hand has shattered the mirror.—

'We are the wellspring from which you draw yourselves, from which you are drawn,' the narrative concluded. 'Our misfortune commands you to take up the thread anew, anew to tie the knot.—You are the bait—we are the line. Alas!'

Regarding the Backside of the Action

'What words!' cried Lumiere, who had watched me read, moving his mouth strangely, like an adult overseeing a child at its meal.—'What resonance,' he cried again, 'when you compare this document with Zerdahel's shoddy efforts—Celldömölk!' he said. 'That was the old name of a town in the south that was completely abandoned for a time—like Ilmücz. "The community is sinking further and further into squalor"—these words hint at the time of the text's origin. It is believed to have been written down in the first two decades of the century before last.—But more important than its time of origin is the twofold delusion to which nearly all succumb when reading it.—Anyone who has acquainted himself even superficially with our scriptures will see it as a document of salvation and, indeed, three apparently irrefutable pieces of evidence point in this direction.

'Let us go through them one by one.

'"Take everything literally," states Gikatilla's commentary on the Vulgata, "and rise to Heaven!" This exhortation has an ironic undertone, for it's in our nature not to take anything literally, to interpret everything. It's a curse, for each interpretation of the word is tantamount to a departure from the word, and thus to a lie, and according to one theory all our scriptures are merely exegeses of one single source which, however, we do not have at our disposal.—"The masters are gone," we say, "the servants expound." Doesn't that say it all?' Lumiere cried again. 'Doesn't that mean that truth wriggles from our grasp, and the longer we contemplate it, the more unreachable it becomes, unreachable like a mountain ridge?—And how else,' asked Lumiere, 'should one view the attempt of a community to link the names of its members (which moreover are always taken from the scriptures) to form one single story, than as the blasphemous attempt to interpret the scriptures and interpolate a new scripture?

'The narrative "was extinguished before Ahura's eyes," the legend says. "He extinguished the flames with the fire" is what we say, or "He wrote with black fire on white fire."—The same thing is meant by the second statement, perhaps still more clearly. "And there shall be no sound on earth," goes one of the last sentences of the augury, and this is hinted at when we read that Ahura's ears closed themselves to the Biereschek.—And the third statement, which most clearly extends and destroys the hope of salvation, is "Ahura's hand has shattered the mirror!"—Who would not think at once of our founding myth? "He has shattered the mirror" means that Ahura himself has done what our founding fathers did, thus absolving them of the guilt of their deed. Here something has happened for the second time, something has been repeated here, and we all know that only HE can do this.

'"Then this statement *is* unequivocal!" you'll say. Then there *is* such a thing as salvation?—Correct. The statement is unequivocal—in two different respects. For in all our peoples' authentic writings they themselves, these writings, are compared with mirrors. And if you read the text in this way, it means that by shattering the mirror, Ahura shattered the scriptures, and with the scriptures all their consolations and promises. However, this would express the opposite of what was said above, and then we could never find salvation. "The two things are all one," we read in Gikatilla, "pilpul—easy and hard!"'—Satisfied with his explanations, the godfather took back two of the sheets he had given me to read. Then he went on.

'"He pulls faces," one of Gikatilla's commentaries says of him who would interpret the scriptures.—"*If words are shadows / shadows become mirrors*"[51] goes the second part of one of our nursery rhymes and it contains a warning which no one should ever forget when reading, for he who reads wrongly sees only himself.—Think, for instance, of the end of the legend of Celldömölk,' said Lumiere, striking the paper on his knees with the back of his hand.

'Here it says, "You are the bait—we are the line."—This passage seems to pose no problems whatsoever, but—beware!' he cried, clapping his hands as though to break a spell. 'It's a trap!—With us the expression "bait" is often used for the dowry which the son receives, while "line" is an archaic term for the daughter-in-law.—And if you read the sentence along these lines, the meaning swings back to its opposite. "Take everything literally and rise to Heaven!"—What sage words!—Only the unequivocal can be taken literally, and there's none of that in our scriptures. When you read them, you often feel you could slip a noose over the necks of the words, so precise do they seem—but attempt it, and you cut off your own breath. For taking literally supposes that you have understood. But if you make the effort to do so, laying your hands on the table of knowledge, it begins to dance like mad.—Only the first, fleeting impression, that brief, barely audible smacking and sighing you hear when you've finished one of our books and closed it again, gives a true indication of what it meant. All else is delusion.—But for comparison's sake, read the second legend. It's the basis for the theory of Inga's which I tried to describe to you earlier,' said Lumiere and pointed at the third sheet which I still held in my hand.

Stays the Same

'In a village not far from here,' the third narrative began, 'lives a man whose sole desire seems bent on becoming so strong that he can stand up to the world in all ways.—Towards this end he employs the following noteworthy method. Upon discovering an object in which he detects a hostile attitude, he plants himself in front of it and waits imperturbably until he believes it has accepted him. Only on achieving this is he satisfied. Though it often takes days, and not seldom a week or longer (during which time the man takes neither food nor drink, neglecting himself, and saying not a word to anyone nor listening to their words), he waits until his adversary has given him an unmistakably conciliatory gesture.

'In this manner,' I read further, 'the man has succeeded in gaining power over humans and animals, solid things and liquid.—Objects in his immediate vicinity are often said to move without discernible cause from their proper places, by snapping his fingers he causes a flurry of sparks, he can set wood to singing.—He was found one day conversing at length with various tools in a shed. They responded loquaciously, rising by turn and knocking together in a euphonious sequence of sounds.

'His own blood is rumoured to run hot and cold.

'Upon entering a room he'd greet all the objects cordially, while indifferent towards people, uncomprehending of their fates.—He'd often fail to recognize even old acquaintances and former friends.—He is said to be helpful and accommodating in every way, though not in a human way, regarding assistance not as a service to distressed members of his community but, rather, grasping their distress as an assault upon him which he must at all costs counter prudently.—In this very fashion, by forcing himself to stare the greatest horror in the eye unmoved and never avert his stare, he manages as it were to transfix it (the horror itself).—He receives thanks from no one for his succour, nor does he appear to expect thanks or reward.

'The view has been voiced that this is a man of false enlightenment. This is unquestionably unjust. Hogy—that is the man's name, meaning "as the case may be", "that" and "how, in what fashion?"—neither boasts of his art, nor have any signs of silent pride been detected in him. But it is through them that the false enlightened one always betrays himself.—Altogether such verdicts are to be treated with appropriate caution.

'At the same time, reinforced by certain circumstances, a different opinion has gained fuel—namely, that his beneficial works in one place are quitted by inexplicable calamity in another. Thus it is told: last year, at the very instant when Hogy, in Kertes, halted a conflagration in a fruit loft merely by rubbing his hands, all the livestock penned on our village pasture dropped dead, a total of twelve cows and thirty pigs.—Another time a tornado of uncommon force descended upon Hetföhely, which means "Monday market" and which we call "Bildein" and tore off the roofs of several houses while he was conjuring a hidden spring from the ground, ezenkivül (what is more) in a place where no water had been found in living memory.'

Regarding the Backside of the Action

Now I handed the third sheet back to Lumiere, and he slipped it into his breast pocket with the others. 'If we knew all the movements of all the particles of a single moment in our history, all future developments, all past states would be deducible. "Each action has its backside," says Inga. It's the corrective injustice, Oslip's see-saw,' the godfather explained.

I flinched.

'What's wrong?' he asked. 'It's an ancient term. "Összelep" is Hungarian, meaning to connect two things at once. "In falling," we say, "you're borne upward." In the very same moment as bliss rushes in your ears and the world sinks beneath you *like a graveyard with its crosses,* the other end of the see-saw strikes the ground, and I, the one carrying you so high in the air, tear off my foot.'

'What?' I cried breathlessly, because I knew he was lying, 'that was you?'

'No, no,' Lumiere said irritably, 'Oslip, of course!—But let me finish now.—"Each slap in the face you get," we Monotomoi say, "deprives the world of the power for a boon.—It's your fault!"—Or, to speak to Inga. "You," he says, "take the blow meant for me. What have you done to me?"'

'We also call it "playing duck, duck, goose",' the godfather added with a laugh.

FOUR

The Interim Aid Society

'Of course, all this is hard to grasp,' Lumiere went on, serious again, and lit another cigarette. 'And I can well imagine that you'll be asking yourself what this has to do with you.—Listen well!' he said and began pacing back and forth again.

'This is the thing—you're the dead man.'* He paused. 'The scriptures warn us against the dead man.—"He sings in the wrong voice," one passage goes, "he eats with the wrong hand."—Straight parents, crooked child. The backside of the action—do you understand? Can you read palms?—The right hand shows what you want, the left shows what you have. You hid the left hand from us, you held out the lying hand!' he said, pointing at me.

'Your uncle died,' he went on. 'You were sent us in his place. Fine. We must learn to cope with that. But that's exactly why we need to know who you are.—Who are you? Where do you come from? What are your plans? Those are the questions.—What do you think the Jew did that first evening without your noticing? He drank from your wine glass. When you

* As the Bieresch call the godchild.

drink from someone's wine glass after him, we believe, you know what he's been thinking.—But your glass was empty. Tough luck.' He stopped at the end of the dance hall. 'So we waited,' he said, his face to the wall. 'And what did we learn in five long weeks?' he asked and turned around abruptly. 'Nothing. You showed us your sweet side. Thanks—now we want a look at your behind.—"Turning the sow on her other side" is what we call that.'

He looked at me gravely.

'So, the interim aid,' he said at last, abruptly.—'You called us, we're here. What can we do for you?'

I gave no reply and closed my eyes to avoid looking at the godfather.

'I tried to explain it to you just now,' Lumiere went on patiently, 'It's a sort of emergency relief organization for young people who, through no apparent fault of their own, have got into difficulties.—I say "apparent",' he interrupted himself, 'because the fault is beyond doubt.—However, the absolute prerequisite for support of any kind is that the recipient proves himself worthy of assistance. That means that he himself must earnestly endeavour to free himself from his plight. Belonging is not enough!' he cried fervently. 'More is called for.—What's called for is *esprit de corps*, community-mindedness, cooperation! That's what matters!—The dead man gratefully taking the hand that reaches out to him, showing that he'll help himself too, if necessary—that's it!'

'I don't want any help,' I said this time, my eyes still shut.

'Yes you do,' the godfather returned, 'you want help.'—And, as though speaking not to me, but to all of humanity through me, he added, 'You want help desperately.'

'There's so much fever in you,' he went on softly, bending close to me. 'All your life it wants to escape you and all your life you haven't let it out.—Touch your head!' he said. 'Do you feel the heat? You've got an unhealthy climate. You came within an inch of dying!'

I looked at Lumiere, who now spoke as though in a fever himself, and shook my head.

'You're singing with the wrong voice!' he repeated thoughtfully.—'What's so important that you so urgently have to hide it from us?—What have you got there behind you, hm?' he asked, now threatening. 'An umbrella? A wheelbarrow?—We'll find it out sure enough!' He scrutinized me.

'You city folks,' he said scornfully, 'you're such masters of the lie! Every innocent word's a lie, that's your guiding principle.—You always take the short-cuts, and when you don't end up where you wanted, you're indignant.—But not with us! With us everyone has to learn how to walk first before he can go dancing about as he pleases.'

Lumiere composed himself and said calmly, 'Now, do you want our help or don't you?'

I made no reply.

'Then you don't?' he asked. 'Will we have to try again differently, then?'

'Do as you think,' I rejoined.

'I already am!' he cried almost cheerfully.—'Lina!'

I gave a start. He'd called my aunt.—What did he want from her?

My aunt came in and stopped in front of the door, her hands pressed flat against the door panel behind her. I noticed for the first time how much she had changed over the past weeks. Nothing remained of her former self-assurance. On both sides strands of hair hung down into her face—the face of a drinker.

'Yes?' she asked, her hands darting back and forth fitfully behind her.

'We're ready now,' said Lumiere. He seemed satisfied.—A memory stirred within me. Had he said these words before today? No. But I was certain I'd heard him say them once. When had that been? On which occasion?—I mulled it over, but Lumiere interrupted my thoughts, addressing my aunt in a sharp, commanding tone.

'Now sing,' he ordered.

'Yes, godfather,' she said timidly.—And then, laying her hands weakly on her hips and swaying clumsily, as though resigned to her fate, she began to sing in her nasal voice. She tilted her head and reluctantly squeezed out her little song:

'*"They'll find us a way!"*

say the blind to the deaf men,' she sang.

'*And who do the blind mean?*' the godfather interrupted, call and response.

'*The lame men!—*'

'*A-men,*' Lumiere concluded gravely.

My aunt wept.—It was a revolting farce.

'What you just heard was the 51st Calypso.—Actually that term is incorrect. It ought to be "klipot"!' I already knew that from Zerdahel.

'But what is the message of this song?' the godfather asked. 'What do the first two lines of the response mean?—You'll understand shortly.'

'We have a prophecy from the late fourteenth century,' Lumiere began his exposition. 'You know it as the legend of Anochi Yglemech, telling of a Bieresch community's disbandment immediately after the unexpected appearance of a stranger. In an addendum to the version you're familiar with, the following passage appears towards the end: "And so they"—meaning the Ilmüczers,' he interjected, 'who made the stranger carry the dog outside the village—"And so they beheld the earth in its true form—as fire!—and the water in its true nature—as blood!"—These words provide the answer. And what is it?' he asked.

They implied, the godfather explained, that the Ilmüczers had seen into the nature of things, an event that according to tradition could occur only when a community was about to disband, which, Lumiere went on, did in fact take place. The inhabitants of the village, the narrative related, abandoned it on advice from an Anochi. Moreover, an earlier text, lost in the previous century, described in detail what had preceded the Biereschek's departure from Ilmücz—in a mirage never before beheld or described, the eye of Ahura had appeared in the southern sky in all its terrible splendour, as a mirror in which the colours of all four elements played at once. In this place the dome of the sky had cracked with a report, audible to none, but casting everyone to the ground, and immediately closed again. This closing had been clearly perceptible to all witnesses, as a noise perhaps best compared to a rapidly pulled up zipper.—'"God zipped his fly" as we sometimes joke,' cried the godfather.—Fiery rain had fallen from the sky, turning as it touched the ground to sand which the four winds scattered, and the hole, grown together again, was visible in the sky for some time longer as a Monyorokérék, as a 'circular hazel bush', a scar.

Whatever one might think of this account, whose inconsistencies in places were confusing for the reader, one thing, Lumiere went on, was undeniable—that the stranger's arrival in the village had, from that point on, been directly associated with the salvation of the

Biereschek. Especially in the time immediately following this text's inception, this had occasioned the most absurd and unfortunate speculations.—'Salvation as such was thought possible!' the godfather cried. 'Think of the manuscript of Celldömölk!'

It was no wonder, he said, that the events in Ilmücz left their mark on the manuscript's style and message, and there was plausibility to the claim that at that time similar incidents were recorded throughout the area east and south of the lake—but in works which must have quickly lapsed into obscurity only to find expression once again in the Celldömölk version. Of course, the disappearance of these links surprised no one, as only authentic accounts could survive intact in the long term.

'This account achieved one thing, at any rate,' said Lumiere. 'A fatal dispute flared up between the Minim and the Malchim. We, said to have been a happy people—"Saturday's olive pressers",[52] they used to call us—destroyed all means of salvation in the following salvation wars.—Salvation,' the godfather exclaimed, 'is something you cry for only when you've just gambled it away.—Happy peoples have no history,[53] they say, and we Monotomoi have resolved to restore this condition.' The godfather was speaking as though to an electoral assembly.

'*We* believe in the uniqueness of every single Bieresch and his irreproducible combination of qualities, and for that very reason we know we can expect nothing from him. His contribution to history is to prevent things from repeating. And that is why there can be no reconciliation between us and the Histrions—Zerdahel most of all!' Lumiere stopped in his tracks and pointed his finger at me.

The way he talked, he reminded me more and more of Inga, whom he had clearly chosen as his role model. And he had taken all his gestures from him. But like a diligent yet talentless pupil who looks up to his teacher and idolizes him, he seemed to have learnt by rote what Inga had pre-digested, without grasping the substance of what he declaimed.

'The Histrions,' he exclaimed, 'would have us believe that salvation is possible through an individual—contrary to the scriptures! When not a single passage in our writings leaves any doubt that the grand design can be restored only *when all the teeth of all the dogs bite together*, as they say, that is, only when all make common cause.—And although everyone knows that, it is always the best among us who prefer the Anochis' life to the bliss of community. In each person the desire for solution and salvation is so overwhelming that our sole wish is to see a stranger carry a dog outside the village, rather than get back to work on the common history of our people together with our brothers and sisters, unperturbed by the story of Yglemech.—Is any of us proof against the stranger and his promises?—The stranger!—When will he come?—What will he be like? What will he do?—"*The old, old stories,*" it's said of these hopes, *"all the books are filled with them, in all the schools the teachers draw it on the blackboards, the mothers dream of it as the children drinks at their breasts. It is the whispering of embraces, the soldiers sing it as they march, the merchants sing it to the buyers, the buyers to the merchants."* [54]—The stranger!—The Biereschek have been blinded by these promises!' The godfather slid the chair closer to my bed and sat down.

'The stranger,' he said again.—'Belief in him brings blindness, and blindness is contagious.—Remember the song your esteemed aunt sang just now?'

I nodded. I didn't want to hear another word, but it seemed he had only just arrived at the point he'd been aiming for.

'The Biereschek—they're the blind,' he said. 'They're blinded by these hopes.—I am the deaf man. Deaf to all promises. And *whom* do the blind expect to lead them, Lina?'

My aunt gave no reply. She covered her face with her hands and sobbed.—I knew what he meant.

'The lame men,' Lumiere crowed. And, as though it were necessary to play this game to the bitter end, he asked, 'And who is a lame man? Whom does the song mean?—What do you think?'

I said nothing.

'You!' Lumiere said solemnly.—'You are the stranger, the lame man. "Light-footed are his words," the scriptures say of him, "let them run away.—He has no weight. Pick him up! If he falls he'll break."' The godfather looked at me eagerly.

'You're alone,' he said.

'I want to go home!' I cried.

He didn't stir.—'You're alone,' he said. 'And believe me,' he added after a brief pause, 'the time when you could run home to hide in the folds of your uncle's coat because of every little thing, just because you pinched your thumb, for instance—that time is over for good!' His words were far too loud.

'I want to go home!' I said again.—What had the godfather meant by the thumb?

Again it seemed to me that I had heard this once before, that his words had flung open a window within me through which cold night air now streamed into my room.—And then I remembered:

One evening during my first stay here I was playing with Oslip and several younger children by the creek behind the carpentry workshop belonging to my girlfriend's father.—Suddenly Oslip called me over. He was standing there bent over a rubbish bin as though there were something special inside. He held the lid in his right hand while rummaging through the rubbish with his left.—'Go sit on top!' he said to me, still busy with the contents of the bin, and proud that he'd chosen me of all people, when he was the universally recognized ringleader and I was new here in town, I'd asked what was going on.—'I don't know, it's really funny,' Oslip replied and asked me once more to sit atop the bin. I did as he said, but nothing happened.—'Wait a minute, you have to do it like this!' Oslip said, standing with his back to the bin. He placed his palms on the lid and swung himself on top of it.—The lid gave beneath his weight with a sigh, but that was all that happened.

'Did you hear that?' Oslip asked, and I said I hadn't.—'I don't believe it! Try it again, and pay attention!'—I tried it again and, clumsy as I was, failed to slip my thumbs from under the lid in time and sat on them hard.—At once two blood blisters rose under the skin, so painful that I cried out loud.

'Do you hear it now?—I think I hear it!' Oslip, who had planned it all, laughed and jeered, and in a canon of malicious glee the other children, standing about us in a circle, chimed in with his laughter.—In my shame and my rage, I dealt the youngest of them, a weedy little boy with thick glasses who hadn't understood a thing but laughed along all the louder for that, a resounding slap. He ran away bawling, and Oslip planted himself squarely in front of me.—'You won't ever touch . . . again!' he yelled, pounding me with his fists to the rhythm of his words. And, as though to prolong his pleasure in this torment, he kept repeating the boy's name and beating me. He didn't stop until my nose was bleeding profusely. 'He's ready!' Oslip said and ran away with the other children.—I tried to remember the boy's name. It had been a peculiar one, a double name or the name of an animal.—And then it dawned on me—'You're Kukmirn!' I said incredulously to Lumiere.

'Exactly,' the godfather returned calmly. 'Kuk-Mirn. Kuk-Mirn.—The little boy with the bird's face.'—As he said his former name, he imitated a cuckoo's call.

'Let's get on with it,' he said impatiently.—'Do you want our help or don't you?'

'All because of a slap in the face?' I asked back without answering his question.—'Are childhood stories your yardstick here?'

Lumiere was silent.

'I don't want your help!' I said.

'Halfway!' my aunt screamed from the door.—I flinched. She had said the name.

The Wheelbarrow

'Leave him be!' the godfather snapped at my aunt.—'It's up to him!' Lumiere stood up.

'Go outside now,' he ordered my aunt.

'Halfway, please accept! I beg you.—Do it for my sake!' she called to me even as the godfather grabbed her by the arm and shoved her out the open door. He shut the door again and stood in front of it as though to keep my aunt from coming back in.

'You will accept. You will accept,' he said firmly, as though to himself. He looked at me, but his short-sighted gaze seemed to fall short.

'You have the choice between Rák, Petty Theft and me.'—I was about to speak but he wouldn't let me.—'It's up to you.—If you choose me, to begin with the least likely option, I'll lend you a hand in Inga's shop as best I can. I won't help you deliver the post, though, because I have a game leg and the doctor won't let me take strenuous walks.—If you choose Petty Theft, you can count on his accompanying you on your delivery runs and pushing the wheelbarrow now and then. Petty Theft has one drawback, though—he drinks a lot, and the last thing you need right now is a distraction from your work. There are mountains of post waiting for you, you're in for quite a surprise!' the god-father interjected.—'So you're left with Rák. We all think you'd be wisest to take him. First, his patience is unflappable. Second, your wheelbarrow belongs to him now (the two of us would have to borrow it from him, and no one likes to loan out a christening gift). So there would be no difficulties in this regard either.—But, as I said, the decision is entirely yours. Make it now, but make it wisely!'

—The wheelbarrow!—'I don't want any help!' I managed to cry. I seemed to feel the windows break, the floor sink a bit beneath my bed.—That had happened once before: it was noon; nothing stirred; the wind could barely be felt, wafting through the whispering leaves. Someone had stepped on the place where later they would bury me. A scream had burst from my breast, a vein ruptured within me, and a second scream followed—but the foot was long since gone.—

I lay as though in a swoon, my hands turned outward. The animal inside me stirred with a rustle.—I thought of the knackerman, and De Selby: Were they raising the spade now to break the ground?—Why had my aunt said nothing about the wheelbarrow?—The wheelbarrow. The christening gift. I screamed.—I was the dead man.

I turned on my stomach and buried my face in the pillow, open-eyed. Lumiere grabbed my ankle and tried to turn my leg around. *'Legs blown askew,'* the words came to me, *'so that I fall into a still deeper pit.'* [55]—Something rose up within me and tumbled down.

'I'm bursting!' I cried.

Lumiere came closer and sat on the edge of the bed beside me. Now he grabbed me by the shoulders and turned me onto my back.—'Turning the sow on her other side,' I thought.—The godfather felt my pulse, bent back my hands, spread out my rigid arms and stretched my fingers which I had clenched into claws.

Something cold ran through me. Only my head was still alive, and my heels. I tried to move. Tears ran down my cheeks.—'A dead man has stirred,' say the scriptures.—From above, like a doctor pursing his lips to whistle through his teeth, I saw myself lying there.

'I'm bursting,' I said again. Then I screamed.

My aunt bolted into the room with several compresses over her arm.

'Vinegar,' I thought. I smelt it. Too late.

'Get out!' Lumiere screamed.

'Vinegar,' I said.

'It'll be over soon,' said the godfather, taking my hand.

'Soon,' I repeated.

'Hush,' said my aunt.

'Yes,' I said.

'Do you have to go already?' my aunt asked the godfather.

'Not yet,' Lumiere said softly.

'Won't he accept?'

'I think he will.'

'Will you accept?' asked my aunt.

'Soon,' I said.

'Who will you take?' asked Lumiere.

'I'll take Rák,' I said.

'Better now?' asked my aunt.

'Soon,' I repeated.

'I'm going,' said the godfather, turning to the door.

'Why are you people doing this to me?' I asked.

'Hush,' said my aunt.

'You really don't know?' asked Lumiere.

I shook my head.

'They have to know who you are,' said my aunt.

'I'm Halfway,' I wailed. 'I'm Halfway.'

'Sleep now,' my aunt said.

'Soon,' I said, and fell asleep.

FIVE

The Second Run

I spent the next day in bed, but the day after that in Inga's shop, sorting the post that had arrived during my illness.

As Lumiere had prophesied, all the postbags filled the little room nearly to the top; only the workbench and my working space in front of it were still clear, so that here at least I could move unobstructed. The half-finished peach-pit was wedged unaltered in the jaws of the vice—clearly Inga had not touched it in the meantime, and more than a month's dust had gathered in the deeper grooves. With difficulty I moved aside a few sacks to reach the hook where my uniform cap hung, freshly washed. My aunt must have brought it back at some point.—Loath to see the beginnings of my uncle's face, I folded up the first empty postbag and laid it over the vice. Then I sorted the circulars.

Inga came in several times that morning, evidently to see how I was getting on with my work. He noticed that I'd covered up his carving, but didn't mention it. No doubt embarrassed, he hardly spoke to me at all.

In the afternoon I was on my own. Inga had locked the shop at noon and taken his leave for the rest of the day, saying that he wanted to play some billiards. I was glad to be left alone. I still felt very feeble, and shortly after he left I lay down on some postbags to take a nap. Turnip, who had stretched out in front of the door, woke me shortly before five with her whimpering.

Then, late at night—darkness had long since fallen—I was done. I had stacked the letters in piles, topping each with one of Inga's advertising flyers. This one bore a different slogan: 'Many greetings, go to Inga's for your eatings!'

I locked the shop door behind me and set out for home with the dog. Inga hadn't returned yet, and I decided to leave the key with the proprietor of the pub next door, assuming I didn't find him there anyway.—Inga was there. He turned around briefly as I walked in and gestured to me to be patient until he had finished his game. He was the last guest in the place, and the proprietor, who sat slumped in one of the niches in his flowered dressing gown, one arm laid on the high upholstered back, seemed to be waiting only for Inga to leave. His eyes were closed, and if he hadn't turned his head slowly towards the door when I came in, I would have sworn he was fast asleep.

Missing a ball at last, Inga leant the cue against the wall, clapped his hands, as I had seen him do the first time, and took the key which I held out to him.

'Put it on my tab!' he said to the proprietor, who, startled up by his clap as though caught at some illicit activity, had hastily wiped off two or three tables. Then he fetched a cover from behind the bar and unfurled it with a flourish over the big billiard table. For a moment the cloth hung in the air as though borne upon the billows of smoke from Inga's cigar, then briefly swelled and sank down on the green table surface. Inga helped the proprietor adjust the cover, and as he fitted the elasticized ends over the corners of the table, he asked me, 'Did you get everything done?'

I nodded.

'Was anyone there to see me?' he asked, straightening up.—I shook my head.—'See you tomorrow, then!' he called to the proprietor in parting.

Together we stepped out onto the street. Without a word Inga gave me his hand, so gaunt that I could feel each separate sinew.—'I have to go to bed now,' he said as though in apology, and took out the bunch of keys to add the one I had returned to him. I wished him a good night, but he no longer heard me. The door was shut, the key turned in the lock—a sound like someone softly grinding his teeth in his sleep.

I headed towards the village. The night was dry and cold, tautening the skin. The grass was hard. It bristled beneath my steps and the padding feet of the dog who jogged along beside me quietly, as though whistling to herself. The houses of the Bieresch seemed pressed by a hand against the hills and into the hollows.—But already I was standing outside the dance hall, and the massive building loomed up implacable, darker still than the faintly moonlit night, not a gleam of light in it, silent as though everything had been settled long ago and there was nothing left to say.—I went inside, breathing rapidly, tiptoeing silently down the corridor whose flagstones Turnip's paws struck like fitful rain.

My aunt was asleep. The door to her room was ajar. As I crept past I saw the woman roll over in bed. The wood creaked with this slow movement, and I imagined I could hear each single bedspring stretch and contract. I paused, as if expecting her to talk in her sleep, but all was still. Quietly, but not quietly enough, I closed the door of her room. My aunt started, stared at me aghast, and as suddenly as though her words were only the continuation of what she had been dreaming she screamed at me, 'Two thirty! A miracle that you've come home at all!—Were you at the pub again?'

She fell back into the pillows. 'They came for the radio-gramophone today,' she said, panting as from great exertion.—I meant to finally ask her why she hadn't told me about the wheelbarrow, but she had already gone back to sleep.

I went to my room.—Not only was the radio-gramophone gone, my books had vanished as well.

Rák

'All the Biereschek's doings are a mystery to me,' Rák said to me the next morning after I had sorted the new post, tied the stacks into bundles and put them in the wheelbarrow outside.—In the intervening time the vehicle's handles had been restored. It was the work of a true artist—I searched a long while before I found the joins where the hands had been glued back on, almost invisible, following the grain of the wood. They felt different than the previous hands. The thumbs were disproportionately thick compared to the other fingers, as though to prevent my breaking them off again.

'You did a fine job smashing up my christening gift!' the godfather said good-naturedly, and only now did I notice what Zerdahel had mentioned: Rák couldn't pronounce the 'sh'; the 'sh', detached from the sentence, seemed to fly from his lips like spittle.

'That cost me two half-days' work,' said the godfather.

I picked up the wheelbarrow. Rák walked a few steps beside me without a word, as though realizing that I'd detected his speech impediment, and then began to speak.

'All the Biereschek's doings are a mystery to me,' he said again. 'I just can't figure out the meaning of it all!—At first glance everything strikes me as somehow plausible and even meaningful but, at the same time, it seems both brazen and devious. It's all like a joke that starts out in good fun but will take a nasty turn.'

Rák turned around, as though to reassure himself that no one was listening.—I said nothing, merely waited.

'I think the reason for that,' he said after pausing to reflect, 'is that, on the one hand, we always think we're capable of giving our all—and we are!—but, on the other, the moment of failure always comes when all would have been necessary.—The swoon of the brain! Think of And Vice Versa!' he cried.

'It's the moment when our brain rises against us and revolts—and then it's more alive than ever. It's as though now and then we have to prove to ourselves that we're capable of failure!'—Now the godfather was striding far ahead of me. His hands were clasped behind his back, and I could see his fingers rise and fall by turns as he spoke, like the hammers of a piano.—'Failure,' he added, 'is the destruction of order required for us to create order. For that at least makes a little sense.—And the result?' he asked. '*"The eternal return of the new,"*[56] one might say.—Where do you suppose that comes from?'

He turned and looked at me questioningly.—I had hardly been listening, trying instead to accelerate or throttle the speed of the wheelbarrow in time to the rhythm of his words. It was that old game again, and only when I realized that he expected a reply did I try to recall what his last words had been.

'Is something the matter?' the godfather asked anxiously. 'Should I take the wheelbarrow for you?'

I shook my head, though sensing that his question was in earnest.—Rák stood where he was.

'You can trust me,' he said sotto voce. 'I'm your godfather now.—I'm not one of the Bieresch, I've never been one of them.—Why? I don't know. Maybe it's Anna—' He reflected. 'But it's not just that,' he said. 'I'm "másként", as we say—different somehow. But I'm good at shamming,' he explained. 'You don't notice at all. I've simply learnt not to stand out.—Do you know what I always say?' asked the godfather.—'I say, "Whatever you do, don't tangle with the unavoidable! School yourself in the avoidable,[57] that's less risky."—Do you understand?'

I shook my head.

'Wait,' the godfather interrupted his deliberations, waving his hand at me, 'I'll take the wheelbarrow for you. It's hot today. That doesn't bother me—on the contrary! I couldn't live without this heat, and when I've got something in my hands, too, keeping me busy, I can concentrate better.—And maybe you'll be able to listen better when you don't need to watch the road.—Here, let me take it!'

'No, it's fine,' I said, though I would have been glad if he'd done it and I'd been able to look around, if only for half an hour.

'As you like!' Rák said politely, and bowed. Then he went on with his speech: 'The unavoidable does what it wants to anyway.—Whereas you can fit in with the avoidable. Only once you've learnt, again and again, to fit in completely with what might have been avoidable, only when you vanish in it without a trace, so to speak, when you know it by heart—only then can you begin attempting to avoid.—One example—' The godfather was completely in his element. 'There's nothing I love more than women with perfect bodies, and after that an artfully prepared meal.' He smacked his lips. 'But as you may have seen, we have little of the one and still less of the other.—But does that make me avoid eating? Do I refuse to take women to bed with me? Not at all.—On the contrary: with downright fervour—albeit not with pleasure—I let my wife sap me, and afterwards I eat like a horse. In other words, I let the avoidable have its way, I eat and sleep badly.—I sense that it might also be right to do something else, but I'm not at the point of actually doing it. So I go on doing that one thing.—Look here: I'm forty-six years old now. I may have another thirty years to live—we die late in these parts. My father made it to eighty, my grandfather to almost ninety. Should I then avoid something today—today, perhaps too soon, avoid something that may need to be done, because it, because *I* am far from ripe for avoiding?—Should I already be transforming some avoidable thing into something else, something that would then definitely be, would have become unavoidable? Now, when I don't know yet?—I don't think so.'

Rák interrupted himself and, as though he knew that it wasn't easy for me to follow his deliberations while pushing the wheelbarrow along behind him, he paused to give me time to think his words over thoroughly.

'You saw my wife at your reception in the dance hall, didn't you?' he asked. 'Well—Anna is not my wife and never was! In fact she's Naghy-Vág's wife, and nonetheless mine, cast by lots into my hands, fallen to me at the dice table. The blow meant for Naghy-Vág struck me. Bad luck, you could say,' said the godfather, but immediately qualified his words. 'But no reason for me to withhold myself, far from it. Nagh is crazy about her—she repels me.—Double bad luck, but that's all it is. As Inga would say, the lives of three distinct persons have crossed in the wrong place, perhaps a completely indistinct place—to the disadvantage of those involved, as it now seems. An avoidable misfortune, that much is clear!—And all the same, no one in sight is avoiding it.—Interesting!' he said thoughtfully.

'So we have Nagh, Rák and Anna. Nagh loves Anna (as I hinted), Anna Nagh.' He glanced at me sidelong. 'And every morning,' he said, 'every morning at ten that hunchbacked ox races up on his blaring motorcycle, dismounts, leans his cycle on my shed, takes off his trouser braces and puts them in his pocket. You take my meaning.' He stressed each word separately. 'I, Rák,' he went on, 'sit in my kitchen, waiting, hoping yet doubting that perhaps this day at least will pass without the obligatory morning disruption which—I admit it—somehow, despite everything, convulses my innermost being.—So I wait. Perhaps I'm wrong, I think, or is that him coming already? Yes, he's coming. I hear it from afar. Anna's cooking cabbage. She doesn't hear a thing. Anna is hard of hearing. She hears him long after I do.—If only the Holy Ancient One had given me her bad hearing, and her mine in its place!' the godfather interrupted himself again.

'On with it,' he cried. 'There he is, then. There he comes. I get the jitters. That deep drone, him waving to us from afar, so to speak.—I want to get to my feet. I'm ready. Not even a beast could stand this any longer!—For heaven's sake, I ask myself, is it humanly possible that she can't hear him yet? It is.—Now I get to my feet. She looks at me (surprised!), so I sit back down again. Those are the rules of the game—I can't leave the house until *she* wants me to. Well then—Anna's cooking, Nagh is roaring around the curve down below, his racket fills the kitchen, I scoot nervously back and forth on my chair.—And now—at last! Now she hears it too!—You ought to treat yourself to the spectacle!' the godfather cried. 'The whole house has to tremble before Anna hears it! Only then—but even now as though somewhere, far, far away, there were a slight suspicious hint of an indistinct, harmless little buzz—only then does she tilt her head to the side, listening, only then does she look at me.—Something in her eyes has changed fundamentally. They have a resolute, self-assured gleam.—Does she even see me still? I ask myself. Am I still among the living? But before I can answer this question, or even think it through to the end, my Anna, as though jolted from a state of distraction, as though struck all at once by something elemental, something of vital elemental importance, says cajolingly, "Could you be a darling and fetch me something from Stitz?"—Fetch "something", she says, she doesn't say *what*! She takes off her apron. In front of me.—I merely nod.—Like a thief caught red-handed, I make off through our back door. There I stand, waiting until it's all over.

'"But why on earth do you wait?" you may ask me,' the godfather interposed. 'A legitimate question, and yet—I beg of you!—Should I put on an act as well? Isn't there enough playacting inside?—No. I stay outside and wait. I hear the front door open. I stand outside the back door. Nagh comes in, stops for a moment warily.—"Is he gone?" he asks. He asks softly, but loud enough for Anna to understand him, which means, he yells.—Of course I'm gone. All he needs to do is look. Well, am I there? No.—I'm standing out here. It's raining, it's hailing, it's cold as a witch's tit. I'm standing out here sweating. I wait, putting my eye and my ear to the keyhole by turns.—"He's gone out," Anna says, "you don't need to worry!"—A fine joke! Nagh is three times as strong as I am.—But what happens next? Well—Rák's standing outside his own back door, Nagh sits down at Rák's kitchen table. Anna, Rák's wife, brings Nagh a plate of cabbage. Cabbage is Nagh's favourite dish.—Rák gets the rest for lunch (he hates cabbage!). No matter. Anna puts a plate of cabbage in front of Nagh. Nagh eats. She sits down at the table next to him and strokes his upper arm with her hand (I can see it through the keyhole).—Anna asks Nagh, "Do you like the cabbage?"—Of course he likes it, but Anna doesn't understand.—"Do you like the cabbage?" she asks him again. Nagh grunts. Anna doesn't hear it (she's hard of hearing!), so she asks him a third time.—"Can't a man eat in peace around here?" Nagh yells and bangs the spoon, *my* spoon, on the table. Nagh is angry. Nagh has had enough.—"Here we go again," I think. She's going to bawl any minute. She starts, and I know Nagh can't stand to watch Anna cry.—"I didn't mean it like that!" he'll say any minute now. Somehow I enjoy that.—Now he says it, but it doesn't do any good. Anna's not that easy to soothe! She goes on crying.—"There, there!" says Nagh.—"Now it's coming!" I think. And then—you hear a smacking noise, as though they were slapping each other, then they huff and puff again.—"What the devil are they up to in there?" you feel like asking. "Are they moving furniture?" But then—boom, boom, boom! They keep time like carpet-beaters. Out here I cover my ears, but it's no good—the thumping gets louder. It sounds like a whole cavalry regiment riding over her. The spoon clanks to the rhythm on the kitchen table. The stool topples over.—Won't it ever stop?—Yes. Now. One more time her skull hits the windowsill. Then silence.—Nagh mounts his motorcycle. Hastily Anna picks everything up and straightens the kitchen as best she can. Then she flings the back door open wide. She acts as though she's looking for me, and is astonished to see me standing in front of her.—"What, you're back already?" she asks.—"How hot you are!" She passes her hand over my brow. "Did you walk the whole way?"—I give no reply, flinching at her touch. But she won't let it got at that. She bends down from the step to embrace me and pulls me into the house. And then it's my turn.

'You mustn't misunderstand me, though!' the godfather interrupted his story. 'I'm not complaining.—My feelings are of no importance in this matter, and I don't take it personally in the slightest.

'It's not about me, any more than it is about Nagh or Anna,' he declared. 'Probably nothing would be easier for the three of us than to avoid these constant indignities.—I'm free! I can go at any time. If I want to.—But do I want to? Or, more properly, am I *allowed* to want to? Wouldn't Naghy-Vág, who's consumed by homesickness for Anna's body, wouldn't he be the one, long before me and much more than I, I who go cold to the core when I hold this woman in my arms, wouldn't *he*, then, be the one with the right to want such a thing? Why doesn't he just move in and leave me his hut? Surely not out of convenience?—*Not* out of convenience, believe me! It's just the opposite, because I've always been this way, but he's had to change himself radically. He used to be perpetually jolly and friendly— today he's brutal and mean!'

Rák now spoke without once turning towards me. Again his hands twitched, clasped behind his back, and he nodded as he went on.

'There's no question,' he said. 'We're allowed to go hungry if we don't like the food!—That's what I wanted to say. But are we really? Are we not *compelled* to eat as long as something edible is there? Are we *allowed* to avoid until we've learnt once and for all to fit in with all conceivable contingencies of the avoidable?—We are allowed to, but we shouldn't.—Believe me, sometimes I dream (fearfully, I tell you), I dream of pleasures that would be free and trustworthy. In these dreams I'm wanton and frivolous, often I even jump out the window from sheer devilment, just to seek this freedom!—And then I think of Anna—my Anna, hard of hearing, hard to budge. And at once I turn back again, back to this square kitchen table. Cudgelled back here by myself, to go on eating bad food, to go on pleasuring Anna who's not bad but physically repulsive to me. And so I go on living the life of one wrongfully used twice over.'

The godfather paused again. Now he turned around and looked at me.

'Were I to go hungry,' he said, 'I'd do so without saying a word. For me, you see, hunger means no more than forgoing bad belly-swelling coitus and forgoing the ensuing punishment by vile belly-rumbling cabbage. And still!—Sometimes, at least, when all this wears me down to the marrow, I think: Perhaps this repulsive offer of menus and bodies is in fact unwarranted? Haven't I fit in with the avoidable long enough? Isn't it sometimes said that the Avoidable suddenly, as it were from weariness at constantly going unused, quite imperceptibly shifts to the Becoming-Unavoidable?—Tell me, is that so?' he cried. 'And if it is—doesn't that mean that all the strange and wonderful things of whose existence so much is supposedly whispered, and which, it is claimed, uplift us, that all that, then, is withering away unseen before my eyes and with my very own approval?—The thought is terrifying.—Listen: I am told there are rivers in South America which flow only six days a week.[58] There are stone rivers, as you can read, where in place of water gigantic boulders tumble with a din—past creeks of sand that flow three days to the south and three days to the north and stand still on the last day because there is no set direction and they don't want to choose the wrong one.—I was born on one such seventh, wrong day—as were you and the others who live here!—We say God created the world on a leap day, and that's true!'

Rák interrupted himself and joined me with a few quick steps, each time crossing his right leg over his left and then dragging his left leg to catch up.—'I walk crabwise,' he said with a laugh.

'Listen: Once I dreamt that my house stood at the foot of a mountain range that towered above me unending. Anthracite crags plunged like waterfalls outside my back door, and inside the house I heard them roaring, raging down. But it seemed every time I got up from my table to fling open the door, they came to a halt—for an eternity of profound, self-immersed silence—and nothing moved. But if I leant back over my desk and my work, or even if I merely looked away, these cliffs began at once to move again, and their depths seethed with tumbling stones.—At last in one such moment I pulled myself together and went out of the house. But the moment I stepped outside I felt how—with a pull that seized all my limbs—the cliffs began irrevocably to usurp my body, how they worked on it to make it stay, how fibre after fibre turned slowly to stone and my movements grew more and more sluggish. And the longer I lingered outside, the stronger, crueller and more fathomless grew the fear and the simultaneous desire to become, at last and truly, the stone I knew I'd long since been.—An impossible sound—like the desperation of a saw unexpectedly coming up against an ingrown stone on its way through solid wood,' the godfather interrupted himself—'this impossible sound rang out each time when, at the last most blissful moment, I managed to leap back into the house, where my liberated bones began slowly to stretch again and the blood to course evenly through my body.—I awoke from this dream with a cramp in my left leg, heavy as though washed ashore, but soon went back to sleep. At once all the blessings and curses began from the beginning.'

Lost in thought, Rák stopped and looked at the sky.

'There!' he cried, and pointed at a flock of swallows that plied the air like something bottomless.—'I told De Selby about this dream once. De Selby has something seductively confidence-inspiring about him,' he interrupted himself again. 'And indeed he immediately came up with one of his crazy explanations. He said he'd read at some point that due to osmotic pressure and the interchanging of atoms, a person who constantly uses one and the same object is gradually transformed into it and that, vice versa, these objects slowly turn into their owners.—"A textbook case of incubus-succubus," he said.—A cyclist, for instance, as the sexton explained to me, could in this way—unbeknownst to himself—turn into a bicycle, and his bicycle into him. At first glance nothing would seem changed, but the change would be a great one, for the soul was more inert and would go untouched by the interchange, meaning that from then on the bicycle would have a soul.[59] No metempsychosis, then—mere transubstantiation!—My dream, De Selby explained, warned me against the excessive use of certain objects—I'd know best which ones.'

'At first, of course, I laughed just like you, but then a sacred terror seized me—I thought of my Anna!' The godfather paused.—'It was the first time I had seriously considered leaving this woman for good.—Since then I've never dreamt the like again, and though I believe that the truth of this dream no longer holds, sometimes its precipices loom black and indomitable before my eyes, relentless as a future of which I've cheated myself only temporarily. No matter,' Rák said again. 'Everything is possible.—It happens, I've read, that people are sometimes transformed into dogs. And the dogs—these big, gaunt, yellow dogs!' he cried, *'these unsuspecting dogs*!—they're transformed into sticks, the kind tossed for dogs to snap up in flight. But once snapped up, the sticks turn into birds that wriggle their way out of the dogs' mouths.—Have you ever seen the birds fly like this?—That zigzag? That quick to and fro?' Rák asked excitedly.—'There! Look at the seam of your uniform trousers! There it is!' he cried.

I looked at him sadly.—He seemed just as lost as the sexton.

'That's how I am,' the godfather went on resignedly. 'Reality runs away with me. Zerdahel always claims I'm an encyclopaedist gone mad.' He shook his head. 'Zerdahel's right.—I—' He stopped in his tracks for a moment. 'I own a unique encyclopaedia that's come down from my mother's side. That's what uplifts me. It's called "The Library of Erudition and Diversion". You can find everything in there!—I'm your godfather,' he cried, enthusiastic once again. 'I'll bequeath it to you!—You'll study these books as I once studied them. There's much in there you won't even believe.—But I assure you, this encyclopaedia contains everything, absolutely everything we need so very much as a contrast to our lives.—Once upon a time, for instance, there were said to be children who were dead on top and alive down below, constantly kicking their little red legs. There were giant women with their right breasts burnt off and their left bleeding milk, with short hair and tiny limbs shod in men's footgear.[60]—You'll find a list of objects and phenomena which are still found today but could be imagined even then as obsolete—men with peg-legs, solar eclipses, the unlit airspace above us at night, the umbrella, mechanical washboards, bridges' prow-like piers, women pushing perambulators![61]—A new constellation appeared in the northern sky when this encyclopaedia was written, De Selby's sign of the zodiac: the Cyclist!—Incredibly valuable knowledge and utterly incredible things can be found in these accounts.—I've read about impressions of the Luggnaggians there.—Do you even know what Luggnaggians are?'

Rák gave me a questioning look.

I shook my head.

'The Luggnaggians and the Struldbrugs! The Houyhnhnms and Yahoos.—There are so infinitely many things in the world the Bieresch have never even dreamt of.—We are told, for instance, that Japan has calamity literally hovering over it—the magnetic isle.[62] It is ruled by a cruel king. He knows the secrets of magnetism, the riddle of the rapid shifts in magnetic fields, the changes in magnetic intensity, the sudden reversal of the poles, the startling fluctuation of magnetic currents under the earth's crust, down to the tiniest, most unremarkable details. This king is a fiend with a beautiful singer as his beloved, and once a year, during the great revolution, he is condemned to die by the sword. When he dies, his beloved sings most beautifully of all, but however bewitching her song, it does no good—the king must die. Or another thing: the story of the honest man and his misfortune. He, too, loved the high art of song! Because the swans sing so beautifully when death seizes them, he'd wade secretly into ponds at night for some swan-strangling.—By God, I tell you, those are the true secrets! Those are what I'm keen on!'

The godfather stopped, his torso swaying back and forth. He ran his hand through his hair. Then he bent way over, as though searching for something on the ground. At last he picked up a small, light, porous pebble and handed it to me.

'Tuff,' he said. 'Volcanic soil. Its age? Roughly ten million years. How did it get here?—The Tortonian Sea once extended to where we are. There were baleen whales, bush pigs, softshell turtles.—I've never been by the sea!' he said sadly.

'It's all so close, but so hidden. The bone is there, the dog knows it, but he can't find it!' he said, tapping the ground with his foot.—'All the things I'm keen on!' he cried.—'But who will satisfy my hunger?—The Bieresch, perhaps? The apostles of Eternal Return?—Not the Biereschek. I'm homesick, that's it. But the homeland has gone into hiding.—You come home, knock—no one's there! They've all flown the coop. So it goes.'[63]

Again the godfather paused.

'Do you know what the Biereschek are?' he asked. 'Hedgehogs. Insect-eating mammals.—Hedgehogs prowling around strange houses at night, moonstruck, milkaholic suction devices concerned with nothing but themselves, rolling up, making themselves as small as possible, vanishing into themselves when you blast your torch in their faces.—The moment something unfamiliar comes along, they show their quills. The moment something rustles in the underbrush nearby, they huddle together fearfully, little pink-grey snouts atremble in the air.—"Do you smell something?" one neighbour asks the other. "I don't know"—and off they go, or they curl up into balls.—That sounds arrogant, of course, but that's how it is,' said the godfather.—'Sometimes I'd love to take a mid-sized steamroller and roll over them good and proper!'

He fell silent.

We had arrived at the first house, and I set down the wheelbarrow to take out a stack of letters. It was his house, Rák's own. He didn't even seem to have noticed.—'I'll have to introduce you to someone who's not a hedgehog, this very day!' he called after me as I climbed up the little hill. 'You'll be in for a surprise!'

But I was already standing outside his door and knocking. Rák's wife opened the door. She was alone. Evidently it was too early yet for Naghy-Vág. She took the post from my hands without a word and waved at Rák, still standing down below, who waved back.

SIX

The Second Run, Continued

As soon as I'd handed the post to Rák's wife, she'd waved to him again, this time peremptorily, brooking no dissent, and the godfather had obeyed this signal on the spot, like a mother's summons. He slipped into the house before her and under her arm, like someone with reason to fear an impending punishment, and she closed the door behind him firmly.

What power that woman had over him!

I waited a while longer in the hope that he'd come back out after all; aside from De Selby, Rák was the only person I liked somehow. In the short time we'd spent together on the way from Inga's shop to his house, I had grown fonder of him than of the sexton, who, perhaps without knowing it, seemed to have given himself up long ago.—I waited, but the godfather didn't come. Once shut, the door stayed shut; he was probably sitting on his stool already, hands darting across the table in agitation, listening for the drone of Naghy-Vág's motorcycle.

I turned and continued on my way alone, the wheel-barrow in front of me like a plough whose wrongly set blade scraped along the poorly gravelled road which in places sprawled without transition into a stony field crackling in the heat.—Time seemed to stand still. Quietly I gnashed my teeth. Again and again it all started over, again and again I pushed my vehicle along this same stretch of road, which always seemed to have been laid down between the low hills just for me, a broad filthy-brown strip of plastic weighted here and there by stones.—As I took the path out of town to the knackerman's dwelling again, I felt gnawed to bits by the rasp of the wheel, ground up between millstones.

From the edge of the hollow where once before I had stood staring down, I saw that no one was home. The dusty, long-stemmed nettles that hung down the slope like wild hair swayed sluggishly up and down, mute, as it were. The door was locked with a big rusty padlock.—I'd been given my dog here, and from up above the shack really did look like a doghouse or—still more so—like an outhouse behind which rubbish had been dumped in a heap that glittered wickedly in the sun. Scattered across the slope which fell down steeply to the hut, empty, burst tins lay amid the nettles and the wild peppermint which was used in these parts to make a sweet, pungent tea.—Sweet, too, was the stench that rose up to me from the hollow, and all around the dark green necks of broken beer bottles glittered venomously.

Somewhere in the distance a circular saw started up—a high, yearning sound, as though whined out by a dog, doubling up in the air when the saw cut the hard wood it was hastily fed, and seeming to stretch out again when one log had been cut and the next was being fetched.—I harkened to this music, but the further I leant towards it, the further it seemed to retreat from me—as though someone were carrying the saw away from my curious ears.

Then, from a great distance, I heard one single blow of an axe and, as though that were the set signal, the town siren suddenly howled out behind me.—The noon train! It had hit De Selby's dog. It had brought me, and after me, day after day, the post for me, which Inga fetched each following morning from the train station with his open lorry.

I remembered my second evening in Zick, when De Selby and I had sat down there with the knackerman on into the night, the dead dog on the table in front of us, and slumped over it the sexton, who had wept and wanted to die himself when Jel Idézö described the funerary rites of the Bieresch. 'A halál kutyái ugatnak ki belöle,' said the knackerman. That means, 'The dogs of death bark from within him.' When a person died, the knackerman went on, the dog would bay. As the soul's former owner, it was the first to claim it, and sometimes the souls of the dead entered dog's bodies shortly after the funeral—which was why dogs were seen as sacred animals in this region.

Earlier that day Rák had hinted at something along those lines.—'Dogs,' I'd read in my almanac, 'are regarded by many peoples as bringers of immortality.'—'They return to their vomit,' Lumiere had said.

Eyes bent to the ground, I hunched over my wheelbarrow.

At the 'Green Wreath'

Rák had advised me to take a short cut on the way back and return to the village across country, by way of the 'Green Wreath'.

When I arrived at the inn, the front door stood open, but both the small taproom and the kitchen behind it were empty.—I put the post down on one of the tables and looked around. The heavy smell of tobacco filled the room. It smelt of old beer, of the century-long hopes and plans of the Bieresch, again and again forged anew and toppled as with the toppling wine glasses, and it was as though they were present, as though they'd merely slipped out for a moment, as though the severed phrases' loose ends still swished through the silence of the room, ready, after this brief interruption, to return at once to their old subject, to ring in what might finally be the last phrase of all, the all-encompassing explanation and salvation.

I turned away.—On one of the two windowsills, between the double panes, lay an old folded newspaper. 'The railway always runs!' it declared in large letters. I read the sentence once more and then said it aloud.—That was the answer. I giggled.

During my first stay I had often stood here waiting for Maria, my girlfriend. At that time it was not yet a taproom, but a tiny kitchen-parlour adjoining her parents' low-ceilinged bedroom, into which Maria had moved shortly after her mother's death, while her father set up a room of his own in the new building which now housed the inn's kitchen and the former cinema hall.

I recalled the last evening before my departure.—We stood in the dusk behind the house, choked by rage at this senseless parting, eyeing each other suspiciously, each solely concerned, it seemed, to wound the other as quickly and irrevocably as possible. The air was moistened, as though by a finger, from the previous day's brief showers, and filled with indefinable noises: a sort of snuffling or soft, snoring groans from all things, which seemed to have sat up in their beds in a fever—'már menöfélben van'.

A sigh wafted towards us from every corner, all objects gazed at us with animal eyes—the barn door stood open like a hand poised for a slap. In a wordless duel we stared at each other hostilely, mute with fury, teeth bared.—Twice Maria had laughed maliciously for no reason, and I had beset her with threatening gestures, filled with treachery and bloodlust. Then, our hands clenched to fists behind our backs or in our pockets, as though to be on the safe side, approaching and addressing each other, we'd stalked aimlessly up and down the yard, we'd stopped and replied with cold gazes, both with separate abysses sealed within us.

To be taller than me, Maria interrupted her wanderings outside the entrance to the cinema and stood on the first step leading to the door. Then she climbed one step higher and her smooth soles slipped. Alarmed, I reached out to hold her or catch her but she angrily pushed my hand away.

Back then, at this impasse, I'd first had the sense of being entangled in something that was stronger than me in every respect. Mortal fear filled me, my arms hung down slack, hung on my shoulders by wire loops, my head projected at a ludicrous angle from my body, like a bird's, my heart was twisted to a knot, and to find some relief, to shake off my weight, I began to make fitful, twitching movements with my hands. Maria watched me a while aghast; then she covered her face with her hands and ran away, weeping.

The next day I went back again, but the house was empty as it was today. At any moment, I feared—still cut and split inside as though by two knives, lengthwise—the white head of my girlfriend's father would lean from one of the windows to curse me and drive me from his land for good. I stood outside the house waiting, with a knot in my heart as the day before, with bird's eyes skipping fearfully, and the feeling of a turkey's beak growing from my face. But nothing happened, and I returned, if possible, unhappier than before.

I did see Maria one more time, at the train station, shortly before my departure. Sitting half in the saddle, her hands in front of her on the handlebars, she was talking to a woman from the village, rolling back and forth on her bicycle in time with the conversation. When she pushed the bicycle forward, she bent her knees slightly, and when she pulled it towards her, she stretched out her leg.—It was a little swinging motion like that of a swaying boat, and at the sight my hands clenched around the suitcase handles as though they could support me.

Without asking my aunt for permission, I set my luggage down beside me and went over to Maria to say goodbye to her. She turned pale as she saw me coming, but as though powerless, she didn't stir, passively letting me stand on tiptoes to kiss her on the mouth. Then, without having said a word, I ran back to my aunt.—A light, fleet fear rose within me as I clumsily stumbled back those few steps, but when I stood beside my aunt again, who scolded me, shaking her head at my behaviour, I felt all at once the wonderful sensation of a victory achieved for all time.

The parting had agitated me so much that on the return trip from Zick to Vienna, my temple pressed against the cool glass, I gazed fixedly out the window—back to the station where perhaps even now, trembling in her innermost being, my girlfriend stood by her bicycle, her tongue pressed motionless to the place where I had just kissed her.

At one in the morning, shivering with exhaustion yet hyper-alert with excitement, I changed in Vienna for the train that would bring me home. I was alone in the car, and I huddled in a corner by the window, still gazing back, trying over and over again to recall Maria's face, and imagining that if I succeeded, she could hear what I said to her in my mind.

One station past Vienna a man got on, and as soon as he sat down he unwrapped his snack and began to eat. By turns I heard the rustle of the sandwich paper, then the noise—rapid, gnawing at me—of his teeth as he split, then crunched up one radish after another.—I had resolved not to fall asleep on the train, but the naturalness, the detachment from the world with which this man, probably oblivious to my presence, addressed himself to his food, had something soothing and, without noticing, I slipped from hyper-alertness to sleep.

Only when the train entered my hometown's main station did I wake up, hoist my suitcases down from the luggage rack as though in a dream, and set out for home, shivering. Dawn was already breaking, but the streetlamps were not yet extinguished, and the empty station square had the spectral look of a brightly illuminated, frozen pond.

One more time I looked around the little taproom. Again the news-paper advertisement between the panes caught my eye. 'The railway always runs,' I said, nodding.—My girlfriend, or so I had learnt from my aunt, had lived since her father's death more than two years ago with a second cousin who had come to Zick from a village in the south as the dead man's proxy. He had a wife at home, and unable to make up his mind on one of them, he travelled back and forth between Zick and his hometown. Maria, enduring this state of affairs no longer, had gone to my hometown shortly before my arrival to spend the summer with her sister and nephew.

And so we had switched roles.

The Way Back

The way back to the village wended its way through low hills, at the bottom of a winding ditch in which the wind was barely felt. The slope on both sides was covered with grass, singed by the sun and nearly withered, the sandy brown soil showing through between the tufts. I thought again of my girlfriend, and how once, in the cinema hall, I had promised to marry her.—Somehow, I sensed, that promise still held today, and the unhappy relationship which, according to my aunt's hints, she had begun with her cousin seemed to confirm this feeling. Maybe, I thought, she had waited all these years for me to return, and when I didn't come to honour my promise, she'd become involved with the other man; or perhaps when my uncle died she had realized that I would come as his proxy, and the thought of how humiliating it would be to see me again following her fiasco had strengthened her decision to go away.

I looked up from my wheelbarrow.—Around me the small, dune-like hills undulated in constant restless motion like an unending ocean, and I wished Turnip were with me now, imagining that the dog, always a little bit ahead of me, would have shown me the way between these humps that jostled together like the backs of herded cattle.

Single blades of grass swayed on the crest of the hill—up here a hot wind blew, burning in the eyes—and a cracking as of dry twigs ran on ahead of me. A high, thin whistling sound, barely audible and always seeming at the point of breaking off, lay in the air. There was a crackling all around; in places the sand, whirled up in slender vortices, rose over the path in wandering columns, and pebbles leapt up and away from the wheel of the barrow like click beetles or sparks come to life.—It was noon, siesta, the time of the mice and weasels who crossed the path in front of me in quick bounds, and sometimes, as though blind from the heat, somersaulting, came running towards me in zigzags.

I glanced up at the sun, which seemed to hang high above like a mirror, lighter than the blue of the sky, trembling within this blue—a mute eye, 'the lesser witness', as they say here, Ahura's second eye.

I thought of the day after my arrival, of the wheelbarrow thrust into the dried-up streambed, the 'monyorókérék' stuck in a crack in the bottom, heralding 'the Wild Hunt'.—That same evening the knackerman had given me my dog, now at home with my aunt, and I'd had to listen to his lament for my uncle. I'd heard Naghy-Vág copulating with Rák's wife, and while I stood by the front door, quivering with shame, Rák himself had probably been out back, watching everything through the keyhole.—'My God, they'll bring us misfortune!' Anna had cried, and I'd taken it to mean that De Selby and I had learnt a secret—which in fact the whole town had known long since. Thus it all seemed to have served the sole purpose of destroying the friendship between me and De Selby, and I bore part of the blame for that.—'You see,' the sexton had said to me at Jel Idézö's, 'See, even Master Knackerman says so: you're to blame!'—And for that Zerdahel had given me a name and father at the 'London'—albeit a father who from the outset had denied any relationship to his scion.

All this was as near as though it had happened just yesterday, separated from today by the thin skin of a single night, preserved in a tiny, transparent capsule which released its contents when pushed around for a time in the mouth.

Under the sweatband of my uniform cap little rivulets made their way through my hair, tickling my nape and neck. As though in greeting, I doffed my cap and ran my hand over my head.—It was a gesture I recalled from my uncle. I winced, as though I'd caught myself doing something wrong, but then made this gesture a second and third time to check the veracity of this discovery, to refute the first impression and ultimately to find myself in it after all. I knew what it meant, but the strangeness remained.—That wasn't me; this gesture was made neither for my head nor for my hand.

I looked up at the sun. I closed my eyes, wanting to sit down on the slope, but couldn't somehow; I merely stood there where I was, while seeing myself standing there, my hands clenched on my uniform cap like my uncle—in the stance of a man with no rights, presenting himself to a new master.

There were two kinds of time, I thought—this slow one here, mine; and a more swiftly passing time, one in which this moment had already been long ago, in which days and years melted away like a substance quick to evaporate, like snow on a hot stone, turning to water, dissipating, a time that raced on, beaten by a quicker heart, while I myself, mute, benumbed and swaying from the heat, went on standing there in the bright noonday as though it were midnight, on the ground before me the wheelbarrow, rooted together with me to this spot.

SEVEN
Litfás

I had stopped in front of the empty, box-like window display—lined with cardboard and then pasted over with faded photographs from old fashion magazines—of a small shop which I took for a former shoemaker's workshop.—For a while I contemplated my reflection, bluish, distorted and bent by the ripples of the window-pane. In it I looked pale, and the irregular ridges of the pane, recalling trickling streams of water, now elongated me at a slant towards the upper right, now pressed out me wide, melting to a puddle at the bottom, my head seeming to vanish between my shoulders.

Rising on my toes in the hopes of finding a place further up where I could see myself as I really looked, I thought I noticed—just above the partition between the window display and the shop, and behind the border of a dirty white, crocheted curtain hanging down to the partition—a small, sluggish movement, barely perceptible, like the wave of a fin, a large fish diving out of sight in an aquarium.—I leant against the windowpane to peer over the partition into the shop's interior, but it was dark inside and I saw nothing.

Behind the panes set into the shop door hung a curtain like that in the window.—I set down my wheelbarrow, stepped into the doorway and pressed my face against the glass to see better, holding up my hand to block the light that fell from the side.

Just as I was about to straighten up to set out on my way again, the door opened and, as though to startle me still more, an old electric buzzer gave its harsh, rasping tone.—I would have stumbled down the shallow step into the store if a strong hand from the side hadn't seized my arm in a flash to keep me from falling.

'Mind the step!' I heard a man slightly behind me cry in warning. Startled, I breathed in sharply through my teeth and turned around, but due to the rapid change in the light I could hardly make out a thing at first. When my eyes had accustomed themselves a bit to the gloom, I began to make out the separate furnishings—the broad counter that spanned the room from one side to the other like a riverbank, on it something which I first took to be a vase, but which later proved, in the light, to be a short-necked, pot-bellied jug; and on my left, in front of the window display, which was half-screened-off with cardboard, a wingback chair, forcibly squeezed into the corner, which must once have served to seat customers.

'I'm locking up now,' said the man at my back who had just propped and caught me, but he held the door ajar as though to give me the chance to slip outside. But I didn't; I stood where I was and watched him bend down to bolt the door from within. And only then did I notice that he was half-undressed. His sole piece of clothing was a capacious white shirt that billowed exaggeratedly with his twists and turns, long as a nightshirt, reaching almost to his ankles and with its sleeves cut off. From the right armhole, beneath the frayed fringe of a badly sewn hem, a stump protruded, amputated just above the elbow, and when the man stood upright before me again, I saw that he had a sparse, nearly white beard which covered his face in irregular patches like down and together with his bald pate gave him the appearance of a faun. This impression was heightened by his peculiar gait, swaggering yet simultaneously almost weightless, and stood in stark contrast to the shy, bashful manner of his speech as the two of us stood together in front of the sales counter.

But the moment he folded up the hinged board that was attached to the wall as an extension of the sales counter, and stepped behind that counter, his tone and behaviour suddenly changed. He was still friendly to me, but now his friendliness had something jovially patronizing, and the gesture with which he removed a dishcloth from one of the drawers to wipe off the counter was more reminiscent of an pub keeper, the proprietor of the 'London' inn, than of the man who a moment ago had been embarrassed by his scanty dress. And whereas just now I had thought he lisped and stuttered, though barely noticeably, his words now sounded persuasive and almost urbane.

'Let's make ourselves comfortable,' said the one-armed man invitingly, adding at once with a laugh, 'if comfort is what we're after.'—And, as though to do his part, he whisked under the counter a plate of leftover food that had stood by the jug and almost simultaneously produced two small cut-glass goblets and a half-burnt candle.

'Turn the light out again!' he said, motioning with his head towards the switch by the door which he'd pressed when I came in.—'No one needs to know we're still here.' He inserted the candle in the neck of the jug, and after deftly removing a match from a box with one hand, he wedged the box under the stump of his right arm and struck the match.—'You see, I'm not the best person for fledgling proxies to be seen with.' He held the match to the candlewick, which refused to burn at first, clogged with soot; little sparks shot off from it, but then it burnt after all. The one-armed man lifted the jug with the flickering taper and handed it across the table to me. 'Put it over there,' he said, pointing at the sill of a small blind window to my left. He watched me set down his strange candlestick; meanwhile, he turned halfway around to a shallow set of shelves built into the wall behind him, broken by a wooden door that led outside, and removing one of five full wine bottles. He pulled out its stopper—a plug of rolled-up newspaper—with his teeth.—'For the poor souls,' he declared without looking up, teeth clenching the roll of paper. He set the bottle down on the counter, lifted up the glasses one by one to check their cleanliness and finally spat the paper out to the side in a long arc.

'Go ahead and take a seat,' he said, as I was still standing by the window, awkward somehow, unsure how to behave. 'But be careful with the armchair, it doesn't belong to me.'—Now, his head at a tilt, he filled the two wine glasses before him on the counter brimful. His actions, and not only them, his words came in a sequence as automatic as though they followed the fixed rules of a game which always had to be carried through according to the same plan, and in which each visitor was made to play the sidekick.—Now the one-armed man carefully took one of the two glasses between thumb and forefinger, so as not to spill a drop, and slid it across the counter towards me. He glanced at me with an inviting gesture, then deftly lifted up his own glass in one sweep and—without touching his lips—downed it.

I watched all his movements closely, and the longer I did, the more I gained the impression that he sought to impress with his dexterity, continually pointing out how well he managed without a second arm, indeed how much more skilfully he used this one arm than others used two.

'And so you're Halfway,' he said at last complacently, and leant back in his chair. He looked at me so searchingly that I lowered my head beneath his gaze. There was a pause. All that could be heard was the flickering of the candle on the sill above me.—'How do you like it here with us?' the one-armed man asked into the silence. His question sounded as though it were meant to encourage me, but I merely went on staring at the full glass, turning it to and fro in my right hand. 'Not very well, hm?' he asked. I shook my head, looking up now, but I saw that he seemed completely indifferent to my answer, or already knew it in advance—evidently he was much more interested in his pointed fingernails, which he examined intently.

He stood up.

'I'm Litfás,' he said, standing next to his chair and bowing slightly. It sounded like the preface to an elaborate explanation he was about to give, having tinkered at length with its phrasing. He couldn't pull it off, however, falling silent again and pacing pensively in the narrow aisle between the sales counter and the shelves. That was fine with me.—Tired from the day, I nestled deeper into the chair and closed my eyes. Now and then I heard him sniff softly; then he'd noisily take a seat again, refill his glass and slurp from it at long intervals like someone suffering from the cold or pondering a difficult problem.—These small, repetitive sounds had something pleasantly soporific, heightened by the occasional absent-minded scratching of his fingernails on the countertop. It was warm here in the shop, and just as I really was about to fall asleep, I heard him raise his voice.

'Now drink,' he said solemnly, as though I were finally in the requisite frame of mind.—I raised the glass to my nose and sniffed. The wine had an outlandish, slightly pungent scent, as of the needles of some unfamiliar tree. I took a small sip.—'Very good,' said the one-armed man and gave me an encouraging nod. I took another swallow and winced involuntarily; the oddly sharp taste made me smack my tongue. I wanted to settle back in my chair but, instead, I leant forward, propped my elbows on my knees, at a loss somehow, turning the glass around in my hands. It was as though some unexpected news had thrown me off balance and confounded me, and miraculously I was wide awake again.

'The wine tastes good,' Litfás observed with satisfaction, and nodded confidentially over the table at me. 'Gyanta,' he explained, 'resinated wine.'

He refilled his own glass and downed it, but held the liquid in his mouth for a time and puckered his lips, sucking in air with a whistle and allowing it to pass over the wine. That was the slurping noise I had heard earlier.—He looked at me calmly. I knew he expected me to speak now, and as I remained silent he launched onto a word or phrase himself, but then shut his mouth again.

'You don't make it easy for a person, Halfway,' he said at last in an earnest but not unfriendly tone. 'Halfway,' he repeated. He cleared his throat.—'Litfás and Halfway,' he began again, 'two fine names.' He tilted his head back and forth.—'Fine name, early grief, isn't that so?' Again he paused. He seemed to ponder something that lay far in the past and, as though from the depths of that time, he said at last, hoarsely, 'I once owned a rabbit with the same name as you.'

It sounded like ridicule.—I looked up, but he seemed completely caught up in his memories. He sat there lost in a dream, head tilted to the side, listening for some sound from above, from a space, as it were, of whose existence I was unaware.

'Do you know,' he went on, looking at me thoughtfully, 'it's desperation that inspires impossible names for impossible things.' His words were a chanted lament. '*"Life is both crazy and meaningful,"* it's said. *"And if you don't laugh about the one thing and speculate about the other, life is banal."*' He motioned vaguely with his stump. '*"Then everything is on the pettiest of scales,"*' he went on with the quote. It sounded final, but in the same tone he added, '*"Then everything yields only petty sense and petty nonsense."*'[64] The one-armed man rose to his feet again and took a few hesitant steps. He turned back towards me: 'Those are dangerous words!' he said warningly. 'Words cried out from the pit of desperation, words that shouldn't be spoken when sober.' He broke off and paced on for a bit. 'They allow everything,' he shouted at the wall, 'they excuse everything!' Just before the wall he stopped. 'At the same time they dump earth over everything.' He turned back again. 'Watch your step,' he said calmly.

'I was at the brink of an abyss when I experienced what I am about to tell you.' He sat down on his chair. Tiny beads of sweat had appeared on his brow, as though anticipating the efforts his story would cost him.—'It happened about three years ago over in Tadten.' He shifted his chair. 'The entire village was astir. We were supposed to go to the fair in Varbalog—it fell on the same date as market day, and of course everyone figured there'd be a huge to-do and a potlatch or two to join in on.—Do you even know what a potlatch is?' he interrupted himself to make sure how much I knew and where to begin his explanation.

'The word potlatch actually comes from the Hungarian,' he elaborated when I replied in the negative. 'The correct form is "potlás", meaning "substitute". There are two kinds of potlatches, the nagypotlás, or the "great" one, and the kispotlás, the lesser potlatch, and when we talk about a potlatch we generally mean the lesser one, since it's more common.—Come here!' He waved me over. 'Give me your glass!'—I obeyed, curious to see what he would do. He took it from my hand and gazed into my eyes.—'But you don't need to stick around if you're not interested,' he interposed. I made no reply, instead returning his gaze until he lowered his eyes and cleared his throat almost apologetically.

'Well then,' he began. 'Put your glass here.' He pointed at the counter in front of him. I did as he said and waited.—'Rest both your hands here and look at me!' He laid his left hand on the hinged board. I obeyed again, and without looking away he picked up the wine glass that stood next to him on the counter, raised it to his lips and took a swallow. As before, he held the wine in his mouth for a while, rolling it back and forth and closing his eyes. Then he swallowed, let a few seconds pass, looked up again and put back the glass.—'Nothing,' he said almost triumphantly.—'You see, the others always claim they can taste from the wine what someone was just thinking.—Funny, I never taste anything at the potlatch!' He looked at me searchingly.—'Have you ever tried it?' he asked, pushing the glass he had drunk from across the counter to me.

I replied in the negative.

'Try it!' he said.—Feeling that what he demanded wasn't right, and that he knew it, I tried to refuse, but he brushed off my opposition.—'It has to be tried,' he said categorically, and pointed at the glass.—'You owe it a try—always!'

I gave in.—Perhaps because I'd had nothing to eat all day, as soon as I drank I felt my stomach contract under the influence of the wine; my torso swayed back and forth as my hands clenched on the hinged board for support. I squeezed my eyelids together to dispel the dizzy feeling and regain my balance, while Litfás, paying no attention to the state I was in, began to tramp up and down behind the counter, talking loudly as though to himself.

'Stop!' he cried without looking up. 'Did you feel anything?' He kept his back turned towards me. 'No?' he said. He knew the answer ahead of time.—'Then you'll just have to try again!' He leant against the wall and pushed off. Two long steps took him to my side.

'Well then,' he said impatiently.—'Hand it over!' He reached out his hand. 'Me first.'

I gave him my glass, but he waved it away and asked for the one he had drunk from first. 'Whatever you do, don't mix them!' he said importantly. 'If you mix them, it's all for nothing.' He held up the glass, the stem between thumb and forefinger, and swirled it a few times.

'Resinated wine,' he said as though reading from an oenology book, 'develops its full bouquet only when thoroughly swirled before drinking.—Only amateurs drink gyanta wine unswirled!'

He looked at me thoughtfully.—'The kispotlás,' he said. '"*May the floodwaters rise before you, may mud rise behind you!*"[65] say the scriptures.—For the second time the waters are divided from the land.' He took a swallow, sweeping his left arm out to the side and, the last two fingers extended ceremonially, lifted the glass almost horizontally to his lips. His upper lip, like a soft beak, stretched far past the centre of the glass as he imbibed the liquid.—'The clear for me,' he said, smacking his tongue, 'the muddy for you!' He held out the glass invitingly. 'Grub in the mud, and maybe you'll find treasure.'

I picked up the glass and sniffed it. This scent reminded me of something, something that had long lain buried within me. I took another swallow, and as I doubled over the sales counter, overcome once again by that nausea, I saw the one-armed man watching me curiously and coldly with his nearly lashless eyes.

—'Are we not compelled to eat as long as something edible is there?—Are we allowed to avoid?' Rák had exclaimed that afternoon, and for a moment I was tempted to fling this question at Litfás but I restrained myself.—'We are allowed to, but we shouldn't,' Rák had answered himself.—I wanted to open my hand to let go the glass, but I couldn't. I only clutched its stem the more tightly.

'Stop!—What was I just thinking of?' I heard Litfás call as though from an adjoining room.

I understood his question but shook my head. It was not meant for me.—I looked down at my trousers, saw the rowisch,* the serpentine line of the embroidered seam whose sight had so excited Rák.—'That zigzag!' he'd cried, 'that quick to and fro!' I bit my lip, closed my eyes. All at once his words made sense.—Where was he now? Why had he broken his promise and not returned to show me the woman he had spoken of?

'Rák,' I said aloud.—From my lips the name sounded like the growl of a dog.

* As the Bieresch call a trouser seam decorated with rickrack.

'What did you say?' asked the one-armed man, staring at me incredulously and drawing his stump to his body like a short wing.

'Nothing,' I said defensively.

'You know' he said, without pursuing it any further, 'our scriptures contain a passage that has momentous consequences for us all.—"*Most of what matters in your lives,*" it states, "*takes place in your absence.*"[66]—It is not the deed that counts, but the image of the deed. Not what we do, but what happens with what we do—that's all that matters. The deed, they say, is the dumb piece of wood in which time is held captive. It is freed only when the wood begins to spin under the whip of hearsay.—And it is not what a deed reveals that counts, but what keeps silence behind it.—The kispotlás!' cried the one-armed man, though his meaning was unclear to me.

'I've seen it a hundred times—that expression of dismay and perplexity that spreads across the victim's face when someone snatches the glass from his hand and cries, "The muddy for me!"—You ought to see the hell that breaks loose! It's like a game of cards where the stakes are eternal beatitude.' Litfás looked at me. 'It's ludicrous, shameless, and yet deathly earnest,' he explained. 'There we are, ten or twelve of us sitting at the table, and every moment you hear someone calling "the clear!" from his corner and the rest shouting "the muddy!" in reply. Everyone sniffs and snuffles over his neighbour's glass until it drives him wild—for the sugar at the bottom of the glass is the dregs of knowledge.—That's what he must drink down to!'

He broke off.

'There is one striking thing,' he said gravely, filling his glass to the brim, 'and it should give pause to those who make fun of the potlatch. However much may be drunk there—no one ever failed to leave the table just as sober as he came.' He pointed to the glass in front of him. 'This wine is not intoxicating!' he declared. 'Our children drink it without harm! Our women!' He looked at me again, and after a pause he added calmly, 'Our women especially.'

'By the way, do you know what I was called as a godfather?' I shook my head, but as though I'd said the name and he were merely repeating it in confirmation, he nodded, '"Seven Lakes and No Water"!—A strange name. Turns up only once every several generations.'—He reflected. 'It's mentioned in a legend,' he said heavily. 'It tells of an Anochi who dug himself a sitting grave and descended through the soul hole to the dead. He spent a year and a day down there, learning from the dead how they managed to live together peacefully.—When he returned from his journey, the other Bieresch asked him what he had seen, but the buried one only repeated these five words: "Seven lakes, and no water!"—No matter.'

Litfás rose abruptly to his feet. Without the slightest embarrassment he opened the back door and stood in the doorway to pass his water.

'You mentioned the name Rák just now, didn't you?' he asked over his shoulder. He shook the last drops from his member and returned. Like a woman, he smoothed the front of his nightshirt before sitting down again.

'Rák,' he said. 'Rák and Anna.' He paused, then asked thoughtfully: 'Do you know what we say when someone loses all he owns in one fell swoop?'

I replied in the negative.

'God thought it over!' he said hollowly, and more as a statement than a question he added tersely, 'You know Anna?'

I nodded.

'Anna used to be my wife,' he explained. 'I lost her at the dice table back at that potlatch in Tadten.'

The one-armed man slammed his wine glass down on the counter-top. I winced. Rák crossed my mind again. 'This woman fallen to me at the dice table,' he'd said to me that morning.

'When I asked you just now what I was thinking of,' the one-armed man broke into my memory, 'I was thinking of Rák—understand!'

Seventh Lengthy Conversation

'The scene, as I said, is Tadten,' he said resolutely, as though he had nothing more to hide from me. 'The Sign of the Cow.—The time: three years ago next fall.' He cleared his throat. 'Since then I've lit this candle every night.' He nodded at the window. 'I'm paying my life back—instalment by instalment.'

I glanced up at the candle on the windowsill. The window was blind, the inner panes, like the lower part of the window display, had been covered with cardboard. The cardboard bore the company logo of a man holding up a bottle in his right hand like a trophy and apparently launching into a sort of jig. Below that stood: 'Egy uj társasjáték'—'a new parlour game'.—I remembered what Litfás had just told me about the potlatch.—The silhouette of the dancer's body was interrupted at regular intervals by small circles like balls or bells sewn to his clothing, heightening the impression of a jester.

—I recalled my secondary school religion teacher. He was a thin little nervous man with a growth the size and shape of a goose egg just below the wrist, which always came into view when he emphasized his words with furious gesticulations.—In earlier times, he explained to us one day, bells had been used to drive off evil spirits; later madmen and lepers had been belled; they were thought to be possessed by evil spirits and people wished to be warned in time of their approach. He told us that this was the origin of our church and fire bells. 'A superstition once exploited by a pope!' he exclaimed, and at the word 'superstition' he motioned scornfully with his right hand, making the ugly yellow growth peek out for a moment beneath his jacket sleeve.

One of my classmates seized on this coincidence to raise his hand lethargically and ask the teacher if he, too, was trying to drive off evil spirits, or if he was an evil spirit, since he had to wear one of those bells on his hand. The teacher stood speechless for a moment, seemingly unable to breathe, but as though in reply to the pupil's jibe he went on to say, facing us, in a high, soft, yet penetrating voice, that at that time there'd been a law in our homeland that a stranger who stepped under the eaves without making noise to announce his coming could be killed from behind with an axe or a club. He said these words in such a sharp, confident tone that the pupil who had mocked him now turned pale and immediately apologized.

I recalled the bell over the door of Litfás' shop. 'Litfás,' I thought, 'has only one arm. He can't defend himself.'—

'It was Wednesday,' he said now, as though to keep me from pursuing my thoughts any further. 'The arrangement was that we men would go to the fair in Varbalog while the women—aside from Anna, your esteemed aunt had come along—would wait for us in the inn with Oslip.—Oslip couldn't come,' Litfás interposed apologetically, 'even then he could no longer stand up on his own.—I don't know whether she told you,' he interrupted himself again, 'and maybe I shouldn't even talk about it, for in the end it's none of my concern, or yours.' He looked at me. 'The others of us hadn't even realized that Oslip was lost,' he said, 'when your aunt had already made him her lover!—Your aunt is a strange woman.' He hesitated, unsure whether to go on, but then decided to do so after all. 'She loves invalids!' he said hoarsely. 'Anna and Lina are like sisters—and Lina loved little Oslip to death!' He gave me an uncertain, sidelong glance.

'Those are the old stories,' he said, and motioned dismissively with his hand as though to unsay what he had just said. 'Everyone knows them, everyone talks about them, and maybe they really would be best buried and forgotten.—The deed and the image of the deed,' he said again. 'Here everyone knows everything about all the others—the latitude left us is not narrow, but it is known, and thus practically non-existent. All that can and does occur, every deed and misdeed, is only a repetition of what has always been. "*The past,*" the scriptures teach us, "*is the stuff from which time is made, and each passing instant must instantaneously return to it.*"[67]—"You people," they say elsewhere, "are innocent only because you know nothing of our guilt. But the fact that you know nothing of our guilt is what makes you guilty."—No matter,' he said contemptuously. 'We have no significance. The future doesn't lie behind us, as some believe, it's simply not on the path we are taking.—Look here!' He opened a drawer under his sales counter and took out a few things—a pair of nail scissors; a small, flat, enamelled jar with a screw-top; and a spool of thread with a needle stuck in it.

None of that seemed to be what he was looking for. 'I wonder what's in here?' he said, having returned the spool and the scissors to the drawer, and shook the jar close to his ear. It made a soft rustling sound.—'Pins?'—He put the jar back too.

'Do you have a cigarette, by any chance?' he asked, glancing at me.

I replied in the negative.

'It doesn't matter.' He resumed his story.

'So, it happened in Tadten.—We'd been at the fair in Varbalog-Szerdahely.—"Szerdahely" means Wednesday market,' the one-armed man explained. 'The market and the fair had fallen on the same day.' He leant down again, clearly still looking for cigarettes, opened the drawer still further and practically stuck his head inside. 'Rák had wanted to buy a saw but couldn't get his hands on one.' It was as though he were talking to the drawer. 'Petty Theft played cards at the inn and lost all his money. The Jew came dragging a ladder he'd won from his father's brother at the nail hammering competition.' Now he shut the drawer. 'Inga, Naghy-Vág and De Selby were there too. Seven people in total, then, myself included—just enough to keep track of.' It sounded as though he were making a statement for the record.

'Just after leaving our wagon outside the "Az Elején" —that's the first inn on the outskirts of Varbalog, meaning "At the Beginning"—just after arriving, then, we separated. Each went his own way, only De Selby and I stuck together, as I said.—You've got to take care of the sexton!' said the one-armed man, glancing at me sidelong. 'He's someone very precious!—No matter. We'd stopped at the marketplace just briefly to take a look around. There was nothing going on, as usual, and I wanted to move right on again, but the fat man didn't want to—he's like a child who never tires of looking, especially at things he knows already. So we stayed for a while. He drank his lemonade, and I was so bored I had my palm read. The palm reader was a gypsy, so I didn't even understand half of what she said, and the part I understood was nothing new to me.—Stop!' he said again.—'At any rate, we were there long before the others and waited for them in the roadside ditch outside the inn until noon had passed. De Selby was restless, maybe he already had a premonition. At any rate he kept leaping up from the grass like a madman and clapping his hands impatiently when he couldn't see the others coming.—At last they did come. Each told his story and showed the things he'd brought, while De Selby, more and more impatient, urged us to head home. Finally we fetched the oxen from the yard. They stood there as we had left them, as though rooted to the ground.—And that set the tone for our journey home!

'We'd all stowed our belongings elaborately on or in the wagon, in a dither as though heading on a trip around the world, as though we feared we'd forgotten the most important thing. Each seemed to believe that he personally had to check the wheels again, the fit of the shaft, the pull of the lines, the fastenings of the luggage. Meanwhile the sun burnt down on us as though through a magnifying glass. An inexplicable hostility had suddenly arisen between each individual's actions and the others'. Each adjustment reversed the predecessors' adjustments, each word was a rebuttal, everything seemed to have a knot tied in it. Only one thing was clear—we wanted to get out of there as quickly as possible.—But quickly was impossible. We could have crawled that distance in the same time!' Litfás was breathing heavily.

'At last we practically collapsed into the wagon from sheer exhaustion,' he went on. 'The Jew clung to the edge of the wagon with both hands to keep from falling over. Stitz leant lifeless against the back wall of the wagon. Inga had sat down on the floor as soon as he climbed in and kept whistling the same toneless melody to himself. It was fear.—Twice the oxen bellowed. Naghy-Vág, who sat up front on the box, flailed aimlessly at them, drunk with weakness, because they balked at going on. No one said a word. You could hear the earth panting in the heat.' The one-armed man looked up. He gazed past me. 'Something evil had happened,' he said. The words sounded lost in the room's silence, as though they'd strayed here from some other room.

'The cart went on strike.—The wheels didn't turn, merely slid somehow across the ground. We all gazed silently into space, and when two did happen to glance up at the same time, and their gazes intersected, it was as though they didn't know each other, as though they were staring at each other across an abyss—with the blood lust of an alien race.—Hatred flared among us in the wagon, and between it and the landscape there lay an alienation such as I'd never experienced. Each seemed to be cursing the others in silence, and searching for words for this curse, fists clenched, staring alternately at the ground and outside, as though despairing that the calamity he summoned with his curses had not yet come to pass.' He broke off again and wiped the sweat from his brow with his sleeve.

'We were stuck,' he said, and dropped his fist on the countertop as though to underline the hopelessness of the situation. 'There was deathly silence in the wagon.—Everything seemed to get out of our way, to shun us—it was as though the earth were suddenly turning away twice as fast beneath us, the trees bent away, and like a guide there rolled along before us, carried by the wind, a tumbleweed, a monyorokérék!—The air was unbreathable.—Glass wool!' Now he looked at me.

'And suddenly I felt I was about to burst!' he cried. 'In this upstarting silence in which we had to stand and wait it seemed as though all stones had come to life, sneaking deeper into the grass on the shoulder, away from the wagon, as though the grain tossed back and forth beneath my glances and the lashes of Naghy-Vág's whip, as though tufts of dry grass, like spiders, skittered about and away before our wheels. A shriek sliced through the air like enormous pieces of metal ground to bits between two drums. Time stood still.—Before me loomed the mirage of a mountain chain that stood far behind us—the massif of Györ!' Litfás paused.—'Everything seemed bewitched!' he cried again. 'This grinding became more and more unbearable, it seemed to come closer and closer. I looked up at the sun—it stood in the sky rocking back and forth with a yellowish gleam, an evil eye, conjured by an evil hand.—Stop!—"The sun has a squint!" I cried.'

The one-armed man had leant forward, remaining in this position as though poised to leap.

'Before the words had left my mouth,' he said, sinking back, 'I'd already seen it—a second, flimsy, paler sun, drifting out from the other like a coloured bubble, on into the sky, where it hung level for a moment and then, slowly, sank. The syzygium! Time and countertime.—It was a revolting sight, a slur upon everything, making me vomit immediately over the edge of the wagon,' he said, adding harshly after a brief pause, 'Retroactively guilty!'

'It's said,' he explained, 'that after the fact things sometimes seek themselves an order that contradicts the sequence in which they occurred.—Cause and effect change places, the other verdict comes into effect.' He swept his hand through the air and left it hanging there for a moment like a heavy object. 'The victim is convicted as the perpetrator.'

'I said, "The sun has a squint!"' said Litfás, and looked down on his hand, which lay in front of him on the countertop, twitching, like something that did not belong to him. 'I heard a soft crunch, the cracking of a shell, the sun burst, and blown out of this egg I saw the yolk of the second sun slowly dissolve, float away, sink.' Distractedly he raised his hand to the bridge of his nose and rubbed it between thumb and forefinger.

'The eye of Ahura!' He dropped his hand again. '"It is clouded as the eyes of the dogs," the legend says.' He closed his eyes. His left hand fell heavily from the table to his lap. 'Litfás is tired,' he murmured. As though of its own accord, his head slid down on his drawn-up shoulders, and a moment later he had fallen asleep.

The Visage of Horror

I waited a few minutes, and when he didn't move, I quietly stood up. The candle had nearly burnt down, and now it was stuffy and hot in the little shop. I made to leave. A floorboard creaked as I stepped on it. I turned around. Litfás sat there like a dead man, his mouth wide open and his head leant to the side on the back of his chair, but as soon as I tried to lift the latch, I heard him move again. 'You're leaving already?' he asked, still groggy. He sounded disappointed. I stood where I was.—'Since Varbalog I can't sleep nights.' It was not an apology—on the contrary: there was pride in his words, as though this insomnia were a sort of war wound which might be unpleasant for him and those around him but of which he had no need to be ashamed. 'I have to steal my sleep here and there,' he explained uncomplaining, and added modestly, 'I'm old, and I don't need much sleep.'

He said it as though in passing, seeming to search for something perplexedly without knowing himself what it was.—'Have another drink!' he invited me, lifting up the wine bottle as though that was what he'd sought. He waved it invitingly, but then saw there was only a little bit left and, without waiting for my reply, poured it into his own glass. 'I sleep standing up, so to speak,' he said to distract me. 'Litfás the elk!' He laughed. He was wide awake again.

'You know—' he went on meaningfully after finishing his glass, 'I pay attention to different things than most people. I know today that life must be viewed with a cold, impartial eye if you wish to learn from it. If you don't, you find out nothing. "*He* suffers without knowledge," the scriptures say. "He doesn't live, he merely spells out life.—He can't read a thing—he's standing too close to the writing."' The one-armed man clicked his tongue.

'Back then,' he declared, 'my life changed radically.—As I stood in the wagon with eyes open wide, suddenly seeing the sun up above, and that twin sun that sloughed it off, sliding downwards, sinking to re-emerge at the other end of our world, I did not yet grasp what this fission meant for me. All I knew was: that is you.—I had waited for that moment all my life—I had spent that life buried beneath the sand, and now I could rise to the surface! That moment was the nexus of my hopes! Until then I had been nothing—afterward, I knew, I would be everything!—I prepared myself for it, filled my lungs with air, let myself be buoyed up as through water, opened all my senses like sluices. "Only *thus* can things be experienced," goes one passage in our scriptures, "with this readiness to forget all that has been!"—And then?' Litfás looked at me questioningly. His left hand, lying on the table, seemed once again, cut off from him, to twitch like an animal.

'I stood there, waiting for the door of that moment to fly open before me, shatter to admit me.—It was as though I spent days and weeks traveling through the sky with this second sun, at the same time standing patiently down below in our wagon, waiting with my hat in my hand, my head bowed as though in prayer.—To this day,' cried the one-armed man, 'my head sometimes sinks into this position as though of its own accord.—And?' he asked.

'Nothing.—Seven lakes, and no water!—I opened my eyes, awaking in a dead, empty world.' He shook his head. 'I was alone, as though I'd woken in the wrong day.—A hot wind skimmed the earth which had lain down beneath the leaden sky as though to die. The first heavy drops of rain came, evaporating on the spot as soon as they fell. Such a silence surrounded me, I thought I'd die. *The blood circulated mutely within me.*—I looked up, gazing deeper into this wasteland than anyone had ever seen. Everything was so transparent, so strange and yet so heart-seizingly close: I was the first human being on our planet, created to release the dead things from their death. Every breath of mine was a mute sigh with which they crowded still closer to me. They seemed to whisper to me, lean up against me. Again I wanted to scream, not wanting this intimacy—but I couldn't scream.—I looked at my hand—it protruded from my coat sleeve like a little shrub, its twigs covered by a tough, silvery skin, the skin of death.'

'Stop!' cried the one-armed man. Again he gave me a penetrating look.—'The visage of horror.'—I looked away. I didn't believe him. Those last words had called to mind something I knew. I thought of Zerdahel but came no further.

'"*Look*!" the legend says,' he said, '"*the raised arm points downward*!"[68]—That was the worst thing, this intimacy with dead things. In one part of my body—here!' He pointed at the centre of his body with his index finger like someone reluctant to touch a still-open wound. '—Here, then, under the breastbone, I felt something stretch to the breaking point, a nerve, an organ never before felt, and then something did break, and at that moment I felt a tug in my arm and my chest as though I were growing a flying membrane.—At the time I didn't understand what that meant. Only at the inn did I begin to, and not even there, but still later, bit by bit, as slowly as though someone were tightening the screw of knowledge twist upon twist—

and yet, I barked as though to give a sign of recognition. I had experienced that once before—dead land, dead land. It was only for this, I thought, that I had risen from my depths—to see this.—As I fell and sprawled on the floor of our wagon, something soared up out of me as from a chasm, a bird circled over scorched earth and took off with a flap of its wings.'

'When I came to,' said the one-armed man, gripping the table edge as though for support, 'I felt that I was waking, torn from a dream, yet simultaneously, as the woken one, that this waking was only dreamt.—I was so weak, I sat down on the wagon bench. The others had ascribed my fall to the swaying of the wagon and thought nothing of it. De Selby, who sat next to me, put his arm around my shoulders, the shoulders of a drowning man. I trembled. Pain raged in my lower right arm. It was bleeding. I knew I was going to lose it.—A small, dark pool gathered on the wagon floor beneath me, and like a face rising inexorably from the depths of this pool, I felt knowledge rise within me.—"Seven lakes, and no water!" It was the knowledge that I had lost everything, that from this point onward everything would reverse itself, that my life from now on would be nothing but the repetition of what had been once before, that it was running backwards.' Again Litfás stood up to go out and urinate. It sounded like the water of life flowing from him.

'I was alone in the world.' He gazed up at the ceiling as at a sky that had closed to him forever, pitiless and grey. 'I was caught in a droplet of time, a primeval animalcule, swimming one-armed back and forth, over and over, along the same marked-off stretch of my life. They all stared at me but no one understood.—With each jolt of the wagon they seemed to feel the spell cast on all things lift a bit more, and each revolution of the wheels meant one more land mile gaping between them and me.—And then came Tadten. The inn beckoned from a distance, kindly as a friend willing to forgive all transgressions.—Stop!'

Litfás braced himself against the counter with his hand as though to keep his memories at arm's length.

'I was the first to enter the taproom,' he said. 'I stopped as though punched in the face. When I saw it, I realized without thinking: Anna was the second thing I had to give back. She sat on Lumiere's lap with her arms around his neck, kissing him as though to suck the life from his lips.—Lumiere!' cried the one-armed man, and laughed.—'"She never kissed me that way!" I thought. I didn't laugh at the time.—A shock passed through my body. I stood there petrified. My arms, cut off from my torso, dangled from my shoulders like bell ropes. I clapped my hands weakly. Next to me Inga stood motionless, as though keeping a vigil. I groped for his arm, seeking support, wanting to lean on him—but at such moments you find nothing to lean on, you grasp at thin air.—I fainted again. I hit the wall hard, fell to my knees. When I woke from my swoon, some unfamiliar thing lay crosswise in my mouth, tasting of iron and salt: my tongue. I had bitten it through as I fell, and tried to spit it out. Blood gushed out, mingling with the blood that flowed from my nose. I saw the black trail on the back of my hand, looked up, saw it again—Anna on Lumiere's lap, his head between her hands, her tongue, quick as a snake, in his mouth.—Kneeling, I crawled towards her. My shoulder blades dug their way up from underneath my skin like shovels, they clashed together, cracking, fusing to a ridge. Warts sprang up like buttons on my chest. Wrinkles and fissures formed around my eyes, my skin turned to horn.—Armoured, I crept onward—a primeval saurian flushed from its millennia-old lair.—Anna left Lumiere's lap in one leap when she saw me coming, fleeing to the furthermost corner of the room.'

Litfás closed his eyes.—'Everything that happened after that,' he said, 'happened as though according to a plan I had drawn up in advance whose execution I now watched unmoved, because I myself had nothing more to do with it.—At any rate, Anna gave me a wide berth from then on. She took the place next to your esteemed aunt and Oslip, near the door, sat there as she always did when afraid—her hands thrust palm-down beneath her thighs—and in this position rocked back and forth.

'Lumiere stood up and relinquished his chair to the Jew. Rák sat down next to him. I was the third man at the table, but I only stayed for a moment and then went out with Stitz, who lent me his handkerchief. I was still bleeding.—I'll never forget that white wall where I stood then, catching my blood and talking away at Stitz!' he interposed. 'Stitz didn't know what had happened, because he was the last to enter the taproom, and I talked and talked. I told him we were in for the surprise of our lives today, but he only laughed—he thought I was still befuddled from falling down in the wagon. I tried to explain it to him. The daddy longlegs flew up the wall and drifted back down again, as though drawing my words on the wall in invisible script as they flew, while I kept daubing the period after their sentences with my bloody index finger, over and over in the same place.—Stitz didn't understand, and I tried again, and water flushing in the women's toilet next to us kept washing into my explanation. It sounded like the sobbing of someone who'd been weeping and resolved to remain for ever in that cold little locked compartment, to be alone with themselves and their pain.

'Maybe it was that,' said the one-armed man, 'and maybe it was because I kept seeking the same words for my explanations, explanations aimed not at Stitz or at anyone else in particular, but at the world, my farewell speech, so to speak, the speech of a dead sailor before whose blind eyes the whole ship has saluted one last time before he slides into his watery grave—at any rate, I suddenly noticed that Stitz had vanished. I turned around, went back into the taproom and heard him laughing in the kitchen with the innkeeper's wife.—No matter,' said the one-armed man.

'I came back and joined Zerdahel and Rák at my table.—De Selby sat back in a corner on the right, apart from the others. He was alone. Inga was playing a slot machine. He had forgotten me completely, engrossed in the game, whispering his calculations for each successive sequence of symbols.'

Litfás cupped his head in his hand and closed his eyes, as though trying to summon up the scene in every last detail. 'Holding Oslip tight, your aunt talked to Anna over his head. Lumiere wandered aimlessly about the taproom as though he'd lost his wits. Nagh was talking to the innkeeper.—Now Stitz came out of the kitchen and, as though at a signal, everything changed. He sat down at the table next to your aunt, so that she and Oslip were sitting between him and Anna. Rák got up and asked for a saw. He sat down next to Anna and started to play. Anna sang along. She has a wonderful voice,' the one-armed man explained.

'Zerdahel talked to me, which he never did otherwise. Nagh joined us and said that the innkeeper was going to make us a fish soup.—Now Lumiere seemed to notice Stitz for the first time and, as though rediscovering a long-lost homeland, he took a chair from De Selby's table and sat down across from Stitz.—De Selby didn't even look up.'—Litfas ran his hand over his bald pate.—'A carafe of wine stood on the table in front of him. Two unpeeled hardboiled eggs lay on a saucer next to it, and a small white jug stood there as well.—I listened to Zerdahel as he launched into another description of how he'd won the ladder from his uncle. He was telling the story to Naghy-Vág, who wasn't interested and didn't even pretend to listen. He knew the story anyway. And then all at once I was holding the dice cup. To this day I can't explain where it came from.

'I looked over at Anna—she was sitting next to Rák, singing. When she noticed me watching her, she stopped.—That made me angry somehow, and I began to shake the cup in both hands and tip the dice onto the table. At first I didn't even pay attention to what I was throwing. I watched Inga pull the arm of his slot machine, and I felt that something about that was wrong.—"When you don't think", our scriptures say at one point, "that's when you start to think yourself!"' Litfás cried. 'And indeed: I threw the dice, and suddenly I saw that each toss of mine resulted in exactly the same sequence of symbols, lining up on the table in front of me as though on a string. The daddy longlegs' writing on the toilet's white wall!—It was a message, a sentence written in a language incomprehensible to me, clearly meant to reveal to me what I'd already suspected—stop!' The one-armed man sat up straight in his chair: '—that my life was now running backwards.—Zerdahel must have been watching me throw as well, for suddenly he interrupted his story, observed me wordlessly for a time and then, as though to mock me, began telling the story of a man whom he'd once met at a fair and who could roll the dice to and fro from a distance merely by looking, and change their pips without moving the dice themselves. Rák had clearly been listening in, and drawn by the Jew's story, he leant his saw in a corner of the room. He returned to our table—the second turn of the screw,' said the one-armed man significantly.

I looked at him questioningly, not understanding how he meant it, but he paid no mind and went on with his account. 'Anna was furious with me—I had driven Lumiere away and spoilt her game,' he said. 'She turned to your aunt, but she was busy with Oslip.—Lumiere had sat there in silence the whole time, staring jealously at Rák and Anna by turns while Stitz talked away at him without getting a response. Now and then he'd angrily raised his hand to his left ear and bent it forward as though to shield himself from Stitz's badgering.—But as soon as Rák came back to sit with us, he leant back in his chair, relieved, and in this relief began absent-mindedly setting up the figures on the chessboard in front of him. When Stitz asked him again whether he'd like to play—you could hear it all the way over where we were!—he actually consented.—I have to say, I was happy about that,' said Litfás. He clicked his tongue.

'The potlatch announced itself,' he said. '"The mule paws the ground" we say when someone breaks an unwritten law, and in this instant Lumiere had done just that. You see, it's forbidden for a strong player to play against a weaker one. It's a breach of good manners,' he explained. 'It doesn't make sense.—And then, not even ten moves into the game, it actually happened.—Stop! Someone proclaimed a potlatch—suddenly, amid a silence that came like the blow of a fist, as everyone stared over at the two chess players, someone cried, "The clear!"—And, as though in one breath, Stitz, sweeping a figure through the air to smash it down on one of the squares, cried, "The muddy!"' Litfás stood up. 'It was as though it had been arranged in advance.—Several of us responded immediately and switched glasses. Your aunt accidentally pushed hers aside with her elbow. It ended up right next to Lumiere's glass, just as he was holding up a figure he'd captured, foot in the air, as though to prove something.'

'And at that very moment, De Selby, who hadn't been paying the least attention to the goings on around him, clapped his hands. "The egg!" he exclaimed. "The egg!"—Still in the middle of the potlatch, but incapable of ignoring a sensation of any kind, everyone yanked their heads around and stared at the sexton. De Selby had peeled one of the two eggs and laid it on the opening of his carafe, in which a little flame burnt. It gave a mysterious bluish light, and for a moment one felt that time's heart stood still while the egg grew thinner and thinner, more and more elongated, slipping deeper and deeper through the neck until at last, with a soft, dull plop, it burst at the bottom of the carafe.'

The one-armed man raised his head as though harkening to the sound.

'It was like a birth,' he said, 'and when it was over, everyone was as relieved as though *they* had been born, emerging at last unscathed.—Wanting to take a sip of wine, Stitz—whether by chance or intent, I don't know—seized Lumiere's glass, while Lumiere, his thoughts focused entirely on the game, reached for your aunt's when he didn't find his own.—In other words, a completely mechanical affair,' Litfás explained, 'and as I say, even in retrospect I can't help feeling a certain malicious glee, though I was probably the one hardest hit that day. First I lost my arm, and later, somewhere amid all the mixed-up glasses, I lost Anna once and for all.—Probably noticing it just as I had, she cried out loud to keep Lumiere from drinking, and fainted. Meanwhile I knocked over the dice cup in the excitement and reflexively picked up the dice from the floor.

'If *I*, not Rák, had come to her aid at that moment, I'm almost certain she'd still be mine today.—However the case may be,' he interposed. 'She hasn't brought him luck. *"She loves the vanquished,"* as they say, *"but she deceives them with the victors."'* He seemed content.

'She lost Lumiere then, because he drank from your aunt's glass, and that's forbidden at the kispotlás. *"He looks up her skirt,"* the proverb goes, *"and now she wears her apron high."* During the potlatch no Bieresch may learn a woman's thoughts, otherwise he falls hopelessly under her spell.'

I thought of Lumiere, sitting on my bed and wheezing with excitement. 'I have a photo of your aunt!' he'd whispered to me. 'Do you want to see it?'

'Lumiere has lost Anna. He can't have your aunt,' the one-armed man went on. 'When he saw Rák rush over to Anna, he realized what he had done, and leapt up, knocking over the table with the chess figures.—He was beside himself. To get some air, he ran to the window and flung it open. He stood there in front of it, water running from his eyes and down his face—but not just from his eyes!' Litfás cried gleefully. 'He pissed himself in front of everyone!'

He pounded his fist on the table.—But checking himself at once, he looked at me and said calmly, 'Both of us lost everything back then!' And after a pause he added with a soft laugh, 'God thought it over, understand!' He shook his head grimly.

EIGHT

The Great Potlatch

Enough of that.

I stood up.—'Lies!' I said. The one-armed man gazed at me in shock, but said nothing. 'I've heard your story from Lumiere. He told it somewhat differently, though—not much differently,' I said, 'but different in key points, and if I asked Anna about it, I'd probably be told a few more lies.' Litfás didn't stir. Nonetheless I felt he was alarmed.—'You're going to see Anna?' he asked.—'Why not?' I retorted, and, as though she were in fact my next destination, I added, 'At any rate, I'm going now.'

I waited another moment, but he made no response, merely shrugged his shoulders as though to imply that he wouldn't stop me.—I turned away. A few steps took me to the door; I bent down, lifted the latch and went outside. The door fell to behind me of its own accord with a soft click like someone carefully shutting a suitcase.

Outside on the pavement, under Litfás' window display, stood my wheelbarrow. It must have rained while I was with the one-armed man, for on the bottom of the wheelbarrow a small puddle had formed, gleaming darkly in the weak reflection of the light that spilt onto the street from the shop window. Something pale, a piece of paper, gleamed in the water. I fished it out with thumb and forefinger and tossed it in an arc into the ribbon of light. It was one of Inga's brochures.

It wasn't raining now. But a fresh, almost autumnal wind blew, sometimes passing through the leaves of a small pollard tree that stood set back slightly on the empty lot next door. From its lowest branch hung a piece of laundry, a dishcloth or a camisole, which kept being flung upwards, as though the wind were snatching at it, but without getting caught in the branches above which seemed to be its goal.—It hung there like a sign meant for me, and I recalled what I'd read in Collin's book about the planting of espalier fruit: that long into the previous century large parts of Europe had venerated a god or spirit of the mountains who was one with the god of the tree, hanging from the branches of certain trees the bed sheets and clothing of invalids and the menstrual rags of barren women to seek relief from illness or the curse upon the barren.—'Similarly,' the book noted, 'in certain regions the possessions of those who had died far from home were either buried in the mountains or hung in trees, so that the dead, returning home, could come only as far as that tree, and no further.'

I recalled the tree outside the window of my sickroom. My aunt had hung out the damp poultices to dry there, and I pictured how—if I had really died—my mother, followed by my three siblings and laden with the belongings I had left at home, would have climbed the ridge of a low mountain by my home town in a small procession to hang them on such a tree or bury them beneath its roots after receiving the news of my death.

I shook myself.—I couldn't let myself think that way; I'd only admit the rightness of everything I experienced here, and I didn't want that. But my gaze returned to the tree and I went on watching the wind's little drama with the laundry, clinging to it like a vision that had detached itself from the world around me, ridiculing both me and the world, when I thought I heard a voice behind me, softly calling my name. I spun around; it had been my old name, the name I'd borne at home and hadn't heard for a long time. No one was there. Only the tree, rustling in a gust of wind.

I picked up the wheelbarrow by the handles. It felt heavy, as on that first afternoon.—In his shop Litfás coughed, began speaking loudly, muttered and coughed yet again.

'This wine is not intoxicating!' he'd said to me at the start of his perorations. The words didn't seem to hold for him, though, for when I climbed onto the narrow ledge beneath his shop window and peered over the partition into the shop from which the small candle's light gusted out at me, I saw the shadow of his head lurching back and forth drunkenly on the shelves behind him.

He began to speak again. He cursed hoarsely, bumped his heavy body against something—probably the chair—and gave it a kick. It careened across the floorboards and crashed into the wall. Then there was a dull bang, probably as he jerked up the hinged board of the sales counter.

Afraid he'd try to follow me, I pushed my wheelbarrow around the corner of the house, setting it down in the shadow of the wall which the light of a streetlamp limned on the pavement. The one-armed man did begin puttering at his front door, but evidently not to open it, as I had believed, for a moment later I heard him shuffle back again. He had merely latched the door behind me, then.—After that it was as silent as before, and instinctively I held my breath, suddenly imagining that he now stood *behind* the wall, perhaps right across from me, listening, like me, only waiting for me to make a mistake and betray my presence out here by a clumsy movement or a noise.

Several minutes passed that way. Nothing happened.—Perhaps he had realized that he was too drunk to have any chance against me, much less head home, and had settled down in the customers' armchair to sleep it off.

Cautiously, so as not to attract his attention, I pushed my wheelbarrow out from the hiding place beside the house, glad that it had rained in the meantime, as the sodden loamy soil swallowed every sound.—But hardly had I taken the first step when I heard a stifled cough behind me, and turning around I saw him standing behind me, his white nightshirt upright and shining like a flame.

'Come back, Hans!' he called softly, and there was something oddly solemn about his summons.

'What do you want now?' I returned, his strange behaviour making me equally quiet and uneasy.

'I need to give you something!' he whispered.

'I don't want anything,' I rejoined.

'It's not for you,' he replied. 'It's for Anna.—You are going to see her, aren't you?'

'Why don't you give it to her yourself?' I asked back.

'She won't accept anything from me.'

I was of two minds.—'Well, all right,' I acquiesced at last, in part to put an end to the strange scene. I set the wheelbarrow down again and went up to take what he'd wanted to give me, but he didn't have it with him.

'It's inside,' he explained in a whisper.

He turned the corner and beckoned with his finger, standing in front of the little wooden door that led into the shop from the back. I followed him and stopped at the two low steps, but he waved me closer, and once I had joined him in the shop—tumbling rather than walking up the steps—he locked the door behind me.

I said nothing, but as though I'd demanded an explanation for his behaviour he cried reproachfully,

'I don't want anyone to know you're here, and you make so much noise!'

This, too, I took without objection.—'Now, where is your present?' I asked.

'Shh, quiet!'—He raised his finger, then struck his palm against a drawer in the counter on which he leant his backside, as though to hint that it was hidden there. He winked at me confidentially.—'I didn't say it was a present!' he corrected.

I'd had enough.—'All right, hand it over!'

He raised his index finger to his lips again and made a placating gesture with his hand as though asking me to be patient for a bit.—Then he elaborately filled my wine glass.

'There, drink up!' he said encouragingly and slid it towards me across the sales counter. He filled his own glass and clutched it for a while, eyeing me thoughtfully.

'Let us drink to our brotherhood!' he declared, now resolute.

The cue had been given and, as though at last all barriers had fallen between him and me, he moved closer and promised: 'Now I'll tell you everything I know!'

It was final.

'You know,' he said, looking me in the eyes, 'you can't hang on to water—it hasn't any hair! That's an old proverb of ours.—A proverb for monkeys.'

He cleared his throat. His breath smelt of garlic.—'And all the same,' he said, 'you've got to hang on somewhere.'

He placed his hand on my shoulder and squeezed it. His chair stood behind me; I felt the edge of the seat at the backs of my knees and sat down. He remained standing.

'When I questioned the others about you,' he continued in a satisfied tone, 'I kept hearing these same three words. Each time it was "Hasn't any hair. Hasn't any hair."' He scrutinized me. 'But I knew better,' he said. 'I'd seen you once before and I knew you're not a bad sort!' He paused for a moment, then added quietly, 'You're just out of your depth.—Rabbit-head!' he exclaimed. His face bent down so close to mine that his breath brushed me again.

I averted my face.—'What?' I asked.

'Watch out for the women, rabbit-head!' the one-armed man said urgently and squeezed my shoulder again.

I looked at him. I didn't understand what he wanted from me.

'I saw you back then in the dance hall,' he explained. 'I was standing outside in the dark and watching you all from a distance. Everyone was drinking and dancing. You sat down at Zerdahel's table, turning your back to me, and I called your name over and over, but you didn't hear me. Just once, when the Jew got up and went out, you came to the window for a moment and looked out at me. And you saw me. You must have seen me,' the one-armed man said firmly, 'because you looked me in the eyes.—But then something happened, and you went away again as if I weren't even there. And then you listened to the Jew all evening as though he were solving the world's mysteries right there before your eyes.—Meanwhile I stood outside, not knowing where to go and what to do, because I wanted at all costs to keep him from telling you his stories.'

'And why?' I asked, now curious.

'Because he doesn't know a thing!' cried the one-armed man. 'Because he doesn't know half of what I know!'

I thought back to that first evening. I remembered everything vividly: all at once, in the middle of Zerdahel's perorations, I had felt an awful, nightmarish pressure upon my chest, as though someone had thrust his arms under mine from behind, clasped his hands and squeezed my ribs with all his might. I had leapt up and gone to the window to shake it off. Leaning on the windowsill and panting, I'd waited for the sudden rush of blood and this pressure to pass. The Jew had taken the opportunity to go out or fetch himself a new bottle of beer. At last I was able to breathe again, and then, through the roaring in my head, I'd heard the high, siren tone, as of yearning exultation, which Anna's index finger made on the rim of the wine glass.—Litfás was right: I had gone to the window—not, as he believed, because I'd followed his summons, but because I was stupefied and breathless from all the strange things I'd experienced that afternoon, and torn to pieces inside from the Jew's endless explanations. And I had returned to the table—not to humiliate him (I hadn't even seen him!), but in defiance, not wanting to forfeit the game so soon.—But as though all those things were mere prevarications, as though he knew better than I and wouldn't allow me to deceive him about how things really fit together, he shook his head and said, 'Anna took you away from me.' He set the wine glass beside him on the sales counter. And, as though this were all that was left to say, and all that had to be said, he added firmly, 'You fell for her—from the very first moment!'

I looked up at him. He was fantasizing.—I shook my head—no doubt he was always this way. He suspected everyone who crossed his path of being an adversary in the battle for his Anna, a battle he'd lost long ago. Everything seemed to revolve round her, and he had no notion that someone else might not share his desires.—And with the single-mindedness of a madman adjusting the evidence to suit his present purposes, he went on.

'You stared at her like an apparition, and because she went like *this* one time with her finger on the wine glass,' he said, making the corresponding motion with his finger on the rim of the glass in front of him, 'you thought she belongs to you.'—I wanted to break in, but he wouldn't even let me speak. 'Yes, you did,' he repeated. 'But that doesn't matter.—She wants you, and she'll get you. One way or other.—Why else do you think she came out of the house herself to take the post from you, even though Naghy-Vág was with her?—Just so she could show you her breasts!—And why did you attack the sexton like that? You were completely beside yourself!' the one-armed man exclaimed as though he'd seen it himself. 'He was in your way! That was it.' He laughed sadly and looked at me. 'Yes, yes,' he nodded.

Suppressed rage at this allegation trembled within me, and more angrily than I intended I yelled at him: 'Is that the only reason you brought me back—to tell me that?'

He shook his head.—'There you go again!' he said, pointing at me and laughing again.

Then he made a dismissive gesture. 'No, that's not why,' he said earnestly. 'Those things are none of my concern.'

The Litfás Tubule

'There's an epilogue,' the one-armed man resumed his speech with a frown, closing his fist round the wine glass on the table beside him as though to say that the crucial part of the evening was only just beginning, 'to the legend of the names. You know the legend from Zerdahel. I'll tell you the epilogue.' He opened his fist again and twirled the glass between thumb and forefinger.

'It is found in just one single manuscript,' he said, 'and even there it's almost illegible, because the author scribbled it in the margin of the page like a sudden inspiration. That may also explain why it was never quite taken seriously, though the force of its message and imagery equals that of our most important scriptures, and it would be the ideal complement to the manuscript of Hetföhely.—But maybe that's just it,' he interposed, 'maybe it's the very compellingness of these images, the authenticity transcending all doubts, that always aroused the suspicions of our scholars!' He pondered. 'And then, of course,' he said, 'there's the fact that this epilogue is couched in the form of a question to the reader, something that makes most of us recoil at the outset, even before reading, because we have enough questions ourselves—what we expect from our scriptures are answers!'

'This addendum, then,' the one-armed man continued his remarks without looking at me, 'this addendum—or, to be more precise, this *text* has two headings. They stand side by side, equal in weight, on one and the same line, without punctuation, separated only by an unusually large space. They are: "However" and "As Ever".—The first heading reflects the introductory words repeated in every sentence, so it is not a title in the real sense of the word. The same is true of the second one. "As Ever" is the oldest known term for the Bieresch, and an insult.'

Again he paused, reflecting.—'This implies,' he said meaningfully, 'that, on the one hand, these two formulae represent the encapsulation of all we can possibly ask—for this "however" signifies that all previous answers have been examined, that their content has been summarized and that each bottom line is the new formula "however"—while, on the other hand, the reflexive "as ever" makes it clear that this question, too, and each further question posed in this spirit, is posed wrongly, and that the nature of the answer given calls upon the questioner to examine his question once again and reformulate it.—Stop!'

Litfás ran his hand over his face and the side of his head. He seemed exhausted.

'According to this text,' he went on wearily, 'it is our task to find out the order of things before the Biereschek laid hands on them, before we even existed.—A difficult, nearly intractable problem,' he said with resignation. 'The world's decline takes place only gradually and is imperceptible, even under constant observation by the trained eye, though of course it cannot be denied and no one really denies it.—For one thing is clear, even to the greatest fool—it can't always have been this way. No human race could stand it!—So this decline does exist, and the world really is going to ruin,' he said, but it sounded as though he were timidly asking a question rather than drawing a rigorous conclusion from his own reasoning.

'We can't prove this decline, as Inga believes, but we sense it.—We register the slightest changes in the status quo!' he declared, and, as though to underline the weight of these words, he knocked on the wood of the countertop with his hand, curled like claws. 'It's as though we had a sixth, yet-undiscovered sensory organ in our bellies, constantly feeding us information on these changes. Here,' he said, pointing, as he had once before, at a place just above the navel outlined under the fabric of his nightshirt as a round, flat depression. 'The Spot of Job!—*"Monkeys think with their bellies,"*[69] they say, and it's true.' Seeming to have shaken off his weariness, the one-armed man began to roam back and forth excitedly behind the counter again.

'Listen!' he exclaimed.—'Once I was sitting in a pub over in Andau, having a glass of beer. It was a summer afternoon in an unusually dry year, and the heat crackled beneath the ground in millions of little fires. A stranger sat down next to me at the table. It immediately struck me that despite the blazing sun he was wearing a soft grey felt hat and leather gloves. He doffed the hat, revealing the finest fire-red hair I've ever seen. We got into a conversation. Playing constantly with the hat on the table in front of him, as though with a beer coaster, he told me he'd spent a long time in Africa, but had been forced to leave the country because every summer a host of army ants had swarmed his house, which evidently lay on their route, and stripped it bare, down to the last edible crumb. Each time he and his wife, for whom this state of affairs had grown unendurable, had to spend three days and three nights in emergency accommodations in the bush before the danger passed. What his wife found so harrowing was the relentless regularity with which this event recurred, predictable down to the day. She had always proved resourceful in unpredictable misfortunes, but this routine annual invasion had unsettled and fundamentally altered her.—

'He'd been back in the homeland for two years now, he told me, but the previous summer something even more awful than the ant episode had happened to him, making him wonder whether he should leave his wife for good, for he believed it was he who brought this misfortune upon her.—One afternoon the two of them had been standing at the window of their suburban cottage, talking to a neighbour who stood in their little front garden below. He was telling the neighbour about Africa and the ants. It was nearly dark, and as he talked he felt an inexplicable agitation rise within him, but he combated the feeling by surprising his listener with more and more new adventures from that continent. "Never before had I been able to tell stories *like this*," he exclaimed,' said the one-armed man, '"and yet I was constantly haunted by the sense that a finger, light but insistent, was tapping the back of my head.—At last I could endure it no longer.—

But you have to endure it! Because if you endure it, it'll pass!" he exclaimed once more.—At any rate, he'd turned around and realized that that tapping had been no illusion. It had sounded faint and distant, like water dripping onto something soft in another room, but when he turned up the lamp he saw that thousands of thin, finger-long threadworms were hanging from the ceiling like fine, curling hair, a living lawn from which at regular intervals a piece broke off and fell to the ground with a soft smack.'—The stranger had cried that he brought it upon himself, Litfás related. But in fact all that had ceased to interest him; he was riveted by something else entirely, something that had hardly anything more to do with the story itself.

'In the midst of it all, while he was telling me about his worms, never ceasing to play with his hat on the table in front of him,' cried the one-armed man. 'I suddenly saw it—his long, wavy red hair waved up and down on its own as he spoke like a thick tuft of grass, and each time he groaned and flung back his head, it was as though fire flared up and licked across the sky behind him, until at last the entire horizon around us blazed as though with one great conflagration.—And just imagine, the next day I learnt that on that afternoon America had declared another war.'

He leant back and tucked his left hand under the stump of his arm.—'I don't mean to claim that I can see the future,' he said, bending forward.—'The future is neither here nor there. Seeing it is an arithmetic problem that might come up one day later on. I'm interested solely in the present and the past—for the quick, barely perceptible motion with which a moment, having barely even been, must return from the present to the past, and yet leaves its traces now, and here and now. This movement!' the one-armed man cried again. 'The trail of the worm, left over here, though the worm crawls over there.' He tapped his belly with his index finger again. 'The light bulb's luminous imprint on the wall when I open my eyes again. The knowledge of what is happening now—but *there*!' He motioned with his head towards the front door, and out into the darkness.

'All that matters in our lives takes place in our absence, I've said—the scriptures say!' he corrected himself. 'And that's a good thing.—The event itself, the fly of the moment, as we call it, is neither here nor there. It is neither good nor evil, for in it, as they say, all forces are released and blameless. The interesting thing is the smear of blood and secretions that is left long after the fly's remains have been swept away.'

Now he slapped his left hand on the stump of his arm, which protruded slightly from under the nightshirt.

'Even at the time, this man's army ants and worms were long gone (even in his story!)—except in that hair! And that clinched it. For me the war was declared through that hair.—My spot of Job!' Litfás cried, 'the Litfás tubules!'

'Stop!' he cried again.

'At all events the addition to the Hetföhely manuscript which I spoke of before demands impossible things of us. We can't imagine how the world was without us! But that's not the crucial thing, for, as always, you must first heed what is marginal, what turns inconspicuous the moment you glance in its direction. From it one may after all be able to infer the main thing.—You see, the passages of this text, often tossed out quite casually, imply that the promise of the disbandment of a Bieresch community that manages to write down its history means more than that alone. This promise, it hints, represents no more of the truth than as much sunlight fits in a cupped hand.'

'"However", begins the addendum, referring to the preceding promise, "what if it"—meaning the recording of the history—"were no more than a step onto the rung of a latter, so hard, so easy?"—Here the text breaks off for the first time, forcing readers to think it through on their own, for here the paths already branch. Either it means that the successful record is nothing but the conquering of a single rung of what is really an infinite ladder—in which case this (though no community has yet managed it, not even the Ilmüczers!) should be relatively easy. But, on the other hand, who would still desire to climb even a single rung if he knew how little this achieved?' Litfás interjected. 'What point would it have? And who wouldn't understand our hesitation?—Or,' he continued, 'there really is only this one rung, and the statement means that by surmounting it, we really would have surmounted everything else as well, and by seizing the tip of the truth we would have seized truth itself—like a flag, so to speak . . . . If that were the case, though, this rung would be so high as to be utterly beyond the reach of our short legs, for despite our hesitation we can claim at least that our entire life is but the constant attempt to climb this one rung.—But be that as it may,' the one-armed man broke off his reflections. He took a swallow from his glass and pressed it to his lower lip for a long time as though lost in thought.

'The second line repeats the interrogatory formula of the first,' he explained. '"However", it says, "what if that meant only a return to the scene of the deed of which it is written that it is not?"'

The one-armed man cast me a quick glance. 'What is the message?' he asked.—'For instance, as I firmly believe, that just as we fail to climb the first rung, it is impossible for us to return to the point at which our endeavour originated!—That we remain eternally suspended between Heaven and Earth, as it were, exposed to the mockery of the world—our standing leg on the ground, our free leg half-floating in the air?'

His gaze dwelled on me—somehow I had resigned myself to the notion of staying here, perhaps for ever. I sat on his chair half-turned to the side, my hands folded on the chair back, my right cheek on the back of my right hand, half-asleep, and agreeing, in this half-sleep, with everything he said.

Sometimes, when my arm fell asleep, I changed position, propped my arms on my thighs and let my head sway back and forth like a weight between my shoulders, listening to him as he went on and on.

His words were a soft rustle; my eyes, open, followed the slow rising and falling of his nightshirt hem which followed the movements of his body that punctuated his speech. It reminded me of the rhythmic beat of waves on an empty beach, and I must actually have nodded off several times during his exposition—it seemed a repetition of something long-familiar, and thus a virtual invitation to sleep—for again and again I felt that Litfás repeated certain sentences twice and more, until at last they turned into images in my mind, lingering for a while side by side and fading only gradually, like the luminous imprint of the light bulb he had just mentioned.

On the History of Barter

'Stop!—You remember the founding myth,' he suddenly said, so abrupt and loud that I started up from my dream and nodded as though it were natural to feel guilty. 'It tells that Ég kicked God in the face after the founding fathers divided the land up among themselves.—Correct,' he confirmed, as if I had just solved a difficult examination question.—But as though at the same time he had to prove that my inattention had not escaped his notice, that he was the teacher and I merely the pupil, and very much so, he immediately qualified his praise again.

'Correct,' he repeated, 'and yet incorrect.' He was satisfied. 'Incorrect because the true sacrilege had happened *before* that point in time and Ég's deed can only be understood as a reflexive reaction to it, admittedly criminal and compounding the sacrilege still more in its fecklessness, but ultimately a somehow innocent attempt to amend the misdeed that had been committed.—What is the explanation for that?' Litfás asked, and once again it was not a question he was asking someone, but merely an empty phrase he had prepared for this moment, a smokescreen behind which he could digress still further.

'The true misdeed,' he explained, 'was the dividing of the land. The oldest, supreme law prohibits us Biereschek from owning land and, thus, of course, any other possessions.—"Isn't, wasn't, won't be" are the final words of the founding myth.—Doesn't that say it all?' he cried. 'Doesn't that tell us loud and clear that we're condemned to failure—once and for all?' He gave me a meaningful look and, as though these words were now meant to warn me, he repeated, 'Isn't, wasn't, won't be.'—'And do you know how the founding myth begins?' he asked. 'It begins with an atmospheric image.—"The industrious hands are at rest," it says,' he quoted, and I gave a start, for without knowing where they came from I had picked up these words somewhere here once before, or had read them and learnt them by heart because they touched me in a strange way. '"Nothing stirs,"' the one-armed man went on, ignoring my reaction and fixing his gaze steadily on the shelves behind me, as though taking the words from one of the cubby-holes. '"The air is smooth as a mirror.—Elsewhere, perhaps, a crime is in progress—all things are so nameless, so nerveless."—These are words like those whispered in embraces, and yet they speak of the moment in which evil smothers good in its embrace.' Litfás paused again.

'"When Ahura sleeps, the world is divided up," we say.' He raised his voice.—'It is the nameless silence of noon, this terrible silence of the sun, destroying all hopes, that makes us ask the forbidden question whose answer this myth gives us and which each generation pays for anew in blood and tears.—Ég, Hal, Jár, Szél,' he recited. 'Back then at that waterhole which we call the Eye of Ahura and which, it is said, never closes, these four men disturbed the sleep of the Holy Ancient One with this question. It is the root of all evil, for it demands an accounting.—"Where do we come from, who are we, where are we going?"—Ask like this, and you receive an answer. They asked Ahura for a sign, and he gave it to them. For a moment the clouds parted, the myth relates, and the light of the sun fell on the men's arms as they crossed over the water in an oath, so that the shadow and the bank merged into a wheel.—The lesser witness! "Shadow that comes in sight"!' cried the one-armed man. *'They let the wheel fall before the cross!'*[70]

He was nearly shouting now.

'And along the shadows of these four arms they divided up the land!' He made the corresponding gesture with his hand. 'That Ég stepped into the puddle then,' he cried again, 'that was just one more thing—the headlong retreat of the first to grasp what had happened, the recoiling after the deed and the attempt to obliterate the traces.'

As though to rally from his perorations, which visibly drained him, Litfás reached for his glass again—but both the glass and the bottle behind him on the counter were empty. And however quickly the agitation had come over him, however it had exhausted him—his face had turned dark red, his hands trembled, sweat poured from his bald pate—it swiftly evaporated again. He composed himself, and I caught the quick sidelong glance he cast at my wine glass, as though he were wondering how to get hold of it. I had closed my hand around it so he couldn't see inside. He shook himself.—'Excuse me,' he said as he took down one of the four still-full carafes from the shelf behind me and the sleeve of his nightshirt grazed the back of my head. As he had the first time, he pulled out the paper cone with his teeth; this time, though, instead of spitting it to the floor beside him, he laid it almost gingerly on the counter next to the bottle and refilled his glass.

'Nothing can be undone,' he resumed. 'Each attempt to expunge what has occurred merely makes everything worse, clouds what is clear.—The clear for you,' he said significantly, 'the mud for me! It is not our deeds that count,' he repeated, 'but what our deeds keep mum about.—No matter.—To the very extent that our forefathers—and in their wake we ourselves—attempted to undo the misdeed, they and we helped increase the old iniquity.—The land once divided stays divided. Ahura does not take back what was stolen from him!' He emptied his glass in one draught and weighed it in his hand.

'At that time, you see,' he said, gazing down at his left hand like a stone at the bottom of a deep lake, 'about a lifetime after that sacrilegious deed and after our founding fathers, each in his own way, had been punished for it, the first reports of the potlatch appear. Of the great one, the nagypotlás!' he emphasized.—'"Potlás" means "substitute", as I said, and it is about substitutes in two respects: on the one hand, the potlatch was intended as an expiatory sacrifice to Ahura, to plead for the forgiveness of our iniquity. On the other hand, however, its sophisticated, twofold design enables all subsequent generations to repeat for themselves, at least symbolically and on a small scale, the crime of our forefathers, namely, stealing what was given them as a gift.—The potlatch!' cried the one-armed man, slamming down his left fist on the edge of the sales counter. 'The house call! The dividing of the loot!—You've experienced it first hand!' he said, and I sensed his gaze upon me but did not look up.

'In a manuscript that sadly has not survived,' he went on, now calm again, 'we are told that Oda Vissza, Szél's son, ceded all his possessions to his wife when their first son came of age, both in penance for his father's murder and in expiation of the crimes his father had committed. Oda's wife in turn, to wash herself free of guilt and do her part towards rectifying the misdeeds of her husband and father-in-law, is said to have invited the clans of the three other founding fathers and, at a feast lasting three days—in the course of which Oda went mad, stabbed her to death with a pair of scissors, and was stabbed to death in return by his own son—divided among the others the legacy bestowed upon her.—The three other clans followed the example of Oda's family, though omitting the patricide, and each wife, upon the death of her husband, gave away the inheritance conferred upon her at the coming-of-age of her firstborn son (the fruits of one generation's labour) to the members of the three other clans, disobeying our second commandment as well, which expressly prohibits either refusing presents or passing them on to third parties, that is, she also passed on the goods that had fallen to their family's share during the last potlások.—Stop.' The one-armed man reflected.

'In this manner a type of barter developed among us, and from it in turn the present-day version of the house calls, that legally protected form of thievery.—Originally, as each person gained a surplus from the looted land and it piled up over time in his barn, he bestowed that surplus upon the others in compensation for their surrendering the rights of usufruct, but kept the land for himself. In this way he could constantly provide for himself through the fruits of his own labour, while at regular intervals the others' potlatches provided him with what he lacked. Later the notion of giving back and receiving gifts was lost—no doubt as the senselessness and hopelessness of these attempts at rectification grew increasingly clear—and greed and rapacity took its place, the desire to enrich ourselves as our fathers did, an undertaking facilitated by the fact that the victim of the robbery was a lone woman whose defencelessness facilitated the men's ever-present, hidden desires for vengeance. For the potlatch had gradually led to a profound shift in our society's balance of power,' the one-armed man explained.

'We owe the division of labour to the potlatch,' he said. 'Men began to devote themselves exclusively to production while women were awarded the sole right of sale. But in this way power passed from the men to the women, and that seemed to have its good side as well, for women are more innocently deceptive by nature and thus more skilled at bargaining.—At any rate, ultimately men counted for nothing, while women counted for everything.

'"The only good son is a dead son," as an old proverb of ours has it. It comes from the time when the potlatch was proclaimed to mark the firstborn son's coming of age. And although we no longer do things that way, the attitude towards men has remained the same. He counts for something only until he comes of age—and just imagine,' Litfás interposed, 'the means mothers used, back when they had everything to lose once their sons left childhood, to postpone and prevent their coming of age, while the other women urged it on however they could!—Once this point has come, it's all over for us. Even today.—However much women value their sons for one reason or the other—their men mean nothing to them. A wave of a woman's hand, and the man must go. One evening he comes home, his toolbox is standing outside the door, next to it a day's ration wrapped in a handkerchief—bread, meat, fruits of the season—and he knows: now he's lost everything. Over. Done with.' He sucked in the air through his teeth. There were tears in his eyes. I looked away. Without asking, I knew that this had been his fate.

'No matter,' he said.

'If we are poor today—' He emphasized each word, setting his glass down on the table and pushing it away from him slightly with his index finger. 'If we are poor today,' he repeated, resuming his previous speech after the digression, 'that doesn't mean in the slightest that the crime of our fathers is forgotten and that we're moving back towards a state of innocence and grace—on the contrary! That we're poor means only that evil has let slip its lovely mask and truth in its hideousness is at last revealed behind it, that we're being shown what we've always fled from: the sight of our greed's bare walls.—Thus all it means is that the time of the true punishment has drawn closer.—The third turn of the screw!' cried the one-armed man.

'"When the storehouses are full," the scriptures say, "beware, for hunger is revelling!"—The ultimate purpose of that first potlatch was not to expiate the criminal division of the land, no, its purpose was to enable it for ever—for ever to capture and divide up booty. And as our forefathers committed that misdeed, so has each subsequent generation repeated their sacrilege with ever-new and ever-increasing persistence and obduracy. But—and this is the mockery, and at the same time already part of our punishment: the more we attempt to possess, the less we seem to succeed at it. Today we have virtually nothing left.'

'Now, perhaps,' Litfás declared, blinking with exhaustion, 'you will understand what the legend of the names is all about and why I wanted to speak to you at all costs on the very first evening—before the Jew could confuse you with his stories: the names of our founding fathers (and the same is ultimately true of our present-day names) were terms of allocation referring to each parcel of stolen land and the booty it brought. Of course, over time our ownership relations and the direct connection to the revenue yielded by each property grew more and more complex, more composite, and thus the naming of the property that had been lost or that had accrued in the meantime became more and more difficult.—What is more: as our population was decimated by our civil wars, the conflict between the Minim and the Malchim, the Histrions and the Monotomoi, and as a result of plagues and famines, the conditions for the proper proclamation of the potlatch worsened radically. For one could not even find a first- or second-born son now, often relatives two or three times removed had to be brought in, and the transfer of legacies took place under auspices that made catastrophe inevitable.—The trustee or caretaker became a proxy, and what had once been right and proper, namely, that the son was divested of what his father had unlawfully appropriated, lost its meaning.' The one-armed man paused and wrinkled his brow.

'Everything became so confused,' he went on, 'that ultimately there was nothing for it but to deduce the name of each newly installed caretaker or proxy from the goods that had been stolen and distributed over the course of the house calls.—Today your name is "Halfway",' the one-armed man summed up, 'and everything seems simple and clear.—But is that who you really are? Do you really belong to Jár's clan, the man who went, as we say?—And is it right that I was once called "Seven Lakes and No Water", descendent of Hal, the fish?' He passed the back of his hand across his brow as though he had a fever.

'Ég, Hal, Jár, Szél,' he recited once again.—'If we really knew the truth about our origins—what would be easier than to climb the first rung of which I spoke? What would be simpler than to write down the history of our community—and thus the history of the ownership relations, the theft relations!' he corrected himself. 'What would come more quickly than the return to the scene of the deed—to those four men at the sacred spring who broke our first commandment as Ahura slept?—But the only thing told of that place is that it is not. And however we may exert ourselves, we can't find the way back to it!' The one-armed man had finished his speech, and with a quick turn of his torso slid from the countertop on which he'd half-sat the whole while.—'The one who proclaims the potlatch,' he said as he came towards me, 'does not abolish the guilt, he prolongs it.—There's perhaps one thing we can do—put back the names, renounce the inheritance, vanish grey amid grey stones, as they say.'

He looked at me.—'Let's get something to eat,' he wheezed. 'I'm hungry.'

I stood up, tired, and without knowing why, light as though tossed in the air. For a moment I had the nonsensical desire to thank him for his words, like a lecturer, and I took a step towards him as though to actually shake his hand.—But he took no notice, bending down instead to push back a sliding door in the sales counter, and rummaged around for a while in the shelves behind it.

'They're not there,' he said shaking his head, probably looking for the trousers and shoes he needed to go out. He opened a second door, but the cubbyhole behind it did not hold what he was looking for either. It contained a toolbox with a long-handled cobbler's hammer, a pair of pliers and all sorts of tools, while pairs of shoes tied together by the laces lay in heaps, completely covered with dust, no doubt from the time when he'd still had two arms and two hands.—At the sight of the toolbox I remembered what he had told me just now about the women who chased their men out of the house when they pleased, and, as though suddenly remembering as well, he sat down heavily on the chair I'd just vacated and shook his head pensively, his brow cupped in his left hand.

But then he stood up, lifted the hinged board, opening the narrow entry to the shop, and slipped through. Two purposeful strides took him to the customers' armchair and he pulled the clothing he sought out from under it.—But as though this had been his actual goal, he now dropped into the upholstered chair and stared at me like a stranger, his thoughts clearly miles away.

'Go alone,' he said at last, as though suddenly recalling his suggestion. 'Go alone.'

I went to the door and was about to open it when he held me back again. 'The drawer!' he cried, and I knew he wanted me to take out his present for Anna. I did as he wished.—It was an illustrated catalogue, evidently a publisher's annual brochure. I read the words set in a broad bar diagonally across the cover. It said *The Library of Erudition and Diversion.*

I remembered Rák, and the promise he had given me before leaving. To all appearances this library was a series of omnibus volumes, regularly supplemented, of which Rák was a subscriber.

Once again I glanced at the cover. A series of captions pompously directed the reader to pages within the catalogue. I read 'South American Adventure' and, next to it, 'The Secret of the Floating Isle'. Another title was 'All about the Yahoos'; a fourth, 'New Compact Lesson in Astronomy'.—These were all things my godfather had rhapsodized about, and for a moment I was uncertain what to think of that.—'I'm your godfather now!' he had cried. 'I'll bequeath them to you!'—Was this what he had meant?

I turned to ask where or from whom he had got this catalogue, but the one-armed man was already sound asleep and, as though in answer to the question I had been about to ask, he sighed deeply and laid his head to the side.

Notes

1 Paraphrase from Gerhard Rühm, *knochenspielzeug* (bone toy) (Düsseldorf: Eremiten-Presse, 1979), p. 26.

2 Franz Kafka, *Gesammelte Werke, Bd. 7* (Complete Works, VOL. 7) (Frankfurt am Main: S. Fischer, 1976), p. 11.

3 Inspired by the eponymous sect in Jorge Luis Borges, 'The Theologians' in *The Aleph and Other Stories* (Andrew Hurley trans.) (New York: Penguin Classics, 2004), pp. 26–34.

4 Genesis 4:6.

5 Inspired by Martin Heidegger, *Wegmarken* (Pathmarks) (Frankfurt am Main: Klostermann, 1967), p. 10.

6 Near-verbatim reproduction of Kafka's story 'Der Kreisel' (The Top). Cited from Kafka, *Gesammelte Werke, Bd. 5*, p. 90.

7 Borges, 'The Theologians', p. 31.

8 Quote from Franz Mon, *Texte über Texte* (Texts on Texts) (Neuwied and Berlin: Luchterhand, 1970), p. 7.

9 Poem quoted from Kurt Vonnegut, *Cat's Cradle* (New York: Random House, 2010), p. 3. The name Bokonon is also taken from that novel.

10 Paraphrase from Borges, 'The Theologians,' p. 31.

11 Adaptation of Hasidic legend in Martin Buber, *Die Erzählungen der Chassidim* (Tales of the Hasidim) (Zurich: Manesse, 1949), p. 6.

12 The term and the following explanation are taken from Flann O'Brien, *The Third Policeman* (Champaign, IL: Dalkey Archive Press, 1999), p. 38. The name of the character De Selby is also taken from the novel.

13 Title of a story by Kafka: 'Die alltägliche Verwirrung', *Gesammelte Werke, Bd. 6*, p. 55.

14 Quote from Kafka, 'Gespräch mit dem Beter' (Conversation with the Supplicant), *Gesammelte Werke, Bd. 4*, p. 32.

15 Quote from Flann O'Brien, *The Poor Mouth* (Patrick C. Power trans.) (Champaign, IL: Dalkey Archive Press, 2008), p. 22.

16 Quote from Hans Arp, 'Sekundenzeiger' (Second Hand) in *Gesammelte Gedichte, Bd. 1: Gedichte, 1903–1939* (Complete Poems, VOL. 1: Poems, 1903–39) (Marguerite Arp-Hagenbach and Peter Schifferli eds) (Wiesbaden: Limes, 1963), p. 98.

17 Paraphrase from a letter by Franz Kafka, *Briefe 1902–1924* (Letters, 1902–1924) (Max Brod ed.) (Frankfurt am Main: S. Fischer, 1975), p. 85.

18 Paraphrase from James Joyce, *Ulysses* (London: Simon & Brown, 2013), p. 42.

19 Paraphrase from Kafka, *Gesammelte Werke, Bd. 6*, p. 83.

20 Paraphrase from Buber, *Die Erzählungen der Chassidim*, p. 501.

21 Quote from Blaise Cendrars, *Moravagine* (Alan Brown trans.) (New York: New York Review Books, 2004), p. 108.

22 Paraphrase from Gabriel Garcia Marquez, *One Hundred Years of Solitude* (Gregory Rabassa trans.) (London: Penguin Books, 1998), p. 80.

23 Quote from Kafka, *Gesammelte Werke, Bd. 5*, p. 192.

24 Inspired by the sect of the Monotonoi in Borges, 'The Theologians'.

25 Quote from Franz Kafka, *In der Strafkolonie* (In the Penal Colony) in *Gesammelte Werke, Bd. 4*, p. 160

26 Paraphrase of Karl Kraus, *In dieser großen Zeit? Aufsätze 1914–1925* (In This Great Time? Essays, 1914–25) (East Berlin: Verlag Volk und Welt, 1971), Chapter 30.

27 Paraphrase from Cendrars, *Moravagine*, p. 57.

28 Paraphrase from Borges, 'The Theologians', p. 122.

29 Quote from Kurt Vonnegut, *The Sirens of Titan* (London: Gollancz, 2004), p. 190.

30 Genesis 27:22.

31 Hasidic legend quoted from Buber, *Die Erzählungen der Chassidim*, p. 278.

32 Oswald Wiener, *die verbesserung von mitteleuropa* (the improvement of central europe) (Reinbek: Rowohlt, 1969), p. LVI.

33 Quote from Samuel Beckett, *Watt* (New York: Grove Press, 1994), p. 43.

34 Paraphrase from Karl Marx, *Das Kapital*, VOL. 1, in *Werke* (East Berlin: Dietz, 1962), p. 86.

35 Paraphrase from Eugen Gomringer, *konstellationen. ideogramme. stundenbuch* (constellations. ideograms. book of hours) (Stuttgart: Reclam, 1977), p. 28.

36 Paraphrase from Urs Widmer, *Das Normale und die Sehnsucht* (Normality and Longing) (Zurich: Diogenes, 1972) p. 61ff.

37 Paraphrase of a song by medieval poet Gautier de Coincy, originally referring to Jews, cited in Léon Poliakov, *Geschichte des Antisemitismus, I. Von der Antike bis zu den Kreuzzügen* (History of Anti-Semitism, VOL. 1: From Antiquity to the Crusades) (Frankfurt am Main: Insel, 1975), p. 47.

38 Quote from Bruno Schulz, 'Tailors' Dummies' in *The Street of Crocodiles and Other Stories* (Celina Wieniewska trans.) (New York: Penguin Books, 2008), p. 39.

39 Quote from Bundesverband der deutschen Standesbeamten e. V. (ed.), *Hausbuch für die deutsche Familie* (Housebook for the German Family) (Frankfurt am Main: Verlag für Standesamtwesen, 1956), p. 9.

40 Hungarian proverb.

41 Quote from Gerhard Roth, *Winterreise* (Frankfurt am Main: S. Fischer, 1979), p. 97.

42 Ibid.

43 Wiener, *die verbesserung von mitteleuropa,* p. *xi.*

44 Quote from Schulz, *The Street of Crocodiles,* p. 100.

45 Quote from Gustav Theodor Fechner, *Zend-Avesta* (Max Fischer ed.) (Frankfurt am Main: Insel, 1980), p. 10.

46 Paraphrase from Kafka's posthumous papers, *Gesammelte Werke, Bd. 6,* p. 31.

47 Jewish proverb.

48 Paraphrase from Ludwig Wittgenstein, *Tractatus logico-philosophicus* (Frankfurt am Main: Suhrkamp, 1963), p. 111.

49 Quote from Arp, 'Sekundenzeiger', p. 98.

50 Quote from Gert Jonke, *Schule der Geläufigkeit* (School of Velocity) (Frankfurt am Main: Suhrkamp, 1979), p. 7.

51 Paraphrase from Gomringer, *konstellationen. ideogramme. stundenbuch,* p. 28.

52 Quoted from Poliakov, *Geschichte des Antisemitismus,* p. 12.

53 Paraphrase from ibid.

54 Quote from Kafka's unpublished notebooks, *Gesammelte Werke, Bd. 6,* p. 250.

55 Paraphrase from Kafka, 'Kinder auf der Landstrasse' (Children on a Country Road) in *Gesammelte Werke, Bd. 4,* p. 22.

56 Paraphrase from Walter Benjamin, *Werkausgabe edition suhrkamp, Bd. 2* (Collected Works, VOL. 2) (Rolf Tiedemann and Hermann Schweppenhäuser eds) (Frankfurt am Main: Suhrkamp, 1980), p. 677.

57 Title of a poetry collection by Alfred Kolleritsch, *Einübung in das Vermeidbare* (Practice in the Avoidable) (Salzburg and Vienna: Residenz, 1978).

58 From Kafka's description of a work by Mikhail Kuzmin in his diaries, 21 December, 1910, *Gesammelte Werke, Bd. 7,* p. 25.

59 The notion of bicycle transubstantiation is taken from O'Brien, *The Third Policeman,* Chapter 6.

60 Paraphrase from Kafka's diaries, 26 July 1911, *Gesammelte Werke, Bd. 7,* p. 25.

61 Paraphrase from Kafka's diaries, 26 December 1911, *Gesammelte Werke, Bd. 7,* pp. 129–32.

62 All references from Jonathan Swift, *Gulliver's Travels* (1726).

63 'So it goes': recurring phrase in Kurt Vonnegut, *Slaughterhouse-Five, or The Children's Crusade: A Duty-Dance with Death* (New York: Delacorte, 1969)

64 Carl Jung, *Bewußtes und Unbewußtes. Beiträge zur Psychologie* (The Conscious and the Unconscious) (Frankfurt am Main: S. Fischer, 1957), p. 42.

65 Hungarian ballad.

66 Quote from Salman Rushdie, *Midnight's Children* (New York: Penguin Books, 1991), p. 270.

67 Paraphrase from Jorge Luis Borges, *Gesammelte Werke,* VOL. 3.2, *Stories, 1949–1970* (Karl August Horst, Curt Meyer-Clason and Gisbert Haefs trans) (Munich and Vienna: Hanser, 1981).

68 Quote from Peter Handke, *Die Innenwelt der Außenwelt der Innenwelt* (The Innerworld of the Outerworld of the Innerworld) (Frankfurt am Main: Suhrkamp, 1969), p. 35.

69 Quote from Kafka, 'Ein Bericht für eine Akademie' (A Report to an Academy), *Gesammelte Werke, Bd. 4,* p. 142.

70 Paraphrase from Borges, 'The Theologians', p. 122.

AFTERWORD

The Closeness of the Foreign I

For Dorle and Eugen Schwarz

My sense of life is one of disorientation.—The first story I wrote was set in a city of a North American cast, a labyrinth of rigorous order (not merely architectural) in which everything was constantly repeated, so that regularity itself induced the sense of being lost, familiarity itself became a frightening enigma. The inkling that a method lies behind life's madness, that, rather like Kafka's marionettes, we are controlled by laws we do not know, and the obvious inference that—they being laws, and ignorance of the law being no excuse—we can also be condemned under them, was a torment, and remains so.

And so my fancy was captured early on by the labyrinthine tale of the lost, presumptuous *drifter* through the land who pretends to himself and to the world that he has been summoned as a *surveyor* of the land to these inhospitable foreign parts, where he must stray further and further until at last he arrives back where he started as a simple *worker* of the land.

I read Kafka's *Castle* as a travel novel.—Kafka proceeds as Swift does, in *Gulliver's Travels*, with the absurd doings of the Academy of Projectors on the isle of Barnibalbi, or Kurt Vonnegut, in *Cat's Cradle*, with the strange rites of the Bokononists on San Lorenzo. The author of *The Castle* uses the outlandish life of the villagers as a background against which the hero stands out as the seemingly familiar and natural, but becomes, in the course of the story, increasingly unnatural, unreasonable, incomprehensible. The utterly strange world of the castle and the village seems to stand on its head—for the sole purpose of standing the hero on his feet. He becomes—in the sense of what Kafka described as the 'good' of self-recognition—what he was from the beginning. Looking back, once his grim story has lapsed into the past, its 'purpose' suddenly turns visible; to speak to Doris Lessing, in retrospect, the unredeemed life—and this is ultimately true for anyone standing baffled before their life story—appears 'steeped' in the 'substance' of a purpose 'that had seemed foreign to it, was extraneous to the experiencing of it [at that time]'.*

As long as I can recall, I have been fascinated by various aspects of that 'literature' which, according to the foreword of Joseph Conrad's *Almayer's Folly*, 'preys on strange people and prowls in far-off countries':[1] here was the depiction of exotic customs and unknown peoples' thought systems, and the character of the aloof traveller, the *scientific explorer* who travels with

* Doris Lessing, *Memoirs of a Survivor* (London: Flamingo, 1995), p. 7.

the intent to see, not 'to intervene in others' circumstances',[2] who experiences and contemplates the foreign in a 'depersonalized' way, to use Peter Handke's diction, and who at last—apprehending this absurd-seeming world, being carried away by it—'becomes other'.

When I began writing my travel novel *Among the Bieresch* around 20 years ago, I was set in motion chiefly by Handke's *Short Letter, Long Farewell* and by Vonnegut's *Cat's Cradle*, with the pidgin English of its San Lorenzans and their forbidden pidgin religion, Bokononism. Kafka's works were constantly on my mind as well, above all *The Castle* and the equally fitting story of the *Penal Colony*.—Yet it had always struck me when reading the *Castle* that K. had not, as he claimed, begun his journey in his 'homeland' and set *out* into 'foreign parts'; rather, his journey led him deeper and deeper *into* his homeland, as though the foreign were home—the *heart of darkness*.

I had a similar thing in mind with my novel.—Rather than send my hero abroad, I sent him, as it were, into the depths—a young lad with the fairy-tale-name *Hans* with whom, and for whom, I sought to gain a different perspective on our situation, an ethnographer's perspective on its hidden exotic, atavistic elements that sometimes emerge unexpectedly in such things as the protective masks of ice-hockey goalies or the little national flags painted on football fans' cheekbones.

I set my novel in a region of Eastern Austria which before the end of the First World War had been known as Transleithania or 'German West Hungary'. Following the Treaty of St Germaine and a plebiscite, it joined Austria as a federal state, with a population structure which even then had all the makings of a double-minority conflict like that in Northern Ireland. Minority and majority had switched places; the 'Alpine dolts', as Joseph Roth described the German-speaking population of the Hapsburg Monarchy, now formed the majority, while the Hungarians formed the largest minority in a mixed population typical of the defunct dual monarchy.

Up until the Second World War, this formerly Hungarian province had been home to a disproportionate number of Jews who had moved there when Joseph II granted them special rights. With a very few exceptions, they all perished in the Nazis' death camps, as did the Roma; the former *Gauleiter* of the Burgenland, who still resides here, played a crucial role in the so-called Nuremberg Laws and was one of the first to call for the annihilation of the Roma. Following the war, a small Gypsy community has settled here once again, as their ancestors did in the past century and even before. And in the south there still live descendants of the Turks and Kurucs left from the wars of the seventeenth century, and, in small, scattered linguistic enclaves, Croats.—But alongside these population groups, the region was home to a social minority, the pariahs of this society, the so-called Bieresch. This group of have-nots—their name derives from the

Hungarian *beres*, meaning 'servant'—was comprised entirely of farmhands who worked, on into the 1960s, for large, formerly Hungarian landowners. Despised by and isolated from the rest of the population, they lived under scandalous conditions in groups of several hundred people on feudal manors known as *pusztas*, forming a fully self-contained, closed-off social subsystem.—It was by chance, through a radio broadcast, that I learnt of the existence of this society within my society, of its living conditions and the customs and rites that had evolved in response to them. I was fascinated by this lost world and decided to set my hero loose in it.

This region, from which the Bieresch, the product of very specific socioeconomic circumstances, have now vanished, has recently seen bombing attacks against ethnic minorities.[3]

The strict rules by which the Bieresch minority organized their social life were the inevitable product of their economic situation, which can perhaps best be described with the term *dispossession*.—Long after finishing my novel, I read the Hungarian writer Gyula Illyés, who had grown up on a *puszta* himself and written down the impressions of his youth. Here the wife of a former administrator at one of these manors opines that the Bieresch had to be treated 'like bees': 'You have to take everything away from them so they'll go on working.'[4]

Thus, what regulated their social behaviour was deprivation.—And then I read in Illyés of that hemmed-in life in which several families often shared one shabby hut, their members moving about the single common room as though according to strict regulations, 'as though along pre-drawn lines', so as not to get in one another's way. He wrote that parents took no interest in their children's choice of spouse, for all potential sons- and daughters-in-law would be equally lacking in property. In this community in which the breaking of a windowpane had more serious consequences than did the cracking of a skull, private property did not exist, and thus little distinction was drawn between *mine* and *yours*—in other words, as Illyés put it, 'They have nothing, and they steal like magpies.'

After all, individuals themselves were mere items of barter which their masters could give as 'gifts' to others, or which could be leased out together with land, carts, machines and livestock or taken over along with them when sold.—In this world, owning something (in an echo of Proudhon's formula) meant that one had stolen it.

This information about the life of the manor dwellers in Eastern Austria fused with my vague knowledge of the gift system of the potlatch* among

*According to Marcel Mauss, 'potlatch' is a Chinook word which 'essentially means "to feed", "to consume"' (Marcel Mauss, *The Gift: The Form and Reason for Exchange in Archaic Societies* [W. D. Halls trans.] [New York: W. W. Norton, 2000], p. 6); according to Franz Boas, in the Kwakiutl language, the word's literal meaning is 'place of getting satiated' (cited in ibid., p. 86).

the Tlingit, Haida, Tsimshian and Kwakiutl Indians on the north-western coast of America, acquired through haphazard reading after my interest was sparked by a study-abroad year in Washington State. In the Native American potlatch, as I later read in Marcel Mauss' famous study of this special type of credit-and-barter system, the act of giving functioned, on the one hand, to return things previously given as gifts, but, on the other hand, it always had an 'element of usury' as well, as the gift put the recipients deeply in debt to the giver.*

This potlatch was a way for the often extremely wealthy Native American host to have his social status within the hierarchy of his tribe reaffirmed by the guests invited to a family celebration marking a birth or a death. To this end he would often give away all his possessions to his guests. In my novel this is mirrored by the total looting of a recently deceased patriarch's household by uninvited, unpropertied members of the community who are seeking 'replacements' for what has been stolen from them—and by a lucky twist of linguistic fate, the Hungarian word for replacement is *pótlás*.

As noted, possessionlessness and dispossession formed the economic foundation for the social system of my manor workers. They were a social minority; they had no particular ethnic identity, but in a variant of anti-Semitism without Jews, which Egon Schwarz

* Ibid.

demonstrates to be a phenomenon of our time,* they were stigmatized and vilified as though they were a specific, odious, worthless ethnic group. Over time this naturally meant that they actually began to see themselves as such, developing their own customs, celebrations and religious and delusional systems.

In my book, their lingua franca is German, although, historically speaking, the Bieresch came from Hungarian-speaking families. Here and there I introduced fragments of Hungarian into their speech, whereby—with no command of Hungarian myself, but emboldened by Vonnegut—I denatured it willy-nilly to produce a pidgin tongue with German grammar and German word order.—Thus they never possessed an ethnic identity; and I robbed them of their linguistic identity.—Nothing should belong to them; all should be merely borrowed or stolen. In this spirit one of my characters says, 'It's not *me* speaking, it's someone else sighing with my voice.' And elsewhere someone boasts, 'I made it my policy not to take my life personally.'

And so the sufferings and sighs of the Bieresch do not belong to them—nor do they themselves. Their identity is defined by the lord of the manor, the large landowner. I once read with regard to the 1921

* Egon Schwarz, 'Jews and Anti-Semitism in Fin-de-Siècle Vienna' in *Insiders and Outsiders: Jewish and Gentile Culture in Germany and Austria* (Dagmar Lorenz and Gabriele Weinberger eds) (Detroit, MI: Wayne State University Press, 1994), p. 54.

plebiscite that delivered the north-eastern Burgenland to Austria that the so-called Seewinkel, that is, the 'province in the east of the Empire' where my novel is chiefly set, joined Austria only because the majority of the local Hungarian-speaking population—the farmhands—was not allowed to vote, because by 'authority' they belonged to masters on Hungarian territory. And Illyés writes in a similar vein, confirming this statement: 'To determine under whose authority a *puszta* inhabitant falls, one does not ask where he was born, and still less where he lives, but, rather, whom he serves.'[5]

In my novel I integrated this phenomenon of self-definition *qua* feudal affiliation by having male adolescents lose their childhood names when initiated into adult society and receive, in their place, the names of ancestors, which, as explained towards the end, were 'terms of allocation referring to . . . stolen land'. These, following a convention of the rural population in our part of the world, were colloquial names, meaning *telling* names—another variant of which I knew from the literature on Native Americans. I gave some of them exotic names in homage to those in Thomas Berger's novel *Little Big Man*, where characters are known as 'Shadow That Comes in Sight' or 'Burns Red in the Sun'. Following my narrator Hans' initiation, I christened him 'Halfway'—a name I'm still pleased with for its hint of seven-league boots, of ground being covered, and because it alludes to Hans' partially successful integration into the society of the Bieresch, who at first seem set solely on robbing him of his identity.

The world and society of the manor workers into which Hans is halfway integrated is at once a counter-world and a complement to the one he comes from.

I have always been a partisan of the view that persecution and extermination is motivated by the perpetrators' unconscious assumption of affinity with their victims; and that, in accordance with the classic dynamic of status within groups, social minorities are accused of character traits which Erik Erikson argues are part of the *negative identity* of the majority, traits which the majority is unable to integrate into its *positive* identity,* which it projects onto the minority and

* See Erik H. Erikson: 'Every person and every group harbors a negative identity as the sum of all those identifications and identity fragments which the individual had to submerge in himself as undesirable or irreconcilable or which his group has taught him to perceive as the mark of fatal "difference" in sex role or race, in class or religion. In the event of aggravated crises, an individual (or, indeed, a group) may despair of the ability to contain these negative elements in a positive identity. A specific rage can be aroused wherever identity development thus loses the promise of an assured wholeness: an as-yet-uncommitted delinquent, if denied any chance of communal integration, may become a "confirmed" criminal. In periods of collective crisis, such potential rage is shared by many and is easily exploited by psychopathic leaders, who become the models of a sudden surrender to total doctrines and dogmas in which the negative identity appears to be the desirable and the dominant one: thus the Nazis fanatically cultivated what the victorious West as well as the more refined Germans had come to decry as "typically German." The rage aroused by threatened

blames it for. For centuries the possessions of the Jews were grabbed with the excuse that the Jews were money-grabbing. Ruth Klüger gets to the heart of the phenomenon in her autobiographical work *weiter leben*, where she notes that the very people who tirelessly propagated the cliché of the gold-hungry Jew Shylock, that is, the Nazis, were the ones who extracted the gold teeth of their Jewish concentration camp victims in an act of unparalleled greed.*

Conversely, I believe, social minorities perform the 'mission' of the majority, that which the majority—in Erikson's words—must suppress and submerge as undesirable or irreconcilable in order to live. And thus, in a cultural sense as well, minorities work for the majority and fill in what the majority omits or spares itself.—One need only recall the notorious and probably unfeigned tears in the eyes of the SS officers at the sound of the concentration-camp orchestras of

identity loss can explode in the arbitrary violence of mobs, or it can—less consciously—serve the efficient destructiveness of the machinery of oppression and war.' *Life History and the Historical Moment: Diverse Presentations* (New York: W. W. Norton, 1975) p. 20.

* Ruth Klüger: 'And so I learnt from her of the perversities of murder and the many ways in which corpses can be desecrated. From her I learnt that the gold was extracted from the teeth of our corpses (I think of that every time I read of Shylock and his fictitious descendants and their fictitious greed), and other things that are general knowledge about the twentieth century . . . .' *weiter leben. Ein Jugend* (Still Alive) (Göttingen: Wallstein Verlag, 1992), p. 117.

Jews and Gypsies who, minutes later, were sent into the gas chambers.

'If we made candles,' says a Jewish proverb which I have borrowed for my novel, 'the sun would shine on us day and night,' and 'if we wove shrouds, no one would die any more.'—I imposed deprivation on the minority in my book. Baffled by the futility and failure of all attempts to live, delirious as it were from withdrawal, they develop complex, lunatic explanation systems for the collective and personal misery which—standardized by the never-changing conditions of their existence—have nothing unique about them, are nothing but a constantly repeated déjà-vu, the echo of the lives of previous generations.—'Only the incomprehensible has meaning,' C. G. Jung writes in *The Archetypes and the Collective Unconscious,* which one of the Bieresch cites, and 'Only one who does not understand requires an interpretation.' They do not understand, and they interpret; they do not live, they are constantly explaining a life incomprehensible to them.*

* 'Life is both crazy and meaningful. And if you don't laugh about the one thing and speculate about the other, life is banal. Then everything is on the pettiest of scales. Then everything yields only petty sense and petty nonsense. Ultimately nothing means anything, for when no thinking human beings yet existed, there was no one to interpret phenomena. Only one who does not understand requires an interpretation. Only the incomprehensible has meaning. Human beings have awoken in a world which they do not understand, and thus they attempt to interpret it.' Carl Jung, *Bewußtes und Unbewußtes. Beiträge zur Psychologie* (Frankfurt am Main: S. Fischer, 1957), p. 42.

In a review of the novel in *Der Spiegel,* Wolfgang Hildesheimer alluded to its repeated mention of a 'Jew' and asked whether I had realized that *all* the characters in the book are Jews.—Hildesheimer's question made me feel that my intent had been understood, for from the time I began writing the *Bieresch,* my concern (in part as the son of a fanatic Nazi functionary) was to trace those intricate paths of thought from which I have profited most in my work and my life, to reconstruct what I have encountered, in the great literary documents of this century, as *Jewish* thought—if it is even permissible to use this term.

The peculiar hatred with which Europe, and especially Austria and Germany, has responded and continues to respond to this complex thinking—a thinking which for me is characterized by unsparing self-doubt and the relentless questioning of even the most laboriously achieved conclusions, and reaches its pinnacle in Kafka's works—this hatred always struck me as also being an expression of self-hatred, and of the abovementioned affinity that bonds the persecutor to the victim. Nietzsche once said that resentment is revenge taken on what has not been understood; it seems to me that there is a second variant as well. In it, revenge is taken on that which, once understood, one must avoid becoming conscious of: one's own frailty, one's own nullity.—It is the revenge taken on Caliban, who seeks to show his face in the mirror.

I wanted to confront my hero with the things which his society suppresses and which manifest themselves in the life of the Bieresch. I wanted him to lose himself as in a labyrinth mysteriously familiar to him.—'Astonishing,' says a Bieresch in a legend, 'it seems that everything repeats, and yet comes as a surprise to me!'

Klaus Hoffer

Notes

1 Joseph Conrad, *Almayer's Folly and The Rover* (Ware: Wordsworth Editions, 2011), p. 5.

2 Franz Kafka, 'In der Strafkolonie' (In the Penal Colony) in *Franz Kafka. Das erzählerische Werk,* VOL. 1 (Berlin: Rütten & Loening 1988), p. 181.

3 Between 1993 and 1997, the Austrian Franz Fuchs (1949–2000) killed four people and injured fifteen in IED and letter-bomb attacks targeting immigrants and ethnic minorities such as Roma in the name of the 'Bajuvarian Liberation Army'.

4 Cited from the German edition, Gyula Illyés, *Die Puszta* (Tibor Podmaniczky trans.) (Nördlingen: Franz Greno, 1985), n.p. Available in English as: Gyula Illyés, *People of the Puszta* (G. F. Cushing trans.) (Budapest: Corvina, 1967).

5 Illyés, *Die Puszta*, p. 18.